SOME DREAMS ARE NIGHTMARES

SOME DREAMS ARE NIGHTMARES

JAMES GUNN

Illustrated by Leonard Everett Fisher

CHARLES SCRIBNER'S SONS
NEW YORK

Fiction is simply dreams written out. Science fiction consists of the hopes and dreams and fears (for some dreams are nightmares) of a technically based society.

JOHN W. CAMPBELL

To Burroughs Mitchell

CONTENTS

INTRODUCTION

*A novel is a prose narrative of
some length that has something
wrong with it.*

RANDALL JARRELL

THIS BOOK CONTAINS FOUR STORIES: one short story, one
novelette, and two short novels. They are related in some
interesting ways, which I will get to a bit later, but one
important thing they have in common is that they are
distilled novels.

The ideal length for science fiction is the novelette.

This is not true of other genres such as the western or the
mystery, whose shorter versions are markedly less successful
and almost invisible; they are known almost entirely for
their novels.

Science fiction, on the other hand, can display hundreds
of great short stories but few great novels. "It's doubtful,"
Anthony Boucher wrote in 1952, "if any specialized field
can lay as much proportionate stress on the anthology as
science fiction does today." More than twenty years later,
the stress is even greater, with hardcover and paperback
anthologies competing with magazines for original short
fiction.

Now that the great, slick fiction magazines are dead and
gone, the last refuge of the popular American short story
may be the science fiction magazine and anthology.

On the other hand, the science fiction novel is often—perhaps usually—a disappointment. Those which avoid the common fate of most science fiction novels are not the purest form of science fiction: that is, they are primarily adventure stories or fantasy stories, or stories of mood or character whose goals and methods approach those of the mainstream. . . .

This brings us to definition—at best a sticky place where one must thrash about to find a place to stand. Perhaps it is sufficient to observe, if we wish to be complete, that science fiction covers a broad variety of fictional forms which may have little or nothing to do with science, that the term "speculative fiction" is a bit more descriptive but has blanketed a great many stories which are related in only the broadest and least meaningful ways, and that the hard core of science fiction is a literature of ideas—unfortunately for accuracy, this also includes fiction which is not science fiction at all, and fiction which is only related, such as the satire and the utopia.

The English critic Edmund Crispin has called science fiction "origin of species fiction" which views Man "as just one of a horde of different animals sharing the same planet. . . . Science fiction's real subject-matter is the present, seen against the perspectives of history. . . . It is about us, here, now—about us as we have been shaped by our genesis, our biology, our environment and our behavior."

What lies at the heart of every hard-core science fiction story is an idea—perhaps an "if this goes on" kind of extrapolation from present tendencies into a future where those trends have come to fruition, perhaps a "what if" kind of speculation about a unique occurrence; perhaps an insight into the nature of man or the nature of his society or the nature of the universe and man's relation to it; or the conflict between man and his creation, between what he can dream and what he can do. In its essence, science fiction is a Platonic fiction dealing with ideals, even in characterization, of which the physical representations we see around us are only imperfect copies; or eschatalogical fiction dealing with last or final things.

The implications of all this are what create problems for the science fiction novel. A hard-core science fiction novel should take for its theme a major problem: pollution, overpopulation, racial survival, social survival, the exhaustion of resources, immortality, happiness, god, man's conflict with his environment, his surrender to it or symbiosis with it, war, progress, superpowers, superman. . . . To these problems or suggested problems there are no easy solutions and perhaps no solutions at all, but a novel, because of the promise of its scope and length, is under some compulsion to provide a solution. The mainstream avoids what science fiction traditionally finds obligatory—explanation—and in a mainstream novel the matter of resolution presents a smaller problem: a resolution must be provided only for a single character or group. Any attempt to resolve larger problems risks the ridiculous; if the larger problems were solvable they would have been solved already. Science fiction writers either take their chances or avoid the danger by one of several expedients. The favorite for many authors is to ignore what they say the problem is and solve some other problem, or allow the problem to be solved by accident.

The best example of this kind of misdirection is Michael Crichton's *The Andromeda Strain*, a novel which begins with the threat of cataclysm: a deadly virus has been brought back from space which will wipe out all mankind unless something is done. The complication of the novel is the gathering together of a group of scientists in an excellently detailed underground laboratory which has been carefully prepared for such an eventuality. The scientists are unsuccessful in coping with the virus, but fortunately it mutates into a harmless form. In other words, everything the author told the reader about the virus and the situation turned out to be unimportant: the results would have been identical if no one had done anything, or, in fact, if no one even had known about the plague. Only two endings would have played fair with the premise (and the reader): either the scientists discover effective countermeasures (which might have been unconvincing) or humanity is wiped out (which might have been too grim for popularity). Two novels which did not shrink from the consequences of their premises are Nevil Shute's *On the Beach* and John Christopher's *No Blade of Grass.*

Another science fiction expedient is to tell the reader something that is incomplete or untrue. An example of this approach is Jack Williamson's *The Humanoids*, an otherwise admirable novel which tackled a major theme and an impossible problem. The origin of the novel is instructive: Williamson submitted to John W. Campbell, editor of *Astounding Science Fiction*, a beautifully conceived and delicately crafted novelette entitled "With Folded Hands . . . ," which was based upon the creation of the ultimate robot (that Platonic Ideal) called a "humanoid." The Prime Directive of the humanoids is "to serve, obey, and keep man from harm." Since they are an ultimate form of the machine, the humanoids, however benevolently, can do everything better than humans, including their arts, and they keep humans from handling dangerous objects or engaging in dangerous activities. When humans become frustrated, the humanoids remove their unhappiness by means of lobotomies. In the end the humans can do nothing but sit with folded hands.

In the ellipsis that followed the title of the novelette, Campbell saw a sequel, a novel that he persuaded Williamson to write entitled ". . . And Searching Mind." It begins with the same premise as "With Folded Hands . . ."

but concludes with humans discovering unique psychic abilities which they now can exploit to the greater glory of mankind. In effect, the author begins by saying that humanoids can do everything better than humans and ends with, "But I didn't mean *everything!*"

Other solutions of the inherent problem of the science fiction novel are the conversion of the problem into a special case which can be solved, or the elimination of a problem in novels which stress adventure, romance, mystery, intrigue, or mere description.

The structure of a science fiction novel, therefore, is almost always the same: 1) a suspenseful situation 2) rising through thrilling incidents to a shattering climax and 3) an anticlimax in a resolution which cannot ultimately resolve. Even those novels which do not dare the impossible, which do not risk a major theme, suffer from the same inevitable pattern of excitement, suspense, and letdown. The science fiction novel starts too high and builds even higher: when what is at stake is racial survival or the fate of galaxies, a society, a nation, a city, or even customs, traditions, or beliefs, the fate of any single individual or group is of relative insignificance.

The science fiction novelette, on the other hand, can reduce its scale to the manageable. Length does not compel it to resolve its themes; the novelette—and its reader—is satisfied with the problem dramatized, not solved. The single case stands for many.

I distinguish between the science fiction novelette and the short story because the short story is too short to encompass an entirely new world. Some science fiction short stories succeed, and succeed magnificently, but those that do depart from the here and now only in small ways; usually the stories take place in our time and involve only a single intrusion of the strange. Only a few can provide greater separation without resort to special conventions which rely on an experience of the reader outside the scope of the particular story.

I include the short novel or novella within my ideal length, although the story that extends much beyond thirty-thousand words begins to assume some of the same obligations—and problems—as the novel.

As a small proof of these controversial statements, let me suggest that the reader pick up a good anthology—I recommend the *Science Fiction Hall of Fame*, particularly the second volume (published, to make confusion total, in two volumes, A and B) which contains only novelettes and short novels. These stories say in fewer and more effective words what the novels cannot say in many. The best novelettes do not develop from smaller ideas than novels. Most are novel-sized ideas distilled into purer form. In the *Science Fiction Hall of Fame, Volume Two*, for instance, the reader will find such classic novelettes as Poul Anderson's "Call Me Joe," John W. Campbell's "Who Goes There?" Robert Heinlein's "Universe," C. M. Kornbluth's "The Marching Morons," Lawrence O'Donnell's "Vintage Season," Eric Frank Russell's ". . . And Then There Were None," Cordwainer Smith's "The Ballad of Lost C'Mell," H. G. Wells' "The Time Machine," Isaac Asimov's "The Martian Way," Theodore Cogswell's "The Spectre General," E. M. Forster's "The Machine Stops," Frederik Pohl's "The Midas Plague," James H. Schmitz's "The Witches of Karres," T. L. Sherred's "E for Effort," Clifford D. Simak's "The Big Front Yard," and Jack Vance's "The Moon Moth." Where in the entire literature of science fiction will one find novels to equal these?

In the same book, incidentally, the reader also will find Lester del Rey's "Nerves," Theodore Sturgeon's "Baby Is Three," Jack Williamson's "With Folded Hands . . . ," James Blish's "Earthman, Come Home," Algis Budrys'

"Rogue Moon," and Wilmar Shiras' "In Hiding." All of these were developed, in one way or another, into novels— and all of the novels were less satisfying, in one way or another, than the novelettes or short novels from which they were developed.

Why, then, does anyone write science fiction novels?

A variety of reasons can be offered, some of them economic, some, artistic. To dispose first of the economic, science fiction traditionally has paid for its stories by the word, and words in a novel come much easier than a comparable number of words in novelettes; and a novel published in book form has a chance of making a great deal more money. Second, the novel is the more glamorous publication: it exists alone, when it is published in a book, and leans on nothing else; it is a single monument to an author's intention and accomplishment. Third, aside from the intrinsic merits of the various lengths, readers prefer novels to shorter stories; most readers wish to immerse themselves in an imaginary world for several hours rather than be forced back to cold reality in half an hour or an hour. My two sons, for instance, were reading science fiction novels long before they could be persuaded to read an anthology of the best short fiction, much less a magazine. As a consequence, serials almost always rank higher than short stories in magazine readership polls. Fourth, as a result of reasons two and three, the reputations and careers of writers are built more rapidly on novels than on shorter stories. The writers of shorter fiction have difficulty reaching the eminence that novelists have thrust upon them. In the fantasy field, for instance, John Collier and H. P. Lovecraft were writing marvelous short stories for years before they were recognized, and the same could be said, in science fiction, for Henry Kuttner and C. L. Moore, Theodore Sturgeon, Cordwainer Smith, and Harlan Ellison. Sturgeon, A. E. Van Vogt, and Robert Heinlein were writing magnificent short stories and novelettes in 1940 and 1941, but Van Vogt also wrote *Slan* and Heinlein wrote *If This Goes On . . . , Methuselah's Children,* and *Beyond This Horizon.*

I was aware of most or all of these arguments for the shorter lengths back in the early Fifties, when I was writing full-time. My convictions were reinforced by the fact that I had written two novels which had not been serialized in magazines and had done poorly in hardcovers. Part of the reason they had not done well could have been the times (no science fiction novels were selling many copies, with the possible exception of juveniles), part, the financial predicament of the publisher; but whatever the reasons the conclusions were clear: if I hoped to be a successful freelance writer I needed to be assured of magazine publication. (From this I derived Gunn's first law for freelance writers: nothing is worth writing if you can't use it at least twice.) When I got a novel-sized idea, I thought of how I could break it into smaller segments which, I felt sure, I could sell to the magazines and later bring together in book form if I was lucky.

A novelette can be developed into a novel in several ways. It can be expanded—I do not use the word "padded," although sometimes it might be appropriate. Usually a novelette is expanded by developing characters and incidents more fully, and by inventing additional incidents. "Rogue Moon" was expanded into a novel in this way, as was Daniel Keyes' "Flowers for Algernon" (available in the *Science Fiction Hall of Fame*), which won a Hugo Award as a short story and a Nebula Award as a novel, and Lester del Rey's "Nerves." A novel can be extrapolated from a novelette, as in the case of *The Humanoids,* or extended with additional stories as was "Earthman, Come Home" (as well as Blish's "A Case of Conscience" and "Surface Tension") and Shiras' "In Hiding" and Sturgeon's "Baby Is Three."

I have the feeling (I could be wrong) that most of these novels were afterthoughts, the result of having written a superlative story and then recognizing its book-length potential. Not in my case: not only was I convinced that the best length for science fiction was the novelette and that the way to obtain the greatest immediate return (not, perhaps, the greatest final return) on my investment of time and thought was by writing the shorter form, but I felt that a novel-length idea treated in this way made possible artistic effects not available to the novel.

(I remember my first editor at Bantam, Dick Roberts, asking me if I thought *The Joy Makers* might be published as a novel, and I said, a bit amazed, "But it is a novel! The characters may change and it may extend over some two centuries, but the hero continues throughout the book—and the hero is an idea: the science of happiness.")

I would not be forced, I thought, to provide any specious solutions to any eternal problems. I could deal with an idea over a considerable span of time and over the lifetimes of several characters. I could dramatize, show the impact of the idea on individual lives, show how it works out for them, and allow the idea itself to complete its destiny, clarified but unresolved, after the book has ended.

I have written five novels in this fashion: *Station in Space, The Joy Makers, The Immortals, The Burning,* and *The Listeners.* They are novels of ideas in which the idea itself is hero: the conquest of space and the ordeals and sacrifices it will require, in *Station in Space*; the science of happiness, in *The Joy Makers*; the implications of immortality, in *The Immortals*; the interrelationship between laymen and the scientists who are beginning to control their lives and shape their futures, in *The Burning*; the difficulties of communication, particularly in the search for intelligent life on other worlds, in *The Listeners.*

The four stories in this book are the beginnings or the

hearts of three novels. "The Cave of Night" was the story that began *Station in Space*. It was published in 1955, and events have dated its projections and proved me a poor prophet: the first satellite was not American but Russia's *Sputnik* in 1957, and the first manned spaceship was Russian, Vostok I, which carried Yuri A. Gargarin into orbit on April 12, 1961, and set a record for dating a book (*Station in Space* was published by Bantam Books in 1958) less than three years after publication. And yet perhaps my prophecy was not all that bad: the American launchings did take place on the east coast of Florida at Cape Canaveral (near Cocoa, Florida), rumors of Russian cosmonauts dying in orbit or possibly not going up at all floated around, and when John Glenn made his first orbital flight on February 20, 1962, the city of Perth, Australia, turned its lights on and off to signal its good wishes (my wife called me—I had gone to work after watching the capsule safely into orbit—and said, "Somebody's been reading 'The Cave of Night' ").

"The Hedonist" is the central portion of *The Joy Makers*, the novella in which is most thoroughly brought out the nature of "hedonism"—the science of happiness—and its inherent conflicts. I got the idea from the *Encyclopedia Britannica*—people are always asking me where I get my ideas (usually, less tactfully, "where do you get those crazy ideas?") and this is the example I often give because I can trace it accurately. I was doing research for another story, and I looked up the *Britannica* article about "Feeling." It was a fascinating piece which analyzed the various ways to be happy: modify, substitute, anticipate, daydream, and delude on one side, and devalue, project, and suppress on the other. One can be happy, that is, by getting what one wants—or by wanting what one gets. The article ended with the statement—like waving a red flag in front of a science fiction writer—"but the true science of applied hedonics is not yet born." Ah, I began to imagine, what if there were a science of happiness so that we could seek happiness directly rather than through the various surrogates we think will make us happy, such as love, fame, success, money. . . .

"New Blood" and "The Medic" are the first and third sections of *The Immortals.* In "New Blood" the reader will meet the Immortal man, a mutation whose blood and circulatory system is improved, whose cells do not age and die, who may live forever, and whose blood can rejuvenate older persons—only there's a catch. In "Medic" the reader will see the result of those facts, a world in which the search for longer life, for immortality, has become obsessive and has warped society into something nobody wanted.

I do not present these stories as proof for my argument that science fiction is at its best in the novelette (I have tried to do that with my other examples), but these stories have been successful. All of them were originally printed in magazines ("The Cave of Night" was included in a best-of-the-year collection), and provided key portions of books which together have sold more than half a million copies in this country and more copies have been sold abroad in translation. Moreover, they have seemed unusually appealing to other media: "The Cave of Night" was dramatized over NBC's "X Minus One" radio series and as "Man in Orbit" with Lee Marvin and E. G. Marshall on television's Desilu Playhouse in 1959; *The Immortals* was dramatized under the title of "The Immortal" as the second ABC-TV Movie of the Week in 1969 and became an hour-long series (alas, short-lived) the following season, with Christopher George; and *The Joy Makers* has attracted the attention of at least three different motion picture producers.

These stories share a common concept: man has dreamed for centuries about space flight, about happiness, about immortality. "If only I could fly to the moon!" he has told himself, "if only I could find true happiness, if only I could live forever . . . then I would be like a god." These stories, however, go on to demonstrate that every dream come true brings unforeseen consequences. The power of man to dream and make his dreams come true is unlimited, but each step forward must be paid for, there is no such thing as a free lunch, and some dreams are nightmares.

James Gunn
Lawrence, Kansas

THE
CAVE
OF
NIGHT

THE PHRASE WAS FIRST used by a poet disguised in the cynical hide of a newspaper reporter. It appeared on the first day and was widely reprinted. He wrote:

"At eight o'clock, after the Sun has set and the sky is darkening, look up! There's a man up there where no man has ever been.

"He is lost in the cave of night . . ."

The headlines demanded something short, vigorous and descriptive. That was it. It was inaccurate, but it stuck.

If anybody was in a cave, it was the rest of humanity. Painfully, triumphantly, one man had climbed out. Now he couldn't find his way back into the cave with the rest of us.

What goes up doesn't always come back down.

That was the first day. After it came twenty-nine days of agonized suspense.

The cave of night. I wish the phrase had been mine.

That was it, the tag, the symbol. It was the first thing a man saw when he glanced at the newspaper. It was the way people talked about it: "What's the latest about the cave?" It summed it all up, the drama, the anxiety, the hope.

Maybe it was the Floyd Collins influence. The papers dug up their files on that old tragedy, reminiscing, comparing; and they remembered the little girl—Kathy Fiscus, wasn't it?—who was trapped in that abandoned, California drain pipe; and a number of others.

Periodically, it happens, a sequence of events so accidentally dramatic that men lose their hatreds, their terrors, their shynesses, their inadequacies, and the human race momentarily recognizes its kinship.

The essential ingredients are these: A person must be in unusual and desperate peril. The peril must have duration. There must be proof that the person is still alive. Rescue attempts must be made. Publicity must be widespread.

One could probably be constructed artificially, but if the world ever discovered the fraud, it would never forgive.

Like many others, I have tried to analyze what makes a niggling, squabbling, callous race of beings suddenly share that most human emotion of sympathy, and, like them, I have not succeeded. Suddenly a distant stranger will mean more than their own comfort. Every waking moment, they pray: Live, Floyd! Live, Kathy! Live, Rev!

We pass on the street, we who would not have nodded, and ask, "Will they get there in time?"

Optimists and pessimists alike, we hope so. We all hope so.

In a sense, this one was different. This was purposeful. Knowing the risk, accepting it because there was no other way to do what had to be done, Rev had gone into the cave of night. The accident was that he could not return.

The news came out of nowhere—literally—to an unsuspecting world. The earliest mention the historians have been able to locate was an item about a ham radio operator in Davenport, Iowa. He picked up a distress signal on a sticky-hot June evening.

The message, he said later, seemed to fade in, reach a peak, and fade out:

". . . and fuel tanks empty.—ceiver broke . . . transmitting in clear so someone can pick this up, and . . . no way to get back . . . stuck . . ."

A small enough beginning.

The next message was received by a military base radio

watch near Fairbanks, Alaska. That was early in the morning. Half an hour later, a night-shift worker in Boston heard something on his short-wave set that sent him rushing to the telephone.

That morning the whole world learned the story. It broke over them, a wave of excitement and concern. Orbiting 1,075 miles above their heads was a man, an officer of the United States Air Force, in a fuelless spaceship.

All by itself, the spaceship part would have captured the world's attention. It was achievement as monumental as anything Man has ever done and far more spectacular. It was liberation from the tyranny of Earth, this jealous mother who had bound her children tight with the apron strings of gravity.

Man was free. It was a symbol that nothing is completely and finally impossible if Man wants it hard enough and long enough.

There are regions that humanity finds peculiarly congenial. Like all Earth's creatures, Man is a product and a victim of environment. His triumph is that the slave became the master. Unlike more specialized animals, he distributed himself across the entire surface of the Earth, from the frozen Antarctic continent to the Arctic icecap.

Man became an equatorial animal, a temperate zone animal, an arctic animal. He became a plain dweller, a valley dweller, a mountain dweller. The swamp and the desert became equally his home.

Man made his own environment.

With his inventive mind and his dexterous hands, he fashioned it, conquered cold and heat, dampness, aridness, land, sea, air. Now, with his science, he had conquered everything. He had become independent of the world that bore him.

It was a birthday cake for all mankind, celebrating its coming of age.

Brutally, the disaster was icing on the cake.

But it was more, too. When everything is considered, perhaps it was the aspect that, for a few, brief days, united humanity and made possible what we did.

It was a sign: Man is never completely independent of Earth; he carries with him his environment; he is always and forever a part of humanity. It was a conquest mellowed by a confession of mortality and error.

It was a statement: Man has within him the qualities of greatness that will never accept the restraints of circumstance, and yet he carries, too, the seeds of fallibility that we all recognize in ourselves.

Rev was one of us. His triumph was our triumph; his peril—more fully and finely—was our peril.

Reverdy L. McMillen, III, first lieutenant, U.S.A.F. Pilot. Rocket jockey. Man. Rev. He was only a thousand miles away, calling for help, but those miles were straight up. We got to know him as well as any member of our own family.

The news came as a great personal shock to me. I knew Rev. We had become good friends in college, and fortune had thrown us together in the Air Force, a writer and a pilot. I had got out as soon as possible, but Rev had stayed in. I knew, vaguely, that he had been testing rocket-powered airplanes with Chuck Yeager. But I had no idea that the rocket program was that close to space.

Nobody did. It was a better-kept secret than the Manhattan Project.

I remember staring at Rev's picture in the evening newspaper—the straight black hair, the thin, rakish mustache, the Clark Gable ears, the reckless, rueful grin—and I felt again, like a physical thing, his great joy in living. It expressed itself in a hundred ways. He loved widely, but with discrimination. He ate well, drank heartily, reveled in expert jazz and artistic inventiveness, and talked incessantly.

Now he was alone and soon all that might be extinguished. I told myself that I would help.

That was a time of wild enthusiasm. Men mobbed the Air Force Proving Grounds at Cocoa, Florida, wildly volunteering their services. But I was no engineer. I wasn't even a welder or a riveter. At best, I was only a poor word mechanic.

But words, at least, I could contribute.

I made a hasty verbal agreement with a local paper and caught the first plane to Washington, D.C. For a long time I liked to think that what I wrote during the next few days had something to do with subsequent events, for many of my articles were picked up for reprint by other newspapers.

The Washington fiasco was the responsibility of the Senate Investigating Committee. It subpoenaed everybody in sight—which effectively removed them from the vital work they were doing. But within a day, the Committee realized that it had bitten off a bite it could neither swallow nor spit out.

General Beauregard Finch, head of the research and development program, was the tough morsel the Committee gagged on. Coldly, accurately, he described the development of the project, the scientific and technical research, the tests, the building of the ship, the training of the prospective crewmen, and the winnowing of the volunteers down to one man.

In words more eloquent because of their clipped precision, he described the takeoff of the giant three-stage ship, shoved upward on a lengthening arm of combining hydrazine and nitric acid. Within fifty-six minutes, the remaining third stage had reached its orbital height of 1,075 miles.

It had coasted there. In order to maintain that orbit, the motors had to flicker on for fifteen seconds.

At that moment, disaster laughed at Man's careful calculations.

Before Rev could override the automatics, the motors had flamed for almost half a minute. The fuel he had depended upon to slow the ship so that it would drop, re-enter the atmosphere and be reclaimed by Earth was almost gone. His efforts to counteract the excess speed resulted only in an approximation of the original orbit.

The fact was this: Rev was up there. He would stay there until someone came and got him.

And there was no way to get there.

The Committee took that as an admission of guilt and incompetence; they tried to lever themselves free with it, but General Finch was not to be intimidated. A manned ship had been sent up because no mechanical or electronic computer could contain the vast possibilities for decision and action built into a human being.

The original computer was still the best all-purpose computer.

There had been only one ship built, true. But there was good reason for that, a completely practical reason—money.

Leaders are, by definition, ahead of the people. But this wasn't a field in which they could show the way and wait for the people to follow. This was no expedition in ancient ships, no light exploring party, no pilot-plant operation. Like a parachute jump, it had to be successful the first time.

This was an enterprise into new, expensive fields. It demanded money (billions of dollars), brains (the best available), and the hard, dedicated labor of men (thousands of them).

General Finch became a national hero that afternoon. He said, in bold words, "With the limited funds you gave us, we have done what we set out to do. We have demonstrated that space flight is possible, that a space platform is feasible.

"If there is any inefficiency, if there is any blame for what has happened, it lies at the door of those who lacked confidence in the courage and ability of their countrymen to fight free of Earth to the greatest glory. Senator, how did you vote on that?"

But I am not writing a history. The shelves are full of them. I will touch on the international repercussions only enough to show that the event was no more a respecter of national boundaries than was Rev's orbiting ship.

The orbit was almost perpendicular to the equator. The ship traveled as far north as Nome, as far south as Little America on the Antarctic continent. It completed one giant circle every two hours. Meanwhile, the Earth rotated beneath. If the ship had been equipped with adequate optical instruments, Rev could have observed every spot on Earth within twenty-four hours. He could have seen fleets and their dispositions, aircraft carriers and the planes taking off their decks, troop maneuvers.

In the General Assembly of the United Nations, the Russian ambassador protested this unwarranted and illegal violation of its national boundaries. He hinted darkly that it would not be allowed to continue. The U.S.S.R. had not been caught unprepared, he said. If the violation went on—*"every few hours!"*—drastic steps would be taken.

World opinion reared up in indignation. The U.S.S.R. immediately retreated and pretended, as only it could, that its belligerence had been an unwarranted inference and that it had never said anything of the sort, anyway.

This was not a military observer above our heads. It was a man who would soon be dead unless help reached him.

A world offered what it had. Even the U.S.S.R. announced that it was outfitting a rescue ship, since its space program was already on the verge of success. And the American public responded with more than a billion dollars within a week. Congress appropriated another billion. Thousands of men and women volunteered.

The race began.

Would the rescue party reach the ship in time? The world prayed.

And it listened daily to the voice of a man it hoped to buy back from death.

The problem shaped up like this:

The trip had been planned to last for only a few days. By careful rationing, the food and water might be stretched out for more than a month, but the oxygen, by cutting down activity to conserve it, couldn't possibly last more than thirty days. That was the absolute outside limit.

I remember reading the carefully detailed calculations in the paper and studying them for some hopeful error. There was none.

Within a few hours, the discarded first stage of the ship had been located floating in the Atlantic Ocean. It was towed back to Cocoa, Florida. Almost a week was needed to find and return to the Proving Grounds the second stage, which had landed 906 miles away.

Both sections were practically undamaged; their fall had been cushioned by ribbon parachute. They could be cleaned, repaired and used again. The trouble was the vital third stage—the nose section. A new one had to be designed and built within a month.

Space-madness became a new form of hysteria. We read statistics, we memorized insignificant details, we studied diagrams, we learned the risks and the dangers and how they would be met and conquered. It all became part of us. We watched the slow progress of the second ship and silently, tautly, urged it upward.

The schedule overhead became part of everyone's daily life. Work stopped while people rushed to windows or outside or to their television sets, hoping for a glimpse, a glint from the high, swift ship, so near, so untouchably far.

And we listened to the voice from the cave of night:

"I've been staring out the portholes. I never tire of that. Through the one on the right, I see what looks like a black velvet curtain with a strong light behind it. There are pinpoint holes in the curtain and the light shines through, not winking the way stars do, but steady. There's no air up here. That's the reason. The mind can understand and still misinterpret.

"My air is holding out better than I expected. By my figures, it should last twenty-seven days more. I shouldn't use so much of it talking all the time, but it's hard to stop. Talking, I feel as if I'm still in touch with Earth, still one of you, even if I am way up here.

"Through the left-hand window is San Francisco Bay, looking like a dark, wandering arm extended by the ocean octopus. The city itself looks like a heap of diamonds with trails scattered from it. It glitters up cheerfully, an old friend. It misses me, it says. Hurry home, it says. It's gone now, out of sight. Good-by, Frisco!

"Do you hear me down there? Sometimes I wonder. You can't see me now. I'm in the Earth's shadow. You'll have to wait hours for the dawn. I'll have mine in a few minutes.

"You're all busy down there. I know that. If I know you, you're all worrying about me, working to get me down, forgetting everything else. You don't know what a feeling that is. I hope to Heaven you never have to, wonderful though it is.

"Too bad the receiver was broken, but if it had to be one or the other, I'm glad it was the transmitter that came through. There's only one of me. There are billions of you to talk to.

"I wish there were some way I could be sure you were hearing me. Just that one thing might keep me from going crazy."

Rev, you were one in millions. We read all about your

selection, your training. You were our representative, picked with our greatest skill.

Out of a thousand who passed the initial rigid requirements for education, physical and emotional condition and age, only five could qualify for space. They couldn't be too tall, too stout, too young, too old. Medical and psychiatric tests weeded them out.

One of the training machines—Lord, how we studied this—reproduces the acceleration strains of a blasting rocket. Another trains men for maneuvering in the weightlessness of space. A third duplicates the cramped, sealed conditions of a spaceship cabin. Out of the final five, you were the only one who qualified.

No, Rev, if any of us could stay sane, it was you.

There were thousands of suggestions, almost all of them useless. Psychologists suggested self-hypnotism; cultists suggested yoga. One man sent in a detailed sketch of a giant electromagnet with which Rev's ship could be drawn back to Earth.

General Finch had the only practical idea. He outlined a plan for letting Rev know that we were listening. He picked out Kansas City and set the time. "Midnight," he said. "On the dot. Not a minute earlier or later. At that moment, he'll be right overhead."

And at midnight, every light in the city went out and came back on and went out and came back on again.

For a few awful moments, we wondered if the man up there in the cave of night had seen. Then came the voice we knew now so well that it seemed it had always been with us, a part of us, our dreams and our waking.

The voice was husky with emotion:

"Thanks . . . Thanks for listening. Thanks, Kansas City. I saw you winking at me. I'm not alone. I know that now. I'll never forget. Thanks."

And silence then as the ship fell below the horizon. We

pictured it to ourselves sometimes, continually circling the Earth, its trajectory exactly matching the curvature of the globe beneath it. We wondered if it would ever stop.

Like the Moon, would it be a satellite of the Earth forever?

We went through our daily chores like automatons while we watched the third stage of the rocket take shape. We raced against a dwindling air supply, and death raced to catch a ship moving at 15,800 miles per hour.

We watched the ship grow. On our television screens, we saw the construction of the cellular fuel tanks, the rocket motors, and the fantastic multitude of pumps, valves, gauges, switches, circuits, transistors, and tubes.

The personnel space was built to carry five men instead of one man. We watched it develop, a Spartan simplicity in the middle of the great complex, and it was as if we ourselves would live there, would watch those dials and instruments, would grip those chair-arm controls for the infinitesimal sign that the automatic pilot had faltered, would feel the soft flesh and the softer internal organs being wrenched away from the unyielding bone, and would hurtle upward into the cave of night.

We watched the plating wrap itself protectively around the vitals of the nose section. The wings were attached; they would make the ship a huge, metal glider in its unpowered descent to Earth after the job was done.

We met the men who would man the ship. We grew to know them as we watched them train, saw them fighting artificial gravities, testing spacesuits in simulated vacuums, practicing maneuvers in the weightless condition of free fall.

That was what we lived for.

And we listened to the voice that came to us out of the night:

"Twenty-one days. Three weeks. Seems like more. Feel a little sluggish, but there's no room for exercise in a coffin.

The concentrated foods I've been eating are fine, but not for a steady diet. Oh, what I'd give for a piece of home-baked apple pie!

"The weightlessness got me at first. Felt I was sitting on a ball that was spinning in all directions at once. Lost my breakfast a couple of times before I learned to stare at one thing. As long as you don't let your eyes roam, you're okay.

"There's Lake Michigan! My God, but it's blue today! Dazzles the eyes! There's Milwaukee, and how are the Braves doing? It must be a hot day in Chicago. It's a little muggy up here, too. The water absorbers must be overloaded.

"The air smells funny, but I'm not surprised. I must smell funny, too, after twenty-one days without a bath. Wish I could have one. There are an awful lot of things I used to take for granted and suddenly want more than—

"Forget that, will you? Don't worry about me. I'm fine. I know you're working to get me down. If you don't succeed, that's okay with me. My life wouldn't just be wasted. I've done what I've always wanted to do. I'd do it again.

"Too bad, though, that we only had the money for one ship."

And again: "An hour ago, I saw the Sun rise over Russia. It looks like any other land from here, green where it should be green, farther north a sort of mud color, and then white where the snow is still deep.

"Up here, you wonder why we're so different when the land is the same. You think: we're all children of the same mother planet. Who says we're different?

"Think I'm crazy? Maybe you're right. It doesn't matter much what I say as long as I say something. This is one time I won't be interrupted. Did any man ever have such an audience?"

No, Rev. Never.

The voice from above, historical now, preserved:

"I guess the gadgets are all right. You slide-rule mechanics! You test-tube artists! You finding what you want? Getting the dope on cosmic rays, meteoric dust, those islands you could never map, the cloud formations, wind movements, all the weather data? Hope the telemetering gauges are working. They're more important than my voice."

I don't think so, Rev. But we got the data. We built some of it into the new ships. *Ships*, not *ship*, for we didn't stop with one. Before we were finished, we had two complete three-stagers and a dozen nose sections.

The voice: "Air's bad tonight. Can't seem to get a full breath. Sticks in the lungs. Doesn't matter, though. I wish you could all see what I have seen, the vast-spreading universe around Earth, like a bride in a soft veil. You'd know then that we belong out here."

We know, Rev. You led us out. You showed us the way.

We listened and we watched. It seems to me now that we held our breath for thirty days.

At last we watched the fuel pumping into the ship—nitric acid and hydrazine. A month ago, we did not know their names; now we recognize them as the very substances of life itself. It flowed through the long special hoses, dangerous, cautiously grounded, over half a million dollars' worth of rocket fuel.

Statisticians estimate that more than a hundred million Americans were watching their television sets that day. Watching and praying.

Suddenly the view switched to the ship fleeing south above us. The technicians were expert now. The telescopes picked it up instantly, the focus perfect the first time, and tracked it across the sky until it dropped beyond the horizon. It looked no different now than when we had seen it first.

But the voice that came from our speakers was different.

It was weak. It coughed frequently and paused for breath.

"Air very bad. Better hurry. Can't last much longer . . . Silly! . . . Of course you'll hurry.

"Don't want anyone feeling sorry for me . . . I've been living fast . . . Thirty days? I've seen 360 sunrises, 360 sunsets . . . I've seen what no man has ever seen before . . . I was the first. That's something . . . worth dying for . . .

"I've seen the stars, clear and undiminished. They look cold, but there's warmth to them and life. They have families of planets like our own Sun, some of them . . . They must. God wouldn't put them there for no purpose . . . They can be homes to our future generations. Or, if they have inhabitants, we can trade with them: goods, ideas, the love of creation . . .

"But—more than this—I have seen the Earth. I have seen it—as no man has ever seen it—turning below me like a fantastic ball, the seas like blue glass in the Sun . . . or lashed into gray storm-peaks . . . and the land green with life . . . the cities of the world in the night, sparkling . . . and the people . . .

"I have seen the Earth—there where I have lived and loved . . . I have known it better than any man and loved it better and known its children better . . . It has been good . . .

"Good-by . . . I have a better tomb than the greatest conqueror Earth ever bore . . . Do not disturb . . ."

We wept. How could we help it?

Rescue was so close and we could not hurry it. We watched impotently. The crew were hoisted far up into the nose section of the three-stage rocket. It stood as tall as a 24-story building. *Hurry!* we urged. But they could not hurry. The interception of a swiftly moving target is precision business. The takeoff was all calculated and impressed on the metal and glass and free electrons of an electronic computer.

The ship was tightened down methodically. The spectators scurried back from the base of the ship. We waited. The ship waited. Tall and slim as it was, it seemed to crouch. Someone counted off the seconds to a breathless world: ten—nine—eight . . . five, four, three . . . one—*fire!*

There was no flame, and then we saw it spurting into the air from the exhaust tunnel several hundred feet away. The ship balanced, unmoving, on a squat column of incandescence; the column stretched itself, grew tall; the huge ship picked up speed and dwindled into a point of brightness.

The telescopic lenses found it, lost it, found it again. It arched over on its side and thrust itself seaward. At the end of 84 seconds, the rear jets faltered, and our hearts faltered with them. Then we saw that the first stage had been dropped. The rest of the ship moved off on a new fiery trail. A ring-shaped ribbon parachute blossomed out of the third stage and slowed it rapidly.

The second stage dropped away 124 seconds later. The nose section, with its human cargo, its rescue equipment, went on alone. At 63 miles altitude, the flaring exhaust cut out. The third stage would coast up the gravitational hill more than a thousand miles.

Our stomachs were knotted with dread as the rescue ship disappeared beyond the horizon of the farthest television camera. By this time, it was on the other side of the world, speeding toward a carefully planned rendezvous with its sister.

Hang on, Rev! Don't give up!

Fifty-six minutes. That was how long we had to wait. Fifty-six minutes from the takeoff until the ship was in its orbit. After that, the party would need time to match speeds, to send a space-suited crewman drifting across the emptiness between, over the vast, eerily turning sphere of the Earth beneath.

In imagination, we followed them.

Minutes would be lost while the rescuer clung to the ship, opened the airlock cautiously so that none of the precious remnants of air would be lost, and passed into the ship where one man had known utter loneliness.

We waited. We hoped.

Fifty-six minutes. They passed. An hour. Thirty minutes more. We reminded ourselves—and were reminded—that the first concern was Rev. It might be hours before we would get any real news.

The tension mounted unbearably. We waited—a nation, a world—for relief.

At eighteen minutes less than two hours—*too soon*, we told ourselves, lest we hope too much—we heard the voice of Captain Frank Pickrell, who was later to become the first commander of the *Doughnut*.

"I have just entered the ship," he said slowly. "The air-lock was open." He paused. The implications stunned our emotions; we listened mutely. "Lieutenant McMillen is dead. He died heroically, waiting until all hope was gone, until every oxygen gauge stood at zero. And then—well, the airlock was open when we arrived.

"In accordance with his own wishes, his body will be left here in its eternal orbit. This ship will be his tomb for all men to see when they look up toward the stars. As long as there are men on Earth, it will circle above them, an everlasting reminder of what men have done and what men can do.

"That was Lieutenant McMillen's hope. This he did not only as an American, but as a man, dying for all humanity, and all humanity can glory in it.

"From this moment, let this be his shrine, sacred to all the generations of spacemen, inviolate. And let it be a symbol that Man's dreams can be realized, but sometimes the price is steep.

"I am going to leave now. My feet will be the last to touch this deck. The oxygen I released is almost used up. Lieutenant McMillen is in his control chair, staring out toward the stars. I will leave the airlock doors open behind me. Let the airless, frigid arms of space protect and preserve for all eternity the man they would not let go."

Good-by, Rev! Farewell! Good night!

Rev was not long alone. He was the first, but not the last to receive a space burial and a hero's farewell.

This, as I said, is no history of the conquest of space. Every child knows the story as well as I and can identify the make of a spaceship more swiftly.

The story of the combined efforts that built the orbital platform irreverently called the *Doughnut* has been told by others. We have learned at length the political triumph that placed it under United Nations control.

Its contribution to our daily lives has received the accolade of the commonplace. It is an observatory, a laboratory, and a guardian. Startling discoveries have come out of that weightless, airless, heatless place. It has learned how weather is made and predicted it with incredible accuracy. It has observed the stars clear of the veil of the atmosphere. And it has insured our peace . . .

It has paid its way. No one can question that. It and its smaller relay stations made possible today's worldwide television and radio network. There is no place on Earth where a free voice cannot be heard or the face of freedom be seen. Sometimes we find ourselves wondering how it would have been any other way.

And we have had adventure. We have traveled to the dead gypsum seas of the Moon with the first exploration party. This year, we will solve the mysteries of Mars. From our armchairs, we will thrill to the discoveries of our pioneers—our stand-ins, so to speak. It has given us a common heritage, a common goal, and for the first time we are united.

This I mention only for background; no one will argue that the conquest of space was not of incalculable benefit to all mankind.

The whole thing came back to me recently, an overpowering flood of memory. I was skirting Times Square, where every face is a stranger's, and suddenly I stopped, incredulous.

"Rev!" I shouted.

The man kept on walking. He passed me without a glance. I turned around and stared after him. I started to run. I grabbed him by the arm. "Rev!" I said huskily, swinging him around. "Is it really you?"

The man smiled politely. "You must have mistaken me for someone else." He unclamped my fingers easily and moved away. I realized then 'that there were two men with him, one on each side. I felt their eyes on my face, memorizing it.

Probably it didn't mean anything. We all have our doubles. I could have been mistaken.

But it started me remembering and thinking.

The first thing the rocket experts had to consider was expense. They didn't have the money. The second thing was weight—even a medium-sized man is heavy when rocket payloads are reckoned, and the stores and equipment essential to his survival are many times heavier.

If Rev had escaped alive, why had they announced that he was dead? But I knew the question was all wrong.

If my speculations were right, Rev had never been up there at all. The essential payload was only a thirty-day recording and a transmitter. Even if the major feat of sending up a manned rocket was beyond their means and their techniques, they could send up that much.

Then they got the money; they got the volunteers and the techniques.

I suppose the telemetered reports from the rocket helped. But what they accomplished in thirty days was an unparalleled miracle.

The timing of the recording must have taken months of work; but the vital part of the scheme was secrecy. General Finch had to know and Captain—now Colonel—Pickrell. A few others—workmen, administrators—and Rev . . .

What could they do with him? Disguise him? Yes. And then hide him in the biggest city in the world. They would have done it that way.

It gave me a funny, sick kind of feeling, thinking about it. Like everybody else, I don't like to be taken in by a phony plea. And this was a fraud perpetrated on all humanity.

Yet it had led us to the planets. Perhaps it would lead us beyond, even to the stars. I asked myself: could they have done it any other way?

I would like to think I was mistaken. This myth has become part of us. We lived through it ourselves, helped make it. Someday, I tell myself, a spaceman whose reverence is greater than his obedience will make a pilgrimage to that swift shrine and find only an empty shell.

I shudder then.

This pulled us together. In a sense, it keeps us together. Nothing is more important than that.

I try to convince myself that I was mistaken. The straight black hair was gray at the temples now and cut much shorter. The mustache was gone. The Clark Gable ears were flat to the head; that's a simple operation, I understand.

But grins are hard to change. And anyone who lived through those thirty days will never forget that voice.

I think about Rev and the life he must have now, the things he loved and can never enjoy again, and I realize perhaps he made the greater sacrifice.

I think sometimes he must wish he were really in the cave of night, seated in that icy control chair 1,075 miles above, staring out at the stars.

THE
HEDONIST

I

Justice is the only worship.
Love is the only priest.
Ignorance is the only slavery.
Happiness is the only good.
The time to be happy is now,
The place to be happy is here,
The way to be happy is to make others so.

ROBERT GREEN INGERSOLL

hedonics (hē·dŏn'ĭks), *n.*; See -ICS. Psychomedical science
dealing with the nature and pursuit of happiness. . . .
hedonism (hē'dŏn·ĭz'm), *n.* **1.** *Ethics.* The doctrine that
pleasure is the only good in life and that moral duty is
fulfilled in the gratification of pleasure-seeking in-
stincts. . . .
hedonist (hē'dŏn·ĭst), *n.* **1.** One who lives in accordance
with hedonism; *i.e.*, for pleasure. **2.** (Since 2005) a
practitioner of hedonics. . . .

THE DAY BEGAN AS more than eight thousand days had begun
before.

"Wake up," it murmured sweetly in the Hedonist's ear.
"The sun is shining. It's a beautiful day. Wake up. Be
happy!"

The Hedonist rolled over and punched the pillow into
silence. He pried one eye open and peered out the long, low

25

window that formed one wall of his cottage. The smog billowed against it grayly like a fat, long-haired cat rolling at the Earth's feet, needle claws sheathed for the moment but ready to flash out and slash if the impulse struck.

So much for realism.

The Hedonist suppressed the thought automatically and sat up. Another day, another pleasure.

He glanced at the pillow beside his and the brown hair flung across it like a silk scarf. He sighed. It was time for that to end, too.

He flipped back the covers and brought his hand down smartly against the youthfully rounded bottom. It smacked satisfactorily. Beth turned over and sat up in one startled movement.

"What's the matter?" she spluttered.

His pajama tops were several sizes too big for her. They drifted down around her like a scarlet tent. She yawned and lifted her arms to rub her eyes. When she dropped them to her sides, the jacket bared one creamy shoulder and threatened to slide even farther.

A smile drifted across the Hedonist's lips. Sleep was so precious when you were young. There was never enough of it. There was never enough of anything. As you grew older you were more easily satisfied. He sighed again. That was a pity, too.

Sleepily, Beth caught the slipping jacket before it left her shoulders completely. "What's happened?" she said in the middle of a yawn.

"Time to get up," the Hedonist said gently. And, even gentler, "Time to go home."

"Home?" she said. She was suddenly awake.

"I'm certifying you today. You can get married whenever you and your fiancé can agree upon a date."

"But—" she began and stopped, wordless.

With the skill of long experience, the Hedonist studied

her face without revealing his interest. Beth's face, normally calm, was troubled. Even troubled, it was the most beautiful face in his ward. He had taken her under instruction with a joy that was not entirely professional. But so young, so young.

His memory, unbidden, offered him the date: February 23, 2035. A Thursday. He remembered it well. Three months ago she had been nineteen years old. He had presided at her birth; now he had prepared her for marriage. Through the nineteen years between he had guarded her happiness. It didn't sit well beside his fifty-three years.

"You still want to get married, don't you?" he asked.

"Oh, yes," she said, her dark eyes steady on his face.

"Then you have my blessing. I have done my best."

"I know," she said evenly.

"The man you're betrothed to—he's from another ward?"

"You know that," she said.

Yes, he knew. He knew everything that went on in the ward: the problems, the worries, the troubles, the sorrows. He knew everybody: their emotional quotients and what to expect from them and when, and how to treat them. . . . Sometimes he even knew their thoughts.

In this ward, he was—in a very real sense—divine. In his knowledge and his power over the lives and happiness of a thousand people, he was a god. But a god can know too much. Knowledge is a burden, and responsibility multiplied a thousand times is enough to bow the shoulders of an Atlas.

But the girl beside him was deep; he could sense that much, even if he couldn't touch bottom.

Touch bottom! The smile that flickered across his face was almost wry. He had touched that one for the last time.

"You must be gentle with him," the Hedonist said. "He may not have had your advantages."

She touched her soft lower lip with her teeth. "I will,"

she said softly. "If—I mean—when we get married, we'll come back here. If he needs treatment, I'll send him to you—"

The Hedonist shook his head. "That isn't wise. Girls are more adaptable than men. You could adjust to another hedonist, but your husband would have trouble. You must move to his ward."

She was silent, looking at him through a silken veil that had drifted down across her forehead.

"Remember," he said with an uneasiness he could not pin down, "your duty—your only duty—is happiness."

"Yes, Hedonist," she said obediently.

"Good-by, Beth," he said. "Be happy!"

He swung his legs over the edge of the bed and walked the three steps to the necessary with cautious dignity. It wasn't because he was fat, exactly, but fifty-three years had thickened him a little around the middle, and there is nothing aesthetic about a middle-aged man's naked back.

Besides, the Hedonist could sense that Beth was watching him.

The necessary door slid shut, and he was alone in the three-by-four foot cubicle. Fifteen minutes later he was ready for the new day and its demands upon him. His beard had been depilated; warm, detergent sprays had cleansed him; hot sprays had rinsed him; icy needles had jabbed his body into tingling awareness. Hot air blasts had dried him. And he was reluctant to leave the comfortable little room.

Womb-symbol? the Hedonist wondered.

He pressed the bottom button on the right. The lights shifted. One wall was suddenly a full-length mirror. The Hedonist looked at himself and frowned. He was not so thick after all. There was no fat on him; he was tall and well muscled. His close-cropped hair was still black, unfrosted.

His firm, definite face was unlined. He looked no older than an athletic thirty.

The last geriatric treatment had been even more successful than usual.

And yet there was something wrong. He had counted six distinct feelings of unpleasure since waking. And there was no reason for any of them.

Quickly, skillfully, he counted his blessings. In a golden age, he held one of the most responsible and rewarding positions possible. He knew his work; he did it well; he liked it. There wasn't the smallest reason for him to be unhappy. And yet he sighed.

As he accepted new underclothes from the dispenser and stuffed the transparent wrapper into the disposal, he told himself that the difference between Beth's age and his was obvious and irremediable. What did he want? A wife?

Nonsense! There was a logic behind the Inconstancy clause of the Hedonic Oath. *"As a hedonist, I shall not love nor wed nor father, but I shall keep my self intact for the proper performance of my duties. . . ."*

A hedonist could not permit himself to become emotionally involved with one person. To the extent of that involvement, his available emphathetic energy was diminished, and his carefully cultivated insight was impaired. The ward would suffer. His dependents would feel slighted. They would stop bringing their problems to him; and, even if they still came, the delicate relationship so vital to his work would be destroyed.

Publilius Syrus said it over two thousand years before: "A god could hardly love and be wise."

And yet— The Hedonist sighed. After ten years of the Institute's rigorous, specialized training and twenty-three years of practice, he still didn't understand the roots of his own unpleasures. How could he hope to treat the unpleasures of his dependents?

"Happiness is indivisible," he told himself sternly and concentrated on the devaluation of the desire.

By the time he had finished the hedonic exercise, his feeling for Beth was no different in kind or intensity than for any other girl in his ward. He felt once more—as he had felt so rapturously long ago—the exquisite beauty of hedonics.

When he came out of the necessary, Beth was gone. He felt a quick, cold sense of loss.

The bed had been lowered into the floor. It would have fresh sheets on it, he knew; Beth was a thoughtful girl. His desk and chair had swung out from one wall; from the wall opposite had come the comfortable diagnostic chair. The room had returned to its spacious daytime dimensions of twelve by twelve.

Devaluation and substitution soon took care of his absurd disappointment, and he realized, as he sublimated the emotion into professional enthusiasm, that he had forgotten to cut the cord cleanly and finally. It was always a delicate operation; he dreaded it. But it was vital to the therapy, and he had never actually forgotten it before.

The relationship between a hedonist and his patient is an unparalleled intimacy; transference is inevitable. And if the hedonist has his problems, the patient's problems are even more serious. And he does not have the hedonist's technical equipment and training for handling them. It was the hedonist's duty to break off the relationship cleanly when the therapy was finished.

He made a mental note to call Beth back.

II

It ought to be the happiness and glory of a representative to live in the strictest union, the closest correspondence, and the most unreserved communication with his constituents. Their wishes ought to have great weight with him; their opinion high respect; their business unremitted attention. It is his duty to sacrifice his repose, his pleasures, his satisfaction, to theirs; and above all, ever, and in all cases, to prefer their interests to his own.

EDMUND BURKE

Habit is a technique for simplifying existence, for saving time and the energy of decision. It is a pleasure tool.

As a creature of habit, the Hedonist had a standing order for breakfast. He pressed the top button on the wall beside the table. A panel slid up into the wall. His breakfast was in the cubicle behind it. It sat on a tray in covered plastic dishes. He drew the tray out upon the table and broke the plastic tab that held the lid on the juice glass. He drank the juice quickly; it was cold and good and acid, as usual.

It had been a good batch; Monsanto was proud of it, and they had a right to be.

The next dish steamed aromatically. The plankton cakes had a delicate shrimpy flavor the Hedonist always enjoyed. They were especially good fried in the new high-fat chlorella oil. He ate them slowly, savoring each bite.

While he ate, he flicked on the news. He punched the highly compressed channel; the words came rattling from the wall like the rare, accidental hail on his plastic roof. The film was compressed only a little, but the time-compression on the speech sometimes went as high as seventy per cent without audible distortion. He understood it as easily as ordinary speech, and there was little enough time, anyway, for everything that had to be done.

The Hedonic Index, which had registered only 85% at dawn (the depressing effect of the morning smog, the Hedonist thought), *had already risen to an acceptable 93% (breakfast), and was expected to go higher as the 0737 shower cleared the air.*

In the corner of the picture, the time was listed as 0736. The Hedonist stopped eating and lifted his head to listen. Over the announcer's voice came a slow, growing spatter of rain on the roof. The Hedonist nodded with satisfaction. Right on time. Through the window, he could see the smog melting away. That was the kind of efficiency that made government a solid, unobtrusive foundation for a nation's happiness.

The Hedonist remembered when some thought it hedonics' proudest achievement: "They made the rains done on time." Now it was a commonplace.

There would be sunshine all day, although the weather bureau had scheduled a brief shower for 1916, just at sunset, to clear the air once more. The temperature would be held steady at 85 degrees until dusk, when it would be allowed to drop to 70.

Interplanetary Authority announced the completion of a new ship in the yards adjoining the Old City port. (It gleamed like a jewel, the Hedonist thought, with the sunlight breaking through the clouds to sparkle in the diamond-drops of water the rain had left.) *The ship would be launched shortly when the emigration complement was filled. At the end of the three months' trip was Venus.*

The Hedonist smiled. *Shortly.* The ship would wait a long time there in the yards. How do you recruit emigrants from the promised land? Where do you find people who will trade peace and plenty and happiness for toil, starvation, and misery? Asylums, maybe, if there were any asylums left. But there weren't. There were few people left who were that crazy—at least in that way.

"The ship," the announcer rattled off, "has been named the Asylum."

The Hedonist started and relaxed, smiling. Someone had a sense of humor. Strangely enough, it was a rarity these days. Well, if that could be attributed to hedonics, it was a small price to pay for the tears that had vanished, too.

The culturing of a new mutation had increased chlorella production by 50%. The protein content of the new crop was high. Chlorelloaf would be on the menu in most wards for several days. Plankton would be more plentiful soon. The scooper fleet reported a layer of zooplankton which promised to be almost inexhaustible. Catch was already within the thousands of tons.

The Hedonist uncapped the Kafi and hoped the boats didn't syphon the sea clear of life. Alga was all right and the synthetics were efficient and often quite delicious, but the subtle flavor of once-living protein could not be cultured or brewed. On the other hand, he reflected, he could be thankful that he liked fish; some people didn't, and they had only the synthetics and the algae or an extensive reeducation therapy.

The latest Teleflush Index, in millions of gallons, placed the sensie LIFE CAN BE ECSTASY 11.7 ahead of ONE MAN'S HAPPINESS. . . .

The Hedonist stopped listening, instantly, completely, and lifted the Kafi cup to his lips. He had no time for the sensies and less inclination. Perhaps they had a certain therapeutic value in some cases, but as a general rule he considered them on the dangerous lower peak of imaginary gratification. They were daydreams made effortless.

He had suggested as much in a memorandum to the Council, but no doubt they were too busy for such minor matters.

The Hedonist shuddered and almost dropped the cup. For a month now, the Kafi had been bitter and acrid. Something had gone wrong in the last synthesis. He supposed the stock had been too great to dump, but he hoped that Du Pont would do better next time. And that next time would be soon.

He braced himself and drank it down without taking a breath. After all, the caffeine alkaloid was in it. It was the only stimulant he allowed himself, and he had a vague premonition he would need it before the day was over.

"The Hedonic Index," the announcer said with infectious joy, "has reached 95 per cent."

The Hedonist switched him off and shoved the soiled dishes into the cubicle and drew down the cover. The lunch menu flashed on, but he turned it off. He couldn't stand thinking about lunch so soon after eating. He would select something a little later when he wasn't so full, he told himself, but he knew he would be too busy. He would forget and be forced to accept the standard meal. Well, that was good enough, and he would be happy with it.

The wall square started blinking at him. A cheerful voice said, "Message for you. Message for you. Message—"

The Hedonist hit the ACCEPT button hastily. The square steadied and filled itself with letters, black on white:

TO: Hedonist, Ward 483
FROM: Hedonic Council, Area 1

You will report to Room 2943, Hedonic Council Building, Area 1, at 1634 for annual examination. Be prompt! Be happy!

You will report, the Hedonist repeated to himself as he brushed the message away with the automatic acknowledgment. The form was standard, and the message was clear enough. But his last examination had been less than six months ago. They wouldn't be recalling him so soon— would they?

There was something ominous about it. A sudden shiver ran down his spine. His adrenals began discharging their secretions into his bloodstream; in response, his heart beat quickened, the blood sugar level rose, the coagulability. . . .

The sensations weren't completely unpleasant. They stimulated him to a condition of awareness and excitation he hadn't experienced in years. But they were also dangerous.

Happiness is basic. Without that, all else is ashes.

The Hedonist suppressed it. He breathed deeply, sitting quietly relaxed. He damped his heart beat, soothed his adrenals. The Council waited to discuss his memorandum on the sensies, he told himself calmly. They stayed within the standard form for fear of endangering a whole day's happiness.

He suppressed the small voice that asked, "How could they forget that your last examination was so recent?"

When the adrenaline was satisfactorily dissipated, he slipped on a short-sleeved shirt and a comfortable pair of tan shorts and glanced down at the day's schedule. According to the microfilm memorandum projected on the desk, he had nothing listed after 1630. He picked up the stylus and scribbled across the desk: *1634—2943 HCB—a.e.*

He read it once, hesitated, and went back to underline the last two letters. He had no reason to be afraid of the examination; he had passed them all easily. There was no reason to let anxiety ruin his day. And with that underlineation the worry vanished.

If he allowed himself fifteen minutes for the twenty-five miles between his cottage and the Council Building, he would have to cancel Mrs. Merton's appointment. Well, it couldn't be helped. The Merton family quarrels would have to wait until Monday for their weekly airing.

It was certain the continual exchange of bickerings was a pleasure activity for both parties. He allowed Mrs. Merton to milk the last drops of emotion from it in his presence. He didn't approve of it, but he wasn't responsible for the warp, either. And, as a pleasure value, it didn't deserve the time necessary to straighten it out.

He flicked the MESSAGE button, scribbled a note to Mrs. Merton on the desk, and sent it off. The desk was clean again. He placed an order for a cab at 1615 and turned to the day's business.

Sara Walling. The Hedonist punched her number on the square of buttons under the edge of the desk. Her case history appeared in front of him, projected onto the desk in numbers, letters, and symbols, a meaningful, condensed description of twenty-seven years of a woman's life. The Hedonist nodded and wiped it away. His memory had been correct, but it was just as well not to depend on something fallible when a person's happiness was at stake.

It was 0800. The milky square on the outside of his door read: COME IN AND BE HAPPY. The door opened. Sara Walling stood there, her dark, thin face unhappy.

The Hedonist was up to greet her in one fluid motion that took him effortlessly the three steps to the door. He put his arm around her and caressed her fondly. "Joy, Sara! Come in, darling," he said gently. "Tell me all about it."

When she was sitting in the diagnostic chair, the Hedonist sat down at the desk and, cocking his head sympathetically, divided his attention between Sara and the desk-top readings.

At twenty-seven, she was a lean, sallow girl, an inch under average height at five feet nine. Her features weren't bad, but it was obvious that she was one of the least attractive girls in the ward. She was unmarried, and she had no lover. That was her problem. Or so she thought. The Hedonist knew, with a flash of guilt, that he had failed her.

From the readings flashed from the chair to his desk, the Hedonist put together another story, just as valid. Muscular contractions, pulse, blood pressure, breathing, volume of limb, but chiefly the electrical resistance of the body—often called the psychogalvanic reflex—gave him a running account of her emotional state. Balanced against her recorded emotional quotient, it was obvious what had happened.

The marriage aspect was only the culmination of several physiological and psychological tendencies which were themselves aggravated by the marriage aspect. . . . It was a vicious, cyclic tangle. He would have believed it impossible except that the constantly increasing demands on his time made periodic review of every dependent an ideal he was unable to realize. But now there was no time to be lost in the long but not hopeless task of untangling this girl's life.

"You have someone in mind, of course," he said.

"Yes," she admitted.

"Has he gone with you to the premarital cottage?"

"Once," she snapped.

"I see," the Hedonist said. It was a misfortune all the way around. He suppressed his empathy; the diagnosis was complete. "Have you any ideas for increasing your happiness?"

She hesitated. "Can't you make him love me?" she said quickly, hopefully. "Then I'd be happy and he'd be happy—"

"Is he unhappy now?" the Hedonist interrupted quietly.

"No-o-o," she sighed.

"Then I can't make him do anything," he pointed out. "You know that. The fact that your desires don't coincide with his is no grounds for compulsion. You're the one who's unhappy. You're the one who needs therapy."

"But that's the only thing that will make me happy!" she wailed.

The Hedonist shook his head slowly, pityingly. "We can't force life into the patterns we draw for it, and if we let our happiness depend on circumstance we doom ourselves to sorrow and despair. Happiness begins at home—inside. Didn't we teach you that?"

"I was taught," she groaned, her teeth clenched, "but it's so hard to learn, so hard to do."

"Have you tried the hedonic techniques?" the Hedonist asked. "Have you practiced suppression? Devaluation? Substitution?"

"I've tried," she moaned. "I've tried so hard. But it's no use. It's too—" She broke suddenly. The Hedonist was ready for it. He caught her against his shoulder and let her cry until the sobs had dwindled into sniffles.

"How long has it been," he asked gently, "since you've had a diagnosis?"

"I don't remember," she said in a muffled voice.

"A year," he said firmly. "You can afford a nickel every week. We're going to bring up your blood pressure, increase your thyroid, tone up your body generally—"

"Will that help?" she asked weakly.

" 'Life is swell when you feel well,' " the Hedonist quoted. "Even the ancients knew that. Humanity is a tangled thing. You haven't felt well. You've been depressed, moody. That has reacted on your relationships with other people. That, in turn, has increased your depression and created psychosomatic conditions. The free expression denied your emotions has fed your moods—those resonating echoes of the emotions. The spiral continues downward. Now we're going to start it back up."

Her thanks were almost incoherent.

"I'm certifying you for minor plastic surgery," the Hedonist added. He studied her drab gray skirt and blouse. "And we're going to get you out of those clothes and into something bright and revealing. Don't worry now. You're in my hands. You're going to be happy."

As he watched her leave, there was a shadow of wistfulness in his eyes. She was happy already. She had shed her burdens. He had picked them up.

The next patient was a man. He had a knife in his hand.

"You filthy kinsey!" he screamed and launched himself across the floor.

III

The world would be better and brighter if our teachers would dwell on the Duty of Happiness as well as on the Happiness of Duty, for we ought to be as cheerful as we can, if only because to be happy ourselves is a most effectual contribution to the happiness of others.

SIR JOHN LUBBOCK

For a fraction of a second, the Hedonist sat in his chair, frozen, watching the revelatory contortions of the man's face as he came close. For all his seeming speed, he approached with incredible slowness. The Hedonist had time for a dozen observations, a hundred thoughts.

He identified the man—Gomer Berns, sixty-two, recently married, a newcomer to the ward. He identified the flashing knife—an antique table instrument, honed down. He speculated about the expression and its probable motivation—

And he was out of his chair, moving with blurred speed, his hand catching the wrist of the hand that held the knife. As he caught it, he twisted. Something snapped. The knife clattered to the floor. Berns sprawled across the desk, unconscious.

The Hedonist bent to inspect the man. He heard a faint, whirring noise, but as he listened, it stopped. He frowned and continued his examination. The wrist was broken; geriatrics was not so successful with the bones. Outside of that, Berns was in good condition. He had fainted from the pain.

The Hedonist straightened up. His pulse was swift and dynamic. The world seemed sharp and vivid around him.

He felt immensely competent, immensely strong, immensely alive. There was no task too great for him.

He caught himself with a sharp thought. The exhilaration was being paid for by Berns. It wasn't worth the physical pain and the mental agony that had fathered it. His emotion was antisocial. He suppressed it quickly.

Effortlessly, he scooped up the body and propped it into the diagnostic chair. The chair straightened into a table. The Hedonist touched the under side of the edge toward him. The shadowy X ray of the broken wrist was projected onto the wall.

A slim, metal arm raised a horizontal half-cylinder over the edge of the table. It picked up the wrist. Gently, firmly, it drew the broken bones apart and fitted them back into position as the Hedonist watched the wall picture. A tiny hypodermic jet penetrated the skin above the break. On the wall, the line between the broken bones grew cloudy. A nozzle spun a short, tight plastic cocoon around the wrist. As the table tilted itself back into a chair, the arm retreated back into the chair's base.

The Hedonist glanced at his watch. Berns would have to wait. The case was serious. It demanded time—a lot of it—and the Hedonist didn't have the time to spare. In five minutes he was due at the school.

He touched the desk. Berns's head twitched a little as a hypodermic forced the anesthetic through the skin into the spinal column. Berns would have to sleep here until he got back.

Outside, the Hedonist looked back. The milky square on the door said:

THE HEDONIST IS OUT
IN REAL EMERGENCY
PUNCH WARD SCHOOL
(RRR 1764)

The Hedonist walked through his ward in the warm, clear springtime, enjoying the pleasant heat of the sunshine on his head and back, feeling a brief moment of contentment. The ward was a field of varicolored mushrooms set in a green meadow; each of the bubble houses had its small but precious lawn.

In the thirty-by-thirty vacant lot, the long-nosed house-blower was spraying plastic over a flat-topped balloon. Eliot Digby lolled lazily in the cab, glancing occasionally at the unwavering dials. As the Hedonist passed, Eliot looked up and waved happily.

The Hedonist smiled. By next week the new house would be ready for the Wayne couple. He would marry them the same day.

Basic School was a cluster of mushrooms in a bigger patch of green. When the Hedonist walked through the broad front door, the pretty ward nurse was waiting for him. The Hedonist smiled at her, thinking that the instruction of the boys was in capable hands.

"Joy," said the Hedonist.

"Joy," echoed the Nurse, but she looked anything but joyful. "We've had more trouble about the dispensers in the necessary."

"The neo-heroin?"

The Nurse nodded.

"How many children have bought it?" A frown slipped down over his face.

"None," she said quickly. "I put a recorder on the dispenser, just as you said, and only one syrette has been purchased. That was by the salesman himself. But he was here this morning complaining that someone was sabotaging his sales. He said he was going to take it to the Council."

The Hedonist shrugged. "If that's all—"

"But the Council has approved the manufacture and distribution," she went on anxiously. "And half the profits have been allocated to the Council. The Council has asked all the wards to co-operate, and we've been doing just the opposite—"

"The Council—the Council," the Hedonist chided. "The Council isn't some unfeeling, prehedonic bureau to be afraid of; it's made up of trained men, hedonists, bent only on increasing the available happiness. But it's not infallible. In this turn toward delusion, it has made a mistake. At the next Congress, the mistake will be corrected." He was about to move on when he turned back and asked, casually, "Did you recognize the salesman?"

She bent her forehead in despair. "I couldn't think of his name. But I'll remember it."

The Hedonist smiled; a poor memory was her greatest sorrow. "Remember: anxiety is the thief of happiness." He patted her fondly and turned toward the first class.

The morning's lessons were like a fairy tale turned upside down.

To the little ones, he said, ". . . And so the world lived happily ever after."

As he left the room, one little girl pressed against his leg and lifted up her shining face. "I love you, Hedonist," she whispered.

"I love you," he said quietly and smoothed her blonde hair.

To the beginners, he said, "What is the greatest good?"
The class answered in unison: "Pleasure!"
"What is the basic freedom?"
"The freedom to be happy!"
"Be happy, then," the Hedonist said.

As he left the room, they were singing the familiar sixth stanza to the old folksong, "Turkey in the Straw":

> *"Sugar in the gourd and honey in the horn,*
> *I never was so happy since the hour I was born."*

To the secondary class, he said, "Who can tell me what I am?"

One boy held up his hand eagerly. "You're our Hedonist."

"And what is a hedonist?"

"He's the man who keeps us happy."

"Once I would have been called many things," the Hedonist said softly. "Doctor, teacher, psychiatrist, priest, philosopher, ward-heeler, God-surrogate, father-image, lover-symbol. . . . But none of these did what I can do. Your definition is the best: I am the guardian of your happiness."

To the intermediate class, he threw questions swiftly. "What are feelings?"

The answers ran around the room consecutively: "Feelings are unique and unspecific." "They can't be analyzed; when we try, they disappear." "They can apply to any mental process." "There are only two: pleasure and unpleasure."

The Hedonist began again. "What are emotions?"

"Emotions are specific; they are connected with a particular tendency to action."

"They are the result of blocked conations; conations are our strivings to get the things we want."

"Our feelings are directly conditioned by the success or failure of our conations."

"And the moral of this," the Hedonist concluded, "is that we should want the right things—the things we can get. That is the royal road to happiness."

To the advanced class, he said, "Once upon a time does not always begin a happy story. It can describe the real world we left behind us."

Exacerbated desire, doomed to frustration. A rapidly diminishing area of possible satisfaction. Inevitable, daily tragedy.

Want more! Be more! The pre-hedonic world puffed stale air into the balloon of desire; people were overpaid to increase demand. Buy! Own! Enjoy! And slyly the frustrations waited with their pins in hand: laws, social pressures, economics, physical impossibilities.

Illusions. "There's plenty of room at the top; only the bottom is crowded." Fallacy. Dangerous, deadly.

"Teach me to earn so that I may buy so that I may ease this torment of desire." And no one could be found to say, "Teach me to live so that I may be happy."

Poor, tortured world! World of tragedy, doomed to periodic violence, priding itself on being free.

Free. Free to make each other miserable. Free to drive each other to insanity and crime. Free to kill in mass and individual slaughters. Free to develop such stress diseases as stomach cramps, rheumatoid arthritis, asthma, duodenal ulcers, hypertension, heart disease, ulcerative colitis, and diabetes. Free to fret themselves into an early grave.

In 1950, thirty-three men out of every one hundred thousand in the United States committed suicide. That was freedom.

" 'The function of government is, and of right ought to be, the preservation and promotion of the temporal happiness of its citizens,' " the Hedonist quoted.

The girl stood up, straight as a young elm. "The Declaration of Hedonism. December 31, 2003."

"What was the April Fool Amendment?"

"The Twenty-sixth Amendment to the Constitution came three months later. It made hedonism the law of the land."

IV

It is not true that suffering ennobles the character; happiness does that sometimes, but suffering, for the most part, makes men petty and vindictive.

WILLIAM SOMERSET MAUGHAM

As the Hedonist followed the winding walk to the Graduate School, the Nurse caught up with him.

"I've thought of the name," she panted happily. "It's Berns. Gomer Berns."

The Hedonist carried the implication with him through the rest of his morning's duties. He stood in front of the Hedonic Mural and turned it over slowly with part of his mind while he went through the discussion.

Hedonics hadn't happened overnight. The philosophical consideration went back more than two thousand years. The Greeks asked themselves the question: What is the greatest good? The answer was "Pleasure." The philosophy was hedonism.

The interpretation differed. Aristippus, of the Cyrenaic School, believed in "pure" hedonism—the sentient pleasure of the moment. But Epicurus, following Socrates and Aristotle, recognized that happiness must be rational; many momentary pleasures led to future pain.

Later came a preoccupation with society. Should a man seek his own happiness or his community's or that of everyone else at the expense of his own? Egoism, Utilitarianism, or Altruism.

Altruism was obviously false. If the agent's happiness was worthless, how could anyone else's happiness be valuable? Without a calculus of pleasures, Utilitarianism was unworkable; there was no way of balancing pleasures. Egoism was the only tenable philosophy; no ethics can be successful which does not begin and end in the individual.

Hedonics was, above all, practical. It worked. But philosophy was only one leg to the stool.

Means had to become available to relieve the great psychological anxieties: death, sickness, hunger, cold, and the social relationships.

Geriatrics had reduced the fear of death. Medical research had largely wiped out sickness. No one needed to go hungry while chlorella surged through the polyethylene tubes and the sea fixed 135,000,000,000 tons of carbon every year. No one needed to go without shelter when houses could be built overnight.

Social relationships had been complicated by antiquated mores and laws; its artificial barriers were guarded by society's policeman, the conscience, which punished the instinctive desires. The barriers were torn down, the laws were rewritten, and the policeman's badge was torn away.

Research into the physiology of the human body brought out the exact relationship between the glands and the emotions and slowly brought them under conscious control: the adrenals, the pituitary, and the hypothalamus. The development of that control into something effective and invaluable was the function of the hedonic exercises; they occupied a large part of the Graduate School curriculum.

But the final development of hedonism as a way of life waited on the discovery of the hedometer, which brought statistical significance into the introspective fields of psychology and philosophy. The simple device, which worked through an application of the psychogalvanic reflex, became an integral part of every room, and its constant reports made possible a nation-wide application of the axiom "that action is best which procures the greatest happiness of the greatest numbers."

The Hedonist stood in front of the Hedonic Mural and explained these things, as he had explained them before and would explain them again. And the wisdom he tried to impart was diagramed upon the wall behind him.

The Hedonic Mural. To the left, a valley; to the right, a mountain with two peaks, one below the other. At the bottom of the valley was a low-pressure mattress; a man was asleep on it, curled into a fetal position. At the top of each of the peaks was a naked woman, her arms held out invitingly, but on the lower peak she was hazy and out of proportion.

They were symbols, of course. The valley was *reduced desire*. The mountain was *increased satisfaction*. There are two ways to be happy: want less or get more. It was simple as that.

There were trails leading to the top of the mountain and paths leading to the bottom of the valley. Signposts pointed out the way; they were hedonic techniques.

Two trails led to the higher peak: *modify* and *substitute*. A man can actually get what he wants by modifying the outer world, or he can sublimate his frustrations into other goals which can be achieved.

The lower peak with the hazy, dream woman on it was *imaginary gratification*. There were three trails to her: *anticipate, daydream,* and *delude*. Anticipation could lead to real satisfaction, but daydream was conscious wishing, and delusion abolished the wall between wish and fulfillment.

There were four paths into the valley. *Substitute*, which pointed up the mountain, also pointed down; it was the route of wanting what we can get. The other paths were: *devalue, project,* and *suppress*. Devaluation, sometimes called the "sour-grapes technique," is seen at its finest in the cat; the moment something is proved unavailable, it becomes worthless. Projection attributed the desire to someone else. Suppression was a means of preventing the desires from reaching the conscious mind.

The valley and the mountain. And the mountain, attractive as it seemed, was relatively worthless. Reality will allow only a very limited amount of modification; population increases, limited as control measures had made them, had rationed the amount to the point of insignificance. If a man allowed his happiness to depend on it, he was dooming himself to frustration.

The lower peak of imaginary gratification was positively dangerous. The mind overcomes obstacles so easily that it seduces the person from all other forms of gratification. For the same reason, narcotics and the sensies were to be avoided. They were not far from madness, and madness—the ultimate retreat for the protection of the organism—was antisocial and nonsurvival, and, therefore, non-hedonic.

In the valley of hedonic discipline was found the heart of hedonics, untouched and untouchable. Its techniques made man independent of environmental vagaries.

"As long as we have these techniques available," the Hedonist concluded, "nothing—no one—can make us unhappy. Like gods, we hold our happiness in our own hands."

Berns was still unconscious, but the neutralizer quickly made him stir in the chair. His dark, deep-set eyes opened and stared blankly at the Hedonist. Slowly, darkly, they drew memory from a secret place.

His face twisted. His right hand groped, lifted. Pain twitched across his face. He stared down at the cast on his wrist. Tentatively, uncertainly, he wriggled his fingers.

The Hedonist stooped and picked up the knife. He looked down at it for a moment. He handed it to Berns, hilt first. "Is this what you're looking for?" he asked politely.

Berns licked his lips. "Yeah," he said. He took the knife and then held it awkwardly as if he couldn't decide what to do with it.

"Why do you want to kill me?" the Hedonist asked reasonably.

"Because," Berns said furtively. "Because of what you done to me."

"And what's that? Whatever it is, if I can help—"

"What's done's done," Berns said sullenly.

"That's a pre-hedonic attitude," the Hedonist said. "It isn't what happens that's important; it's how it affects us. But what are you talking about?"

"My wife," Berns said. "I'm talking about her."

The Hedonist remembered. Just before moving to the ward, Berns had married one of his dependents—a young girl, not quite out of her teens. There was nothing basically wrong with that. Geriatrics had kept Berns's body young. Hedonics should have done the same thing for the man who lived inside. And yet, Berns had attacked him with a knife. That wasn't a sane thing.

Dani Farrell. The Hedonist remembered her. A quiet girl, a quick, interested student. With her, hedonics had worked well. She was a happy woman, not deep but sound. He had never expected complaints.

"What's the matter with Dani?" the Hedonist asked.

"You know." Berns's eyes slid away.

"She's made you unhappy?" the Hedonist asked, puzzled.

"Not her—*she's* all right!"

"Then what *is* the matter?"

"She knows too much," Berns blurted out.

"You're complaining about that? See here," the Hedonist said with sudden suspicion. "Is there something wrong with your sexual adjustment?"

"Nah," Berns said darkly. "That's what I'm complaining about. With my first wife, it took years. Dani didn't come to me—well—innocent!"

"Innocent!" the Hedonist exclaimed. "You mean 'ignorant.' You're objecting to her education!"

"Some things," Berns said, glowering, "a man should attend to personal."

The Hedonist's face grew stern and then was molded by compassion. The man was sick. He had missed the benefits of a hedonic education, and his previous hedonist had been lax or overworked.

He straightened up. These ante-hedonics cases were tough, but he had cracked them before. "What you want," he said slowly, "is the right to make yourself unhappy and Dani miserable for an outmoded, demonstrably false set of values."

"Well," Berns asked defiantly, "what's wrong with that?"

The Hedonist glanced down at the desk and back up. Given the man's emotional state, he was telling the truth. Or, at least, part of it. "It's antisocial," the Hedonist said quietly. "Society can't permit it."

"This is a free country, ain't it?" Berns demanded. "A man can be unhappy if he wants to be, can't he?"

"No!" the Hedonist thundered. "That myth was exploded fifty years ago. The basic freedom is the freedom to be happy. Society must preserve it above all the others, because without it the others are worthless."

"The way I look at it," Berns said sullenly, "it ain't a freedom unless a man can do something else."

The Hedonist shook his head slowly, patiently. He would have to start from the beginning. "If people had the right to be unhappy, they would threaten the happiness of everyone else. Men don't live in a vacuum. Fundamentally, perhaps, everyone has the right to go to hell in his own way, but there are boundaries beyond which a man can't go without injuring his neighbors. That's society's business—establishing those boundaries and setting watchdogs to guard them. When a man crosses them, he becomes a criminal."

"Maybe," Berns admitted grudgingly. "But that don't explain Dani."

"Be sensible, man," the Hedonist demanded. "Would you have us teach a girl all the domestic and marital accomplishments except the one that's most important to the happiness of her marriage? Vital training like that can't be left to anyone. You're no hedonist. What are your qualifications as a teacher?"

"I'm going to file suit," Berns muttered. "You've infringed on my happiness."

The Hedonist exploded. "You've got no grounds. What's more, you've committed a criminal act. For what you've done today, I could certify you for surgery. In fact, that's my duty."

Berns looked bewildered. "You're going to operate on me?"

"You're obviously unhappy," the Hedonist pointed out. "According to society's standards, you're insane. You should be treated and converted into a happy, responsible member of society. A transorbital lobotomy is the quickest, surest method. Those who can't learn suppression must have it done for them."

Berns struggled to his feet, his face twisted with fear. "No!" he said. "You can't. They won't let you—"

"They?" the Hedonist asked. "Who are 'they'?"

"People," Berns muttered.

That was a lie. "You wouldn't argue with society's right to treat the insane. But I didn't say that was what I was going to do. I owe it to myself, as well as to you, to make your treatment as positive as possible. To do that, though, I need your help."

Berns mumbled something indistinguishable.

"To do that you need to understand my job," the Hedonist said. "Like me, you grew up before hedonics became part of everyday life. Like me, your training for happiness began too late, when you were already past the formative years of your childhood. For the new generation, happiness will come easy; they have been prepared for it. We have to work for it."

"How do you mean?"

"For me, it meant ten years of specialized training in the Institute of Applied Hedonics. Since then it has meant a job that is never done, the guardianship of the happiness of a thousand people.

"For you, it means study, beginning this afternoon. As a salesman, I presume you can take time off?"

Berns started and then nodded. He's afraid, the Hedonist thought in amazement.

"Then this afternoon," the Hedonist said, as he installed Berns in the necessary on the one seat available, "you're going to observe."

But as the Hedonist left the sliding door a little ajar and returned to his desk, he thought: Why did the man register fear when I mentioned his business?

As he engrossed himself in the file of the next patient, he had not found an answer to the question.

V

Happiness is like time and space—we make and measure it ourselves; it is a fancy—as big, as little, as you please; just a thing of contrasts and comparisons.

GEORGE DU MAURIER

After the unusual beginning, it was a usual sort of day. The stream of patients was unending, and the variety of their needs touched the Hedonist often with pathos. A man who was not a god should not have such power nor be burdened with such responsibilities.

And he wielded the power and shouldered the responsibility.

Medical treatment was easy and fast; the diagnostic chair fixed breaks and scrapes, gave immunization and curative shots, adjusted endocrine balances, prescribed diets, treated or removed cancers and tumors, tinkered with faulty organs. . . .

The complaints and applications were more difficult. Three oldsters complained about their pensions and the high cost of living. Two parents wanted public jobs for their children just come of age; the Hedonist helped them prepare applications and added his own recommendations after they had left. There was one case of technological unemployment; the Hedonist arranged to have the man re-educated and reassigned and vouchered the cost to the industry concerned. There were five applications for pregnancy certificates; the Hedonist put them off as best he could: the year's quota for the ward was already exhausted.

But the ones that took time, patience, and skill were the hedonic cases.

Case No. 1: Unfulfilled Ambition (to write tragedy)

Therapy: Devalue and Substitute ("But, if that is impossible, write if you must—I will read it, and then we will burn it together; you can't be permitted to make others unhappy")

Case No. 2: Accidental Death (of a father)

Therapy: Suppress ("Don't let causal events determine your happiness; that is something for you alone to control")

Case No. 3: Jealousy (of a husband)

Therapy: Suppress ("I can prepare an infringement suit if you like, but I ask you to think: How many times have you been to the post-marital cottage?")

Case No. 4: Envy (of a neighbor's new red house)

Therapy: Devalue ("Old houses are the best houses; they are machines adjusted to your way of life")

Case No. 5: . . . .

They were all simple—in theory. They were all difficult in

application. Not one of the cases was classic. Each one was individually complicated. Each one needed individual therapy.

It was a usual sort of day. As usual, it made no difference that he had not ordered lunch; he didn't have time to eat it anyway.

Only one incident was disturbing. During a treatment he felt a sudden moment of dizziness. He concealed it from the patient, but he got a quick diagnosis as soon as she was gone. All the readings were normal. He was in perfect condition. He shook his head uneasily.

As 1600 approached and passed, the unease grew. The Hedonist couldn't locate it. Then, with a start, he remembered his appointment with the Council. He would have to leave in a few minutes. Why, he wondered, had he forgotten?

He remembered, too, the call he had forgotten to make. He punched Beth's number. Her mother's face appeared on the wall. A beautiful face. Only an inner maturity distinguished it from Beth's. She smiled inquiringly at the Hedonist.

"Beth," the Hedonist said. "Is she there?"

"Why, no!" She started to frown. "Beth hasn't been home for days. I thought—"

The Hedonist erased the anxiety hastily. "Of course. She has been here. But she went out this morning. Perhaps she's with her young man—"

"Young man?" The frown returned. "Beth hasn't any young man."

"She hasn't?" the Hedonist said blankly. "That's strange." And then, hurriedly, "Of course. How stupid of me to forget!" His face cleared. Almost magically, the mother's frown was wiped away.

The Hedonist stared at the blank wall for a minute after she said good-by. He could deceive her, but he couldn't deceive himself. Beth had lied to him. There had to be a reason for it. After a little concentration, he began to believe it.

He walked to the necessary in two strides and slid the door back. The cubicle was empty. He stepped into the little room and turned around dazedly. There was, obviously, no one in it except himself. No one could have squeezed into the room when he was there.

And yet Berns was gone. The man was gone, and the Hedonist had not left the room, and Berns could not have brushed past him in getting to the only exit unless he was invisible—

The Hedonist remembered the moment of dizziness.

A time-lapse grenade!

He hunted around on the floor until he found the few shreds of plastic left from the explosion of the gas container. He turned them over slowly in his hand.

Berns was gone. Why? He had obtained a time-lapse grenade. How? He had used it to leave the room without being seen. Why? When? The Hendonist estimated the time he had felt dizzy. It had been almost an hour ago.

For once the hedonic techniques were no good. This was no time for suppression, devaluation, substitution. He had to think and think clearly. Very soon he might have to modify the outer reality, and he needed facts to guide him.

But there were so few facts. The rest was assumption. Berns was only partly what he seemed to be. His story was only partly true. He had some relationship with the Council, and the Council had summoned the Hedonist on the day that Berns had attacked. Berns would have to be reported and certified.

The Hedonist filled out a certification form and backdated it to the time Berns was installed in the necessary. He hunted through the cabinets behind the wall panels until he found what he wanted. He pressed them against his chest and back under the shirt, slipped a small disk into his pocket, and turned toward the door.

The idling cab was waiting two feet above the street. It was 1615, as the Hedonist looked back at his door to check the milky square:

THE HEDONIST IS UNAVAILABLE
FOR EMERGENCY TREATMENT
SEE WARD 482 HEDONIST

He climbed up into the helijet. The rotors sighed overhead.

"Where to?" the cabbie asked softly.

"Hedonic Council Building," the Hedonist said, staring curiously at the red cap covering the cabbie's head.

The cabbie swung around. "Great sorrow, man! You aren't going there!"

The Hedonist stared at the cabbie's face, stunned.

It was Beth.

"What are you—I mean—how did you—?" the Hedonist spluttered.

"I rented the heli—"

"But you're underage!"

"I forged an IDisk," Beth said impatiently, her dark eyes brilliant.

"Forged!" the Hedonist repeated slowly. He rejected the word automatically. He couldn't believe that one of his young people could have committed a criminal act, and it was impossible to forge an identity disk. The plastic locket with its radiation-sensitive heart of phosphate glass could not be duplicated. Or so he had always believed.

"See here," he said, struggling to get off the defensive, "you said you were getting married—"

"I am," she said with quiet determination.

"Your parents don't know about it!"

"Oh, I haven't told *them.*"

"I suppose," the Hedonist said with quiet sarcasm, "that you haven't told the man, either."

"He knows," she said softly. "But he doesn't believe it yet."

"You lied to me." In spite of himself, the Hedonist's voice sounded hurt.

"You poor, blind fool!" Beth said desperately. "Look! It doesn't matter. Not now. The only thing that matters is to stay away from the Council. Don't keep that appointment!"

"The appointment!" the Hedonist exclaimed. He looked at his watch. It was 1620. "I've got to hurry."

"That's what I'm trying to—"

"Are you going to take me?" the Hedonist asked, "or shall I call another cab?"

"Oh, I'll take you," she groaned, swinging around to the front. She punched the buttons expertly. With a muffled roar, the heli rose vertically. When it reached two thousand feet, the jets cut off at the rotor tips and the rear jets cut in. They streaked toward the Old City; it rose like a picket fence on the horizon.

The only sound in the cabin was a gentle vibration. The Hedonist sat silent, turning words over and peering under them: forgery, deceit, disrespect. Was the younger generation capable of this? His world rocked as he considered the possibilities implicit in what Beth had done. If these hedonically trained young people were not free from immoral and criminal tendencies, then hedonics was a failure.

It was impossible. The Hedonist shook his head vigorously. Hedonics worked. He was the failure.

"How did you know," he asked without a quaver, "that I was going to the Council Building?"

"I've been watching all day," Beth said casually.

"Spying!" the Hedonist said with horror in his voice.

She shrugged. "If you want to call it that. A good thing, too."

He didn't intend to ask, but the words were seduced from his lips. "What do you mean?"

"That man. The one who called himself Gomer Berns. He was an agent of the Council."

An agent. The Hedonist tasted the word gingerly. It had extensions and implications. "How do you know?"

"He's been watching you for days. And I've been watching him. He's talked to the Council secretary three times, once in person. Then, today, he staged this scene."

"How do you know what he was talking about?"

"I wired the cottage days ago," she said disgustedly. "When he tossed out the grenade and sneaked away, I was afraid it might be something more deadly. Then I realized what it was. I followed him, but I wasn't quite quick enough."

"For what?"

"He'd already dropped the tape into the mail tube."

"Tape?"

Beth reached onto the seat beside her and flicked something over the back of the seat into the Hedonist's lap. He picked it up and frowned at it. It was a flat, opaque, plastic box about half an inch deep, two inches wide, and three inches long. The back was sticky. He turned it over. Projecting a fraction beyond the box was Berns's clear, plastic IDisk.

He turned it back over, bewildered. Something clicked and moved under his fingers. The box fell open. Inside was a tiny, empty reel; there was a spindle for another. Printed circuits were a maze against the plastic.

The thing was a miniature recorder, equipped to pick up both sight and sound. The lens—for some reason—had been disguised as an IDisk. Gomer Berns's IDisk.

"Where did you get this?" he asked suddenly.

"Where do you suppose?"

A sudden flash of apprehension turned the Hedonist's stomach cold. "You said he *was* an agent. What did you—"

"He's dead," Beth said calmly.

Before, the world had rocked. Now it revolved wildly. For a moment, the Hedonist wondered whether the heli had plunged out of control, and then his hedonic reflexes caught him and set him firmly back in place. His pulse slowed, his adrenals stopped discharging. . . . "You killed him," he said.

"Yes."

"Why?"

"It was an accident, I suppose," she said thoughtfully, "although I can't say for certain. I was mad enough to kill him. I tried to stop him from dropping the tape, you see, and he pulled out a knife. The cast made him clumsy. When I twisted his arm, he stabbed himself."

"Go back! Quick!" the Hedonist shouted. "He might still be alive."

She shook her head. "He's dead all right."

The Hedonist groaned and passed his hand over his face. "I'll have to certify you for surgery," he heard his voice saying distantly. "No!" he told himself, sitting up straight again. "I can't do it!"

The weight on his shoulders seemed to shift a little.

Beth sighed. "I was hoping you would say that. It's all right. Nobody saw me."

The Hedonist shuddered. He couldn't believe the immorality he was hearing. "You'll have to undergo treatment," he said nervously.

Beth laughed. "All you want."

The Hedonist looked down at his hands. He still held the recorder. He shuddered again, pressed the button that reeled down the right window, and tossed the plastic thing through. He watched it spin through the air until it disappeared below. He wiped his hands on his shorts as if to cleanse them of an invisible stain. *Forgery, deceit, theft, and murder.* But the stain would not come off. It was his fault. It was his duty to protect the bewildered girl.

"Now," she said, sounding not at all bewildered, "you see why you can't keep that appointment with the Council."

"Because you killed Berns?"

"No, because he was their agent. Can't you see what they're trying to do? They want to certify you—"

"They can't do that," the Hedonist protested. "I'm not unhappy."

"When they get through with you, you will be," Beth said grimly.

"But why? They've got no reason—"

"When have they needed a reason? They want to get rid of you. Why, I don't know. But there could be a hundred reasons. For some reason you're dangerous to them. If you want to stay alive, you've got to stop judging everyone else by yourself."

It was a web of nonsense. The Hedonist didn't believe a word of it. Beth had lied to him before without raising her blood pressure a fraction of a point. She was capable of anything. It had to be lies.

But there had been gelatin fragments on his floor. And he had held a miniature recorder in his hands, and it had a lens shaped like an IDisk. Or had he? Was it delusion?

He glanced at his watch: 1629.

The Council Building was a flat-topped spire a thousand feet below. He could see the large *HC* painted across the roof. Around it were the deep, darkening canyons that separated the building from its shorter neighbors.

The Old City was little frequented now. Industry was decentralized into small, automatic factories near their markets, and the population had spread far out into almost autonomous suburbs. The parts of the Old City left standing were used only for the functions and services which could not be decentralized: government, major hospitals, and interplanetary commerce.

"Take me down," the Hedonist said.

"But—" Beth began, swinging around frantically.

"Down!" he repeated firmly. "I have an appointment in four minutes. I'm going to keep it." He had to accept it as reality, not delusion. But he was ready for the Council, if he could get Beth away and out of danger.

She sighed hopelessly. "All right." She punched buttons savagely. The rear jets cut out. They dropped in a long, swooping descent that clutched the Hedonist's throat, but at the last minute the rotor's tip jets caught and the heli dropped lightly to the roof.

The little devil! the Hedonist thought. She did that on purpose. "Go home!" he said, stepping down from the cab and standing on the roof. The rotors twisted slowly above his head. "Tell your mother to give you an alibi for the time of Berns's death."

"An alibi?" she asked. "What's that?"

The diabolical innocent! "A statement that you were home at that time. She's to lie about it. Tell her I said to. And tell her to make herself believe that it's true. As for you— Don't worry! I'll take care of everything."

"Yes, Hedonist," she said obediently.

"Now get out of here!" he said brutally. "I don't want to see you again."

He stepped back before he could see the expression on her face, and he watched the heli lift from the roof. The rear jets caught quickly with an orange flame that swiftly turned blue and then became a mere wavering of the air.

Except for him, the paved roof was empty. The Hedonist turned and walked to the elevator housing. As he approached, the doors slid open. He stepped in, turned to face the front, and the doors began to close.

"Twent—" he began, but before he had finished, the car started down.

The Hedonist counted the floors as they flashed by. He counted backward from seventy-five, swiftly, for the drop was faster than the one in the heli. When he reached thirty-two, the car slowed suddenly. "Thirty-one," he counted. "Thirty. Twenty-nine."

On that number, the elevator stopped. The Hedonist considered the implications. Without instructions from him, the elevator had brought him to the twenty-ninth floor. That was true efficiency. But then the Council was efficient.

The door remained closed. It refused to open. The Hedonist looked at his watch: 1633. When the sweep second hand reached the top of the dial and went a little past, the doors parted.

Real precision, the Hedonist thought, and stepped out into a deserted hallway. The resilient floor felt springy under his feet. It was an old building. There were windows at both ends of the hall.

The Hedonist walked quickly to one of them. It was made of glass, not plastic. Far below, the streets were empty. They had a green tinge where the grass had taken root.

There were doors on both sides of the corridor, but 2943 was opposite the elevator. There was a sign on the door. Like his own, it said COME IN AND BE HAPPY.

On the door at waist-level was a button. The Hedonist shrugged and pushed it. The doors slid open. The room beyond was an ordinary waiting room, well lighted, neat. Chairs lined each wall. Beside an inner door was a desk. The room was deserted.

The place was silent. Completely, absolutely silent. The only sound the Hedonist could hear was his breathing and the internal workings of his body.

He stepped into the room.

VI

The life and liberty and property and happiness of the common man throughout the world are at the absolute mercy of a few persons whom he has never seen, involved in complicated quarrels that he has never heard of.

GILBERT MURRAY

The sound was deafening. That was the first thing he noticed. Or, no, it wasn't the first thing. The sound was even louder because his eyes had squeezed shut automatically at the first flash of brightness. He waited and felt behind him with one hand. The wall was smooth. The door was closed.

The noise, he thought, was a recording of every sound ever made. He could hear drums, hammers, a chorus of machines; he heard raspings, scrapings, gratings, screeches, horns, explosions, voices, screams, shouts. . . .

He concentrated on identifying the sound, not shutting it out. It seemed to cover the whole range of audibility, from 15 cycles per second to more than 20,000 cycles. It was loudest, though, in the middle high tones. That was natural enough. The ear was most sensitive for those frequencies.

Question: Was the sound objective or subjective?

Unless it had been set off by his stepping into the room, it had to be subjective. Not even the finest interrupter could phase out everything. And he hadn't heard a sound.

Ordinarily, the tympanic muscles would have contracted reflexively to protect the inner ear. They hadn't. Presumption: His sensitivity had been increased or the receptors of the inner ear themselves were being stimulated.

He concentrated on the 1000 to 4000 cycle range and reduced the sensitivity of the ear. Slowly the sound diminished. What he had been hearing was actually the molecular motion of the air particles.

He could hear the voice now. He tried to distinguish the words. Slowly he made it out.

"This is a test," the voice said. "Find your way to the inner room. When you open that door, the test will be over. The test can be discontinued any time you wish. If you desire to do so, lie down on the floor and cover your eyes and ears."

The Hedonist did not even consider the possibility. It was not only against his nature to surrender, but he suspected that passing the test was vital. It was something new. He withheld judgment on it until the purpose became clearer.

Slowly he opened his eyes, squinting to keep down the intolerable glare. But the light had dimmed. As he opened his eyes wider, the light flared up, and the eyes snapped shut. He opened them a slit; the light was dim and gray. He opened them a little wider; the light blazed. The light—or his sensitivity to it—was keyed to the width his eyes were opened. After a little experimentation, he discovered the optimum width which admitted the most light without risking blindness.

The room had changed. It was no longer a waiting room. It was his own room, and he was leaning so far backward that he was going to fall over into the necessary. He caught himself and straightened up and almost pitched forward on his face.

Illusion, he told himself. The room's tilted, not me. But it was more difficult to convince his eyes of their mistake.

Which way had the inner door been when he looked into the room from the corridor? If this was the same room, and his senses brought him only illusions, the door was directly in front of him about four paces. He hadn't moved.

He felt behind him again to make sure. His hand dipped to the wrist in semiliquid slime. He smelled a strong odor of decay.

He pulled out his hand, resisting the impulse to shake off

the slime, and took one step forward, concentrating on the testimony of his semicircular canals and the sense organs in the muscles, tendons, joints, and skin. The room blinked and changed.

He was on a blue desert. The sand was harsh and gritty under his feet. The scorching wind picked it up and threw it against his face and into his eyes. He could taste it, strong and alkaline, between his teeth. Overhead a huge, orange sun burned down on him.

The Hedonist ignored everything. He didn't blink or rub his face or eyes or try to cover his head. He knew now what he was experiencing. This was the sensies without the cumbersome equipment that they needed. This was sensation transmitted to the nerves themselves. But as long as he refused to believe in the reality of the illusion, he had beaten the tests.

Question: What would be the next scene?

Something stirred behind one of the blue dunes. The Hedonist didn't wait to find out what it was. He took another step, concentrating again on the kinesthetic report of his leg and hip muscles to keep him moving in a straight line.

The floor rocked under him. It quivered like gelatin. It was insecurity. There were tall buildings all around him. They were tumbling. He could smell dust in the air. Great masses of masonry were shaken from the buildings by the earthquake, and they fell toward him, turning, growing larger. . . .

He took another step. Now he was falling. He was turning and twisting through the air, hurtling toward the distant pavement. Air became resistant, buffeted him, tugged at his clothes. The pavement came up to meet him. . . .

He took another step. Everything went black. He stood still, trying to see and there was nothing to see, trying to pierce the meaning of the illusion. Or was it an illusion?

The fears the test had played on had not been the learned fears but the old fears, the instinctive ones: the familiar twisted, the completely alien, things dropping and the firm Earth shaking, falling. Baby fears, never forgotten.

What now? Only the dark?

Close to the floor, something hissed. Something moved over his foot, slowly. Something long and thin. There was a second hiss. A third. Things brushed against his bare legs.

Snakes! the Hedonist thought. Snakes in the dark!

Slowly they became luminescent. They glowed in the darkness, lifting in front of him, weaving wickedly. They were all colors: green, red, blue, violet, yellow, orange. . . . The Hedonist stopped listing them. One of the snakes was poising itself to strike.

The Hedonist reached out and pressed its diamond-shaped head.

The door opened.

Three men were sitting at the far end of a long table. They looked young, but the youngest of them, the Hedonist knew, was ten years older than he was. They had been the first men elected to the Council; they had held office ever since.

The room was big and windowless, paneled in dark, imitation wood. On the right wall was a door, which should be a necessary. There was a faint glimmering in the air in front of the Council. It could be nothing else but a missile-barrier. It would be airtight, too. The Council was being very careful.

The chairman sat at the very end. He had a pleasant, blond face. He was a simple, not particularly intelligent man, who could never have become a hedonist except by legislation.

To his left was the treasurer, a dark, brooding man of unfathomable moods. The Hedonist would have liked to have had him in his diagnostic chair for a few minutes.

To the chairman's right was the secretary, a blank, nondescript, expressionless person, but the Hedonist received a subtle impression of tremendous control. He was the one to watch.

"Joy, hedonists," the Hedonist said cheerfully. "I hope I haven't kept you waiting."

"Not at all," the chairman said. "Right on time. Joy to you."

The Hedonist stood in front of them, waiting, smiling pleasantly.

"What did you think of the test?" the treasurer asked finally.

They had mentioned it first. It was a small victory, but it was important. "Very interesting," the Hedonist responded. "What was it supposed to test?"

"Sit down," said the treasurer, motioning to the chair that faced them.

The Hedonist had the answer he wanted. It was a test, not of happiness and mental balance, but of intelligence and self-control. What was the purpose? To drive him into insanity?

"A hedonist," the secretary said tonelessly, "who cannot control himself, cannot help his patients."

"A truism," the Hedonist agreed.

"Look," the chairman said, and moved his hand.

The Hedonist was looking at himself. He was standing just inside the waiting room, his eyes closed. He opened his eyes, blinked several times, and leaned forward and then upright. A little awkwardly, but not too slowly, he walked across the floor. He reached out and pressed the button on the door. He vanished. The experience had taken less than a minute.

The Hedonist looked at the Council. That was it, then. They had wanted evidence for a sanity trial. There was no indication of outside stimulation. If he had reacted to the illusion or if he had given up, he would have been lost. But they had won nothing.

"Are you happy, Hedonist?" the chairman asked.

"Certainly," the Hedonist said. "I presume that this is being recorded."

The chairman nodded curtly.

"What kind of job have you been doing in your ward?" the treasurer asked. "In your opinion?"

"A man is his own worst critic," the Hedonist said modestly. "But if you must have an answer, I think my work has been adequate. But you have better indicators than that. What has my ward averaged on the Hedonic Index? For the record."

There was a moment of silence. "Ninety-seven," the secretary said.

The Hedonist was surprised. "So high? I've done a better job than I thought."

"You haven't certified anyone for surgery in more than a year," the treasurer pointed out.

"There you're mistaken," the Hedonist said. "I certified someone this morning." He glanced casually at the three faces at the other end of the table. "A man named Gomer Berns." At least he had that on the record.

Two faces were politely interested; the secretary blinked once, impassively. "So?" he said. "We haven't received the certification yet."

"No doubt it's being processed," the Hedonist said easily.

"No doubt," the secretary said. "An interesting state-ment, in view of this." His hand slid along the arm of his chair.

This record wasn't as realistic as the other. The film flickered, and the sound wavered. But it was interesting. It was a record of the Hedonist's day as seen through the IDisk of Gomer Berns.

It started with Berns's entrance and ended with his

departure under the cover of the time-lapse grenade. The Hedonist watched himself at work with a trace of self-consciousness, but he didn't have to suppress it. It vanished before the realization of the fantastic speed with which the Council had acted. The record had been edited skillfully, almost damningly.

"Interesting, eh?" the secretary asked.

"Very. Especially as evidence of infringement of happiness. Consider this notification of intent to file—"

"Nonsense," the chairman interrupted. "The Council is immune to suit—"

"Since when?" the Hedonist asked quickly.

"Since February 18, 2054," the secretary said flatly. "You received notification of the legislation, just as every other hedonist did. If you had attended the last Congress, you would have taken part in the voting."

The Hedonist was silent. There were only so many hours in a day. It had seemed better to let the interminable Hedonic Record tapes go unheard than to leave a patient untreated and unhappy. It had seemed preferable to skip the usually uneventful Congress than to leave his ward untended for several days.

"You have abrogated the basic principles of hedonism," the Hedonist said slowly, evenly, "and hedonism cannot long survive. The moment one man or group of men is raised above the laws, the laws become worthless. The basic freedom is the freedom to be happy. Anyone who infringes upon it is a criminal, not above but beyond the laws—"

"You may stop mouthing these phrases," the secretary said quietly. "We are the guardians of their meanings. Besides"—he shrugged—"the recorder had been cut off for several seconds."

"How then," the Hedonist asked patiently, "do you hope to establish the record as authentic?"

The chairman's eyes opened, wide, blue, and innocent. "We will certify it. How else?"

Above the law, above the law, the Hedonist repeated endlessly to himself. It was an accompaniment to the sound of his world collapsing around him.

"Just," the treasurer growled, "as we will certify you."

"On what grounds?" the Hedonist asked quickly.

The treasurer shrugged. "The necessary grounds. Unhappiness, maladjustment. Malfeasance, misfeasance, nonfeasance—"

"I'll fight it," the Hedonist told them calmly. "You can never justify the charges. Not with the Hedonic Index of my ward."

"When a prima facie case of illegal therapy, distortion of legal therapy, or disregard of proper therapy, can be made on the basis of direct evidence," the secretary said dryly, "the Index is inadmissible and rebuttal is worthless."

"The definition of legal and proper therapy is that therapy which is contained in the *Journal of Hedonics*?"

"Obviously," the chairman said cheerfully.

"You've revoked the principle of autonomy, too," the Hedonist observed. He shook his head. "You can't standardize happiness. Every person is an individual case, just as every feeling is unique and unanalyzable. The best we can do is approximation, and that is best done by the person qualified to understand the needs of their individuals, the ward hedonist. Publilius Syrus said it a long time ago: You can't put the same shoe on every foot."

"It seems," the secretary said, "that you haven't read the May *Journal*, either. It explicitly analyzed, contradicted, and exposed the fallacy of your argument. Please don't waste the Council's time by making us repeat it. The official position of hedonism has been laid down: hedonics is a true science, not an art."

"You've discovered a calculus of pleasure?"

"It's the corollary of the process you just experienced," the treasurer said darkly. "We can reduce pleasure to a common denominator by intrinsically reliable physical means. No longer do we have to be content with ninety-seven per cent happiness. We can achieve one hundred per cent happiness any time we wish for as long as we wish."

"By machine."

"That is the beauty of it," the secretary said. For the first time there was life in his voice. "The means are one hundred per cent controllable, one hundred per cent reliable. The sensations you experienced were real and horrible; the sensations we can project can be real and wonderful. We don't need to reduce desire any longer. We can increase desire and match it with increased satisfaction. We have reached the millennium."

"Horrible, perhaps. Wonderful, perhaps. But real, no." The Hedonist shook his head grimly. "Systematized delusion. Madness mechanized. Now, I suppose, you will have no use for the lobotomies?"

"You suppose wrong," the treasurer said harshly. "It will still be used in criminal cases. The projector is a reward not a punishment. It will be saved for those who deserve the absolute happiness it guarantees—"

"Deserve?" The Hedonist picked it up quickly, his head lifting. "When did that word creep back into the vocabulary of hedonics? We all deserve happiness; that is the basis of hedonism. 'Reward—punishment.' Oh, I see what you intend. You are bringing back the two-valued world. On the one side, the hell of the mindless, on the other, the heaven of the mad. I wash my hands of it, gentlemen—I no longer call you 'hedonists.' I'm through with you."

"But," the secretary said evenly, "we aren't through with you. Because of your services to hedonism, we are going to be kind. You are going to have your choice of happiness: you may have your desires reduced by surgery or your satisfactions increased by the projector."

"Hobson's choice," the Hedonist muttered. He looked from the dark, brooding face to the happy, blond one to the blank one. They were determined to get rid of him. "But why?" he burst out. "Tell me that!"

The chairman looked inquiringly at the secretary. The secretary nodded. "It's off," he said.

"You've infringed on our happiness," the chairman said simply.

"I?" the Hedonist exclaimed. "How?"

"One," the treasurer said, "you've cut off your ward's trade in neo-heroin. The income is vital to the proper functioning of government—"

"It's dangerous stuff," the Hedonist interrupted. "It leads to unpleasure and a reduction of real happiness—"

"Two," the treasurer continued as if the Hedonist hadn't spoken, "you have been nominated for a place on this Council. If elected, you would replace one of us—and that would be unpleasure, sir!—and you would upset our plans for the future happiness of Earth—"

"But I had no idea—" the Hedonist began. "I haven't even been to the Congress—I don't want any such—"

"Your lack of ambition is unimportant," the secretary said, shrugging, "except as it affects your own happiness." He moved his hand along the chair. "We have given you an opportunity. Choose!"

"And what if I should tell you," the Hedonist said suddenly, "that I have been recording this discussion, that the record is in a safe place, and that it will not be used unless this proceeding continues?"

"It wouldn't matter," the secretary said, unmoved. "This room is shielded." He cocked his head as if he were listening. "At any rate, your cottage has just been destroyed."

"I suspected as much," the Hedonist sighed. "And so I didn't try." His face suddenly grew pale. "Gentlemen—I find that—this discussion—has suddenly—made me ill. If you will—indicate—the necessary—?"

Automatically, in the face of the Hedonist's obvious distress, the chairman nodded toward the door in the right wall. The Hedonist pushed himself up, cupped his hand to his mouth, and staggered toward the door.

The secretary followed him with unreadable eyes. "Don't forget," he suggested, "that this is the twenty-ninth floor."

VII

Happiness makes up in height for what it lacks in length.
ROBERT FROST

The Hedonist nodded dumbly, miserably, slipped through the doorway as the door slid aside, and turned to close it behind him. The room, almost twice as big as his cubicle at home, was decorated in antiseptically clean white tile. But the door had no lock on it.

The Hedonist's face had returned, miraculously, to its normal, healthy color; his breath came quickly but easily. His hand came out of a pocket. The thin, flat disk was in it. He moved it quickly around the edge of the doorway, stopped, slid it back a few inches, and pressed it to the wall.

When he took his hand away, the disk clung to the wall. He pressed the button beside the door. The door didn't budge.

The Hedonist turned around. As he had suspected, the room had a frosted window. He slipped off one shoe, wrapped his hand in the shirt he had removed, and swung the shoe against the window with all his strength. It shattered explosively.

As soon as the pieces had stopped falling, the Hedonist looked through the jagged hole. The sun was gone; twilight was settling over the Old City; the canyons were dark, shadowed places of mystery. He knocked loose some of the lower pieces and looked down. The street was a narrow ribbon below. He shuddered and drew back.

Someone started hammering on the other side of the door. They were shouting. The Hedonist couldn't make it out. Then one word came clear. The word was: *murder.*

The Hedonist turned back to the window and cleared it and the narrow sill of the sharp fragments. He slipped off his other shoe, tied the two together, and hung them around his neck. There were two large flat circles on his chest and two more on his back. The Hedonist dug a finger under them and pried them loose. They left red circles on his body.

He put the shirt back on and, holding the geckopads in his hand, stepped up onto the sill. He fitted the pads on his hands and feet, making sure that they fit securely and there was no dirt or glass among the fine, rubbery cilia that made a deep-piled velvet on the underside.

He slipped his right hand and foot around the edge of the window and pressed them firmly against the smooth, outside wall of the building. He supported himself by his left foot and reached out with his left hand. When it was stuck, he hung by the three pads and brought out his left foot, feeling in his back the sudden, cold weakness that was recognition of the long emptiness beneath.

He slapped his left foot against the chilly magnesium surface and hung there for a moment like a misshapen lizard. In a moment he had controlled his adrenals. He stopped shivering.

He released his right-hand pad with an upward roll and

moved it—up. His left hand followed it and then his feet, one after the other. It was forty-six stories and over five hundred feet to the top; he hunched toward it like an inchworm on the utterly smooth, vertical, building face, broken only by the occasional shallow inserts of window wells.

In spite of the greater distance, in spite of the greater effort, he went up. They would be looking for him below, but they wouldn't find his body there. Before he could reach the pavement, they would be waiting with their men and restraints and surgical knives and wires. His only chance was to climb.

After a climb of five stories, sixty feet, he stopped to rest. He glanced down over his shoulder and saw the lights below. They milled in the remote darkness like fireflies churning in a fantastic dance. Occasionally one slanted up the building face, but it never rose any higher than the broken window on the twenty-ninth floor.

At the thirty-fourth floor, the Hedonist had forty-one stories to climb. Almost five hundred feet. His muscles ached and trembled from the short climb he had made and the continual downward pull of his body as it was supported from the pads at an unnatural angle.

He wished he were thirty years younger. In spite of geriatrics, the years told on a body when a man asked too much of it.

The Hedonist sighed and slowly, painfully inched his way upward again. They would think of helis soon enough. The first one sped by him as he reached the fortieth floor. It rocketed through the dark, narrow canyon on its tail jets. Its exhaust was only a few yards away, and one of the idling rotors almost brushed him. He turned his head to watch.

Perilously, the heli stood on its side at the corner and zoomed out of sight. The Hedonist hung from the side of the building and waited for the thunder of the crash. It never came. He would have to change his plans. The helis had found him.

It would soon be back. Before then he would have to be off his exposed wall where he was like a fly waiting to be swatted. He sidled toward a window.

When he was beside the shallow well, he loosened his right hand from its pad and undraped his shoes from his neck. There was no chance of untying them; he didn't dare let loose with the other hand. One shoe dangled as he beat against the window with the other.

The taps were feeble and ineffectual. The extra shoe bothered him, and from his suspended position, he couldn't get any force behind the blow.

A muffled roar came from behind him. He turned his head and looked back.

Fifteen feet away a heli hung from its rotors. It couldn't get much closer without battering the rotors against the building. They whirred and roared only a couple of feet from his head.

The Hedonist tried to see into the darkened cab, but the strain only made his eyes water. Then the lights came on inside. The pilot stared out at him with wide, lovely, frightened eyes. It was Beth.

Hopelessly, they looked at each other, separated by a gulf fifteen feet wide. It might as well have been fifty. The hedonic techniques were no good here; suppression, projection, devaluation, and substitution were worthless. The only thing that could make him happy was modification, and there was no way to modify the impassable fifteen feet that divided them or the five hundred feet of emptiness that stretched below or the hardness of the street at the bottom.

Beth made impatient motions at him. What did she want him to do?

The Hedonist couldn't figure it out. He looked down toward the distant street. A large searchlight was sweeping the width of the lower stories. Soon it would work its way up here, and they would spot him.

Longingly, he looked back at the heli. Beth was still gesturing, frantically. He understood her now: *Come here!*

Gladly, the Hedonist thought. Give me wings, and I will fly to you.

Beth's lips were moving. She swung open the door and motioned down at the frame. The Hedonist studied her lips, incredulous. Again and again they framed the same word: *Jump!*

Jump? Fifteen feet? Maybe. On the ground. But fifteen feet over five hundred is another thing entirely. As a fraction, it expressed his chances of reaching the heli and hanging on. Three chances out of a hundred.

On the other hand, his chances of escape were zero if he stayed where he was. Beth was right. Three chances were better than none. The watchdogs wouldn't get him.

He redraped his shoes around his neck and walked sideways across the smooth magnesium until the geckopads were clinging to the clear window glass. He wasted only a moment on a glance down the long, bare, unattainable corridor. Break the window now, and he would fall with the shards.

He slipped his feet out of the straps and onto the ledge. He released his right hand and caught the strap and got his left hand free. Slowly, holding tight to the straps, he turned himself around.

The pavement was a mile below.

The Hedonist shuddered and squeezed his eyes shut. He opened them and looked out toward Beth. *Please!* she said with her lips. And: *Hurry!*

The searchlight finally jumped past the twenty-ninth floor. As it swept by, it caught the Hedonist, silhouetting him against the bright window and the brighter walls, like a dark, clinging beetle.

The Hedonist blinked blindly. Gradually he made out the heli again, the lighted cab and the dark outlines around it. Slowly he bent his knees until his arms were stretched full length below the pads. He let the straps go and crouched lower.

Now he was toppling forward. The action was irreversible. He was committed to jump, and the only thing between him and the distant pavement below was the doorjamb of the heli. He straightened his legs abruptly. He hurtled through the air.

He rushed toward the heli, and the heli rushed toward him. He realized that Beth had rocked the ship to bring the cab a little closer to the building. Closer, but not close enough.

His agonized fingers missed the doorjamb by inches. And he was falling, falling through the darkness, falling toward the distant pavement and death.

Beside this, the Council's illusion was nothing. It was irony that he had time to think of that. This was reality; it was bloodcurdling, terrible, and final. A man plunged through the thin, cold air toward the Earth that rushed up toward him to deliver the last, deadly blow. . . .

His arms hit something, slipped down past it. His clawing hands caught it, held it while his body fell and came to a jerking, swinging stop that almost tore the hands loose.

The Hedonist dangled above the emptiness and looked up because he could not look down. The heli was above him. He was clinging to the tubular metal landing skid. Beth's face was framed in the door above. Abstractly, he watched the play of emotions across the face—horror changing to relief and joy and back again to concern and terror.

The Hedonist swung on tiring arms and felt the heli dropping with his added weight. Beth's face disappeared for a moment. The heli lifted, leveled off. Beth leaned out again. She stretched far down from the door, but her reaching hand was two feet short of the skid.

She'll fall! the Hedonist thought, and he had a strange sensation in his chest as if his heart had turned over. He shook his head desperately.

With a sudden burst of adrenalized energy, he pulled himself up until his arms were over the skid. He clung there, gathering strength. In a moment he raised a leg over the skid, sat upright, and caught the edge of the doorjamb.

Beth's hand was surprisingly strong as she caught his wrist and helped him into the cab. He collapsed into the seat beside her and closed his eyes. Rapidly his breathing slowed and became regular.

"Let's get out of here!" he said.

He felt the rear jets kick in and boot the heli forward. He opened his eyes. The dark walls of the artificial canyons reeled past.

"I thought I told you to go home!" he growled.

Beth's hand, which had been reaching toward his hand, jerked back. "That's gratitude!" she said indignantly.

"Gratitude?" The Hedonist's eyes widened. "Where did you pick up a word like that? And when did you learn to expect it? Happiness is a man's right in this world, and if he has that, what's left for him to be grateful for?"

Beth was silent. Finally, distantly, she said, "I came back because I thought you might need me. You did, apparently. I couldn't go home because the watchdogs are after me. They found Berns's body."

"So I gathered," the Hedonist said thoughtfully. "Watch out for the jog!"

Beth swung her eyes to the front just in time to swerve the heli around the building that loomed up in front of them. The new canyon turned a thirty-degree angle. Slowly the buildings got lower and shabbier. They were getting farther into the Old City.

"I lost them when we reached the City," Beth said scornfully. "They didn't dare follow me down. Which way shall we go?"

"The way you are," he said absently.

"But we're almost to the ruins," she objected.

"That's right."

The heli flew on in near silence. An eerie glow grew bright on the horizon, like a low aurora polaris. The luminescence was mainly green and blue but there were flickerings of violet and purple.

"You weren't as confident as you sounded," Beth said suddenly. "You had those geckopads with you."

"I'd have been a fool not to prepare for the possibility," the Hedonist said casually. "If I hadn't I would be mindless or insane by now."

"Lobotomy I can understand," Beth said. "But what do you mean by 'insane'?"

"Induced delusions," the Hedonist said heavily. "The Council has perfected the sensies. Now, they're realies. The Council is going to make Earth one hundred per cent happy."

Beth shook her head slowly. "Poor, happy Earth," she murmured.

The Hedonist glanced at her silently. What did she mean by that? He knew it was wrong, theoretically, but the wrongness wasn't obvious. The goal of hedonism was to make people happy. Why not the happier the better? Because, as in everything else, a man had to be rational. It was inevitable that a man choose happiness, but he could—and had to—forego some immediate and momentary pleasures in order to insure future happiness.

Anything that decreased a man's capacity for pleasure was wrong. Delusion did that. It ruined a man for reality.

Anything that took a man's happiness out of his own hands was wrong. Happiness wasn't a gift to be bestowed. It was a grail, a purely personal goal, which could only be described in general terms. A man could do that, and he could train someone else for the quest and sometimes help that person over the barriers, but he couldn't do it all. He couldn't find happiness for the other person and he couldn't give it to him.

The mile-wide crater swung under them, glowing phosphorescently. Mostly, as it had been on the horizon, it was blues and greens, but there were flickering patches of purple and violet, and here and there flitting wisps of yellow and orange. The crater was almost two hundred feet deep; after fifty years, it was still deadly. For three miles around the crater, the shattered spears of buildings stretched mutely above rubble, weathered a little now, its sorrow blunted.

"Take it down," the Hedonist said.

"Here?" Beth exclaimed.

"On the other side. Hurry. There's no time to waste."

The heli hovered above the rubble, lighted obscenely by the luminescence behind. Beth and the Hedonist stood a few feet away.

"I thought you set it for homing," the Hedonist said, frowning.

"I did. But I had to give us time to get out."

In a moment something clicked inside the cab. The rotors speeded up, and the heli lifted itself into the sky. It went up fast. When it was high enough, the rear jets cut in. They watched it streak off toward the rising towers they had left.

Distantly, over the City, it exploded and fell in a shower of sparks.

"They shot it down." The Hedonist sighed. "I thought they would. That will give us a few hours."

Beth had pulled out the IDisk that hung like a locket from a chain around her neck. It had begun to glow in gentle sympathy with the crater behind them. "Look!" she said.

"Don't worry about it," the Hedonist said. He fished two large pills out of his pocket. "See if you can get this down without water."

"What is it?"

"Cysteine. An amino acid. A radiation protective. It'll last long enough to get us out of here."

She choked down one of the pills; he swallowed the other easily. "Let's go," he said.

They walked away from the crater across the rubble. Soil had blown in, and the rock had weathered down. Seeds had drifted down or been dropped by birds. They had sprouted. Most of the rubble was already covered by a kind, green blanket. In fifty more years, this part of the Old City would be gently rolling meadows.

"How it happened I don't understand," the Hedonist said, "but somewhere you've picked up a poor opinion of hedonics."

"No—no," she protested. "You don't understand—"

"This is what it saved the world from," he said, sweeping his hand from the ruins back toward the glowing crater. "For the warped conations of a twisted world it substituted the only real goal, happiness, and it taught man how to find it and how to keep it."

"What is a man profited," Beth said quietly, "if he shall gain the whole world, and lose his own soul?"

The Hedonist stared at her in astonishment. "Where did you learn that?"

"I read it," she said. "In an old book."

"I know that. But where did you find one? It isn't on the proscribed list, exactly, but it isn't approved, either. I haven't seen one in twenty-five years."

Beth shrugged carelessly. "There are things that even the Council knows nothing about."

"So it seems," the Hedonist said thoughtfully.

Side by side, not touching, they walked in silence over the silent mounds of the troubled past.

VIII

A wise woman never yields by appointment. It should always be an unforeseen happiness.

MARIE HENRI BEYLE (STENDHAL)

Beth was the first to speak. As the buildings around them slowly changed from broken stumps to dark, hollow shafts, she said, "What do you intend to do?"

"Get you someplace you won't be picked up immediately," he said slowly.

"Don't worry about me," she said impatiently. "I can take care of myself."

"Don't be foolish," he said. "I'm your hedonist. It's my duty to look after you. Do they know your name?"

"The watchdogs? Not yet, maybe. But they will. They're getting smarter."

"Getting?" the Hedonist repeated puzzledly. "Since when?"

Her furrowed face smoothed out magically. "Since recently. But what I want to know is what you're going to do. You're the one they're hunting. You're the one they want. You're marked and condemned. That trick with the heli won't fool them for long, only until they run a proteinalysis on the wreckage. Then they'll be after you again."

The Hedonist lowered his head and studied the ground. It was more than he cared to admit, but there was no evading her logic. "That's true. And there's no place to run. I'll have to get the Council overruled and its policies—"

"Folly!" she burst out. In the silence, the word was loud and startling. "How many times have you yourself pointed out the fallacy of altruism?"

"True," the Hedonist admitted. "But I am a hedonist. That makes all the difference. My life is making people happy. Would you have me turn my back on all that now? That's my happiness. I could no more stand aside and see others unhappy than I could eat while others are hungry."

"And how many times," she said quietly, "have you pointed out the fallacy of special cases?"

The Hedonist was silent. The streets had become discernible. They trudged along them, and the silent shapes of the past shouldered close. The Hedonist's eyes were watchful.

"Once," Beth said, "this was misery's last hiding place. Rebellion haunted the streets by night and hid in rats' nests by day. Here was the final stand of violence, grief, pain, sickness, rape, murder. . . . If we'd been here then, we'd be dead by now. The watchdogs cleaned it up."

The Hedonist stared at her with curious eyes. "So much for the Council."

Beth sighed. "I suppose so."

They passed into an area where the buildings were sound. Among the dark, looming warehouses, light, occasional and feeble, was evidence of occupation. Twice they had to dodge the sweeping searchlights of mechanical watchmen. They were approaching the spaceport and its complex of warehouses, yards, hotels, and fun houses. They stayed close to the sheltering walls until they emerged, suddenly, into a brightly lighted cross street.

There were people here, walking briskly on business or pleasure, dressed in shorts or slacks or dresses. Some of them reeled and some of them wore masks covering their whole faces and some of them had faces like masks. No one looked at Beth and the Hedonist as they joined the traffic, even though they looked cautiously at everyone who passed.

This was the Strip. Here three worlds met to share their secrets and pool their pleasures, and nothing was taboo. Along this colorful, incandescent street anything could be purchased, anything could be sold.

Beth and the Hedonist stared at the riot of brilliance and color stretching into the distance and forgot, for a moment, that they were fugitives from happiness.

In jumping, sparking letters, the nearest of the signs said:

JOY FOR SALE!

ALL KINDS

YOU NAME IT—WE'VE GOT IT!

THREE WORLDS FUN HOUSE

Licensed, Hedonic Council

Except for individual variations in color and design, the others were much the same. Farther down the street were the more modest signs of hotels, restaurants, and shops. Towering above them was the blood-red sign MARS HOUSE.

"What now?" Beth whispered. With fascination, the Hedonist noticed that she didn't move her lips.

"First, food," the Hedonist said. "I haven't eaten since breakfast, and the sensation, suppressable as it is, is distinct unpleasure. Then rest, which is necessary to future pleasure. I prescribe the same for you."

She frowned and then sighed. "All right," she agreed. "You're the hedonist. But what are you going to do about that?" She pointed to the IDisk on the breast of his shirt. It was glowing brilliantly.

The Hedonist slapped his hand over the telltale IDisk. "I didn't think we'd get so much." He took his hand away; the disk was gone.

"You can't walk around without one," she said.

He put his hand back to his shirt, and the disk was back. It wasn't glowing any more. Beth looked closer. The disk was opaque, and the identification on it was meaningless.

"Turned it over," the Hedonist muttered. "Don't attract attention. It will fool anything except a close inspection, and I don't intend to get that close. Drop your locket inside your blouse."

As she obeyed, he turned her toward the door of a modest Foodomat. It was almost deserted. There was a couple at the back, but they were engrossed in each other. At the side, against the wall, a man teetered idly in a straight chair. The Hedonist inspected him with a casually sweeping glance. The staring pupils told their story. The man was deep in the fantasies of neo-heroin. He was locked up tight in his own, private paradise.

The Hedonist took Beth's arm again. "Come on." They entered the necessary together. It was big enough for three or four people at a time. "Got your false IDisk?" he asked. She nodded. "Coins?" She nodded again, puzzled. "Go into the di-booth. Bring me the tape."

"But won't it be reported to the local hedonist?"

"Don't think so," he said. "Not in a transient area like this. But in case it is, your fake disk should confuse the matter long enough to make it unimportant."

While she went into the booth, the Hedonist took care of his own necessities and was waiting for her when she came out. She handed him the six-inch tape. He scanned it quickly.

Height, weight, temperature, BMR, urinalysis for sugar and the keto-steroid indicators of adrenal activity, refined Papanicolau cancer test—he gave them no more than a glance. He skipped over the section dealing with the external senses and the sensory network, scanned the X-ray report and the electrocardiogram, and barely noted the E.Q. The blood cell count was what interested him, the red, white, differential, and hemoglobin.

His sigh was heavy with relief. He crumpled up the tape and threw it into the disposal. "Let's eat."

"Wait a minute." She put a hand on his arm. "So the radiation didn't do me any damage. What about you?"

He shook his head. "Can't take a chance. I haven't got a false IDisk. But if you're unharmed, I can't be in any danger."

She frowned but didn't say anything.

Inside the Foodomat, they walked quickly down the glass-fronted serving line, slipping coins into the slots. The Hedonist went to a table with a tray of planked plankton steak with a high-vitamin chlorella sauce and a hot milk-substitute. Beth chose a lighter meal, chiefly low-fat chlorella patties and Kafi. They ate quickly and in silence, glancing frequently at the door. The couple at the back finished and left, but no one came in.

Beth and the Hedonist got up, stuffed their dishes into the disposal, and walked through the doorway. The door slid shut behind them.

"Where now?" Beth asked.

"You're going to rent us a room."

Beth's eyes met his levelly. "One room?"

"Of course," the Hedonist said, surprised. "How many do you think we need?"

When they were within fifty yards of the slideway into the magnificent portal of Mars House, the Hedonist drew Beth suddenly out of the stream of traffic and into a shadowed niche. "Pretend to be interested in me," he muttered. "Put your head on my shoulder."

She put her slim arms around his neck and buried her face in the base of his throat. Her lips moved against it. "What's the matter?"

The Hedonist felt his pulse quicken. "Not so—" he began. "Not so—"

"What?" she asked in a muffled voice.

"Oh, never mind. The clowns are only a few yards away."

"Watchdogs?" she whispered.

They passed in motley, vivid and gay, but their faces were young and sharp and intent. In their hands were the subduers modeled after the ancient electric prodders. They searched the faces on each side of them, lifting masks, inspecting IDisks. There was something horrible in the contrast between their unsmiling purpose and their dress.

So passes power dressed in the clothes of joy, the Hedonist thought suddenly. And, Is this the generation that Hedonics fathered?

And then they were gone; the Hedonist felt his body relax. Once more he became conscious of Beth. "Stop that!"

Her lips stopped moving against his skin. "What?" she whispered innocently.

"That! Listen, now. We won't take chances. You'll register for a single, using your false IDisk. I'll sneak into the room later. The clerk will want to know your business." He paused and thought swiftly. "Say that you're volunteering for the new Venus colony. Got money for the deposit?"

She shook her head. Her lips slid deliciously across the base of his throat, and her silky hair brushed against his cheek.

"There's a pocket inside the shirt. Money in it. Take it."

Her hand was cool and slow and sensual as it fumbled the money out of the pocket and withdrew. In spite of the Hedonist's efforts at suppression, his breathing quickened. Then she was gone, and he felt suddenly alone, suddenly cold and deserted.

She walked quickly, youthfully, to the slideway and stepped onto it. She disappeared through the rose portal without a backward glance.

"Old fool!" he said savagely, and he walked slowly toward the hotel.

The lobby was remarkably spacious. It must have been at least twenty feet square. The red resiloid floor was sprinkled with red sand that grated underfoot, and the walls were the realistic depth murals of Martian landscapes. The lobby was lighted by a Mars-sized sun suspended invisibly from the ceiling. Periodically, the Hedonist understood, the sun faded out and Deimos and Phobos raced across the dark blue dome of the ceiling, the swift inner moon twice a day from west to east.

Beth was standing at the desk, talking to the clerk; as the Hedonist passed, she slid her IDisk under its scanner. The Hedonist fed a coin into the newsfax dispenser. A sheet of paper slid into his hand. He took it absently and wandered over to the elevator. It was a crude-seeing openwork model in a rough, tubular frame; behind it the wall curved shinily like the outer hull of a spaceship. The Hedonist sat down on a mocked-up luggage carrier and hid his face behind the news sheet.

Hedonic Index at 2000: 94%. Weather for tomorrow: same as yesterday, sunny and warm after the early morning shower. News bulletin: the flash noticed over the Old City at 2009 has been identified as a meteor. . . .

Meteor, the Hedonist thought with sudden clarity. Unhappiness has been exiled from Earth. The unexpected, the unpredicted, and unpleasant? Deny it; suppress it. Does it flash in the sky? It comes from space. It is an alien.

The Hedonist looked back at the sheet. The rest of it was hotel advertising. One of the ads said:

Visit the Exotic MARTIAN ROOM
(in the penthouse)
Against the Outré background of the *CRATER*
Taste
Strange *LUXURIES* and Stranger *DELIGHTS*
"A pleasure experience without compare"

At the bottom of the sheet was the notation: *Hedonist on duty at all hours. Press 11 for therapy.*

A breeze touched his face with a familiar fragrance. Something small and light landed on his outstretched hand. Beside him, the elevator climbed quietly. The Hedonist looked up. The cage was disappearing through the blue arch of the sky. In his hand was a crumpled corner of paper. Behind the cover of the news sheet, he smoothed it out. There was a number on it: 3129. He squeezed the paper into a ball and slipped it into his pocket.

When the elevator returned, he threw the news sheet into the disposal beside the chair and entered the cage. "Mars Room," he said.

The penthouse turned out to be on the thirty-fifth floor, but it was a quick trip. The only light in the room came through one wide transparent wall; it was the phosphorescence of the crater. Wavering blue and green fingers clutched at the room and the huddled shapes in the dark corners. The Hedonist stood there for a moment listening, in spite of himself, to the oddly stirring atonal music, smelling the pungent alkaloids and incenses. But when a tall, thin shape glided out of the shadows toward him with a whispered question, the Hedonist turned quickly, found the fire door, and ran down the steps.

The stairs were dark and deserted. The Hedonist wondered if they had ever been used. Within a minute, he was outside a door marked 3129.

The corridor was empty. He rapped gently and the door slid open. He stepped inside quickly and shut the door behind him.

The room was empty.

The Hedonist searched the room frantically, but there was no possible place for her to hide. There were only eighty-one square feet to the room, and she was on none of them.

His stomach suddenly felt cold and empty, as if the meal he had eaten only a little while before had suddenly been teleported away.

"Hedonist?" she asked. There was alarm in her voice. "Is that you?"

He jumped and then sighed with relief. "Yes," he said. She was in the necessary. Now he could hear the muffled spatter of the sprays behind the door.

"I'll be out in a minute," she said.

She was. The door opened. She was dressed in something black, lacy, and clinging, and she was brushing the damp ends of her hair. The Hedonist had never seen her look so desirable. Suddenly he wasn't tired any more. He felt young and alive again.

"Where did you get the clothes?" he asked.

She brushed past him; it was an upsetting experience. She pushed the button that folded the chairs and tables into the wall and raised the bed through the floor. "Ordered them," she said carelessly. "There was money left. We need clothes that won't be recognized. There's some for you, too."

She motioned toward the luggage door. It slid open at his touch. In the compartment behind were two boxes. The Hedonist opened the top one. Inside was a dark-blue tunic and a pair of slacks. He never got to look in the other one. A thump on the floor drew him around.

On the narrow strip of floor beside the bed was a pillow. He looked at Beth, startled. "What's the reason for that?"

"That," she said sweetly, tossing a blanket down beside the pillow, "is where you're going to sleep."

"I don't understand," he said in bewilderment. "We've been sleeping together for almost a week now—"

"But that's over," she said, wide-eyed and innocent. "You said so this morning. And this is scarcely the time for therapy. Unless it's a question of *your* happiness—"

His happiness? Of course not. That was absurd. "Of course not," he said, frowning. "Only—"

"Only what?" she asked when he didn't finish.

"Nothing," he said and settled himself on the hard floor.

He turned over and over in the darkness, trying to find a comfortable place for his hip and shoulder bones. There weren't any.

Absurd, he said to himself. Beth was acting very strange; not like herself at all. He yawned, and a wave of relaxed weariness swept out toward the extremities of his body. Definitely not hedonic.

The bed was plenty big enough for two. . . . It was soft . . . molded itself to a tired body . . . . and Beth was softer . . .

IX

Even in the common affairs of life, in love, friendship, and marriage, how little security have we when we trust our happiness in the hands of others!

WILLIAM HAZLITT

The Hedonist woke up. He stared into the darkness above him and tried to figure out what had awakened him. There was no sound, no movement, no odor. And yet something—indefinable—was different about the room.

When he identified it, it was only a little thing. He couldn't hear Beth's soft, even breathing.

He sprang up, grunting a little from the pain of sore, stiffened muscles, and switched on the lights. The bed was empty. Beth wasn't in the room. The little cubicle of the necessary was empty, too.

Beth was gone.

He slid the door open and glanced up and down the hall. It was dark and deserted. Slowly he let the door go shut, walked to the bed, and sank down on the edge.

Gone. Beth had left him. Silently, in the middle of the night, without a word, without—he glanced with sudden hope around the room, but it turned to disappointment—a note. Gone. It was a dismal word; it seemed to fit the way he felt—a cold, drawn-out emptiness.

Maybe she was better off on her own. Maybe he was dangerous to her. But she might have said something. He wouldn't have tried to keep her. He would have—

He suppressed the anguish, devalued the importance. She was gone. The question: What should he do now?

He glanced at his watch. It was almost midnight. Three hours since he had laid down on the floor. He had slept, he supposed, for a little more than two of those. Now, he was still tired, much stiffer, but there would be no more sleep. He felt sure of that.

He got up impatiently and paced the room. Three paces. Turn. Three paces. Turn. It annoyed him, having to sidle around the bed. He lowered it into the floor and kicked his pillow and blanket after it before the floor closed over it.

It was better, but not much. His pacing was still profitless. He shrugged, stripped off his underclothes, and stepped into the necessary. Steamy jets loosened his muscles; icy jets refreshed him. When he was dry, he inspected the dispensers on the wall.

Ethyloid, one of them was labeled. Three positions were available: Scotch, bourbon, gin. The Hedonist shook his head. He wanted to improve his ratiocinations, not dampen them. That meant, too, no neo-heroin and no mescaline. He located the spigot labeled *Coffee.*

Not Kafi? he thought in surprise. He shrugged. No doubt it was part of the Mars House scheme of décor. He filled a cup with the dark, steaming liquid and sipped it. It was the most delicious stuff he had ever tasted.

That was one consolation, he thought wryly. Du Pont had brewed another batch, and it was the best the laboratories had ever done.

He told himself to forget about Beth. He told himself several times. He had to concern himself with important things. . . . Eventually the hedonic exercises were almost successful. Although Beth was not forgotten, she was pushed into a corner of his mind and imprisoned there where she could not scatter his thoughts in an unwary moment.

He concentrated on the problem of survival.

Decision: His survival depended on the overthrow of the Council.

Question: Was his survival worth the price?

Answer: No, not alone; but it isn't the life that's important; it is Earth and hedonics.

While he had been occupied with individual therapies, the Council had turned off the main road. They were in full cry down the wrong trail. The rabbit they were chasing was an illusory rabbit. It is not correct to say that the quarry is unimportant, the chase is the thing. Unless the rabbit is real and worthwhile, the chase becomes unreal and worthless.

The tricked hound soon loses his eagerness for the hunt.

The Council had turned to pure hedonism. It had gone far back, to Aristippus and the Cyrenaic School: the only good is the sentient pleasure of the moment; the true art of life is to crowd as much enjoyment as possible into every moment.

It was false, just as every extreme must be. Happiness had to prepare for the future, or there was no future for happiness. Every moment is important, not just for the happiness it contains but for the happiness it leads to. Every moment must make a man readier to understand happiness, to recognize it, to seize it, and to hold it.

That was what illusion couldn't do. Imaginary gratification dulled the senses and pushed every other type of satisfaction farther out of reach. It even failed itself; eventually unreasoned gratification becomes meaningless.

The only road was the middle road. The only hedonism was rational, the hedonism of Epicurus, Socrates, Plato and Aristotle.

Eventually Earth would realize that. Pure hedonism could not endure. But it was important to save Earth the long detour which might, eventually, discredit hedonics itself.

But how to discredit the Council!

The Council had maneuvered itself into a position of near invulnerability. 1) It had placed itself above the law—even though that meant the inevitable downfall of law itself. And 2) It had legislated hedonics into a science, which is like legislating a sow's ear into a silk purse. It didn't make it one, but it punished everyone who called it by the wrong name.

But it was only *near* invulnerability. There was always the Congress. The names of fifty hedonists on a petition could call an emergency session, and while the Congress was in session every hedonist was immune from arrest and any proceedings against him.

What the Congress had done, the Congress could undo.

The Hedonist's only problem was to get fifty names on a petition. It was not a small problem: he was a hunted man.

He couldn't do it alone. He needed help. He could, he felt sure, get help from the dependents in his ward, but he couldn't drag them into what could be considered illegal activity. The logical choice were the hedonists themselves; they were responsible for the situation, and they could do the most good.

He considered the hotel hedonist for only a second. He didn't know the man, and couldn't take chances. The first poor chance he took would be his last. He closed his eyes and ran over the list of the hedonists he knew. Suddenly he snapped his fingers and moved to the phone.

He consulted the directory on the panel beneath the screen, punched a two-digit number, waited until the screen flickered and buzzed approvingly, and punched a seven-digit number. There was one man he could trust: Lari.

They had gone through the Institute together. Ten intimate years of living together and mutual analyses and shared confidences had exposed a bedrock of character. Their chance meetings at conventions and Congresses had been infrequent, but the understanding and affection couldn't change.

He knew Lari better, the Hedonist thought, than he knew himself.

The screen got gray and defined itself into patterns of dark and light. Lari looked up wearily from his desk, his face lined, his eyes large and dark. The Hedonist stabbed a button. The screen went dark.

"Yes?" Lari said. "Something seems to be wrong."

"It does indeed," the Hedonist said in a deep voice. "That is why I have called you. Lari, this is—this is—" For a frantic, impossible moment, he groped wildly for the name. He had not been a name for twenty-three years; he had been a position, a manipulator of people's happiness. Then he said, "Morgan. This is Morgan."

"Morgan?" Lari's voice was twisted and strange.

The Hedonist frowned, wished he could see Lari's face, but he couldn't risk his own face on the screen.

"Where are you?" Lari asked.

"Never mind," the Hedonist said. "That isn't important. I need your help."

"Yes," Lari said heavily. "I guess you do."

"You know then?"

"Yes. Go on. What can I do?"

"Meet me. I've got to talk to you."

"Where?"

The Hedonist thought swiftly. "Interplanetary Strip. There's a fun house called the Three Worlds."

"How'll I find you?"

"I'll find you," the Hedonist said. "Will you come? Now? I wouldn't ask you if it wasn't—"

"I'll come. It'll be about half an hour."

"Good. See you then."

The Hedonist turned off the screen and looked around for his clothes. They were gone.

He found his IDisk on the floor beneath the disposal; it had stopped phosphorescing. He held it in his hand and stared around a room that, except for the discarded underclothes on the floor, was as bare as he was. Then he thought of the luggage compartment.

The door was a little ajar. Inside there was one box. In it were the blue tunic and slacks and sealed packages of disposable underwear, socks, and shoes. He slipped into them quickly. In his preoccupation, he almost didn't hear the noise outside the door.

It was a scuffing sound. The Hedonist stared at the door and silently flicked the button that locked it. He scooped up the box and his discarded underclothes and stuffed them down the disposal. He noticed the cup, and that followed. He noticed the IDisk in his hand and stuck it on the tunic, backward again.

Now to get out. He stopped, stricken. There was no way out. Mars House was newer than the Council Building. The hotel had no windows; even if it had, his geckopads were gone.

Someone tried the door and found it locked. The Hedonist glanced frantically around the room. He could, he supposed, hide in the bed, but the floor recess would be searched.

"Open the door," someone shouted. "In the name of the Council. Joy!"

Watchdogs! In two silent steps, the Hedonist was beside the luggage compartment. He slid back the door and wedged himself into the box, his knees doubled up against his chest like a fetus. He let the door slip shut until there was only a hairline crack letting light and air in to him.

There was a moment to think. How had they found him? The only answer that came to him was Beth!

No! He refused to believe it. Not Beth. And yet—Beth had sneaked away while he was asleep. But if she wanted to turn him in, why should she have rescued him from his precarious position clinging to the outside of the Council Building. Unless—she had changed her mind and had decided to turn him in to save herself.

No! Not Beth! And yet—she had deceived him before.

The odor of burned plastic drifted into the box with him. Something slammed nearby. Feet tramped into the room. Bright motley crossed in front of the crack. It turned, searching the room. There was a subduer in its hand, like a two-foot ebony club.

The brief whir of machinery told him that the bed was being raised. The feet clomped impatiently, in and around. The Hedonist watched the crack intently, hardly daring to breathe. Suddenly, very close and huge, appeared fingers, reaching . . .

The Hedonist jerked his hand back. The door clicked shut. The box fell out from under him. He dropped, fast. He clutched his hands tight against his sides. They could be scraped off against the wall of the chute. He fell in utter darkness. He was afraid.

A giant palm pressed him down, forced the breath from his body, flattened him against a hard, smooth board, tried to mash him, squash him, break him. The darkness turned red and then became black again. . . .

The Hedonist opened his eyes. His legs were dangling into emptiness. There was a little light filtering past them, and he twisted himself around so that he could look out of the box without committing himself to leave it.

He was at the bottom of the chute. Radiating out from the box in all directions were endless rubberoid belts, lighted only by the dim radiance of machines looming beyond. He was in the service cellar.

Something pressed against his back, pushing him out of the box. He grabbed the edges and tried to hold back, but it was futile. Unceremoniously, he was dumped onto one of the belts. It complained at his weight, but it started him toward a distant and unknown destination.

The Hedonist slid his legs over the edge and dropped to the floor three feet beneath. He stood still for a moment, studying the pattern of moving belts and chattering machines. One of the machines had lights flashing inside it. They flashed in sequence, and it clucked to itself as if it were counting.

The Hedonist looked it over quickly. There were thirty-five bulbs, and the one that was lighted for a moment was nineteen from the end. He grabbed the handle of the heavy switch on the front of the machine and pulled it open. The machine went dark and silent. He hoped that it had controlled the elevator.

The service cellar was a maze. Tunnels and narrow passageways led here and there with apparent aimlessness, ending abruptly, twisting, turning. The belts took up so much floor space that the Hedonist spent most of his time crawling under or climbing over. The cellar wasn't meant for men.

At last he found a stairway that wound upward in a tight spiral. He ran up the steps quickly. After two turns he saw a glowing button in the curved wall. He pressed it. The wall swung aside. The Hedonist walked into the hotel lobby.

It was dark and empty. The sun had set. Phobos was moving swiftly across the sky toward the east.

He was beside the elevator framework. Distantly, he heard a ghostly voice. "Hel-l-l-l-p!" it said. ". . . stuhuck!"

The red sand gritted under his feet as the Hedonist smiled and walked out into the brilliant night.

Money was a problem. Beth had taken all the money he had. The Hedonist solved that one by picking up a dime on the street. He walked into the glittering entrance arcade to the Three Worlds Fun House and studied the slot machines for a moment. Finally he slipped the coin into a dexterity game.

The machine was an enclosed cylinder separated into ten horizontal compartments by transparent, bright, colored disks. In the center of each disk was a hole diminishing in size from the bottom to the top. At the sloped bottom was a hollow plastic ball. Three jets of compressed air lifted it through the holes in the disks, and the intensity of each jet was controlled by a key on the front. The object of the game was to raise the ball as high as possible before it toppled into one of the compartments.

The first time the Hedonist got back his dime. The second time he worked the ball clear to the top and hit the jackpot. He scooped the dimes into the tunic pocket and walked to the next machine. It was a tone analyzer.

Within the range of the machine, the Hedonist could hear a compound tone. It was faithfully duplicated on a screen by a swirl of colors. As the Hedonist analyzed the tone into its components of frequency, intensity, wave form, and phase, the colors separated into a prismatic layer arrangement. A multiple of the winning could be obtained by identifying the overtones and their intensity.

By the third trial, the Hedonist had corrected for the machine's inevitable distortion and collected the jackpot. The whole business had taken five minutes.

It was not as difficult as it seemed. The machines were shills for the more expensive pleasures inside; they weren't set for a high return. Being public, too, they would never be approved by the Council if they produced too much unpleasure. Most significant, however, was the Hedonist himself. Sensory analysis and its corollary, dexterity, were his business. He had spent years on more difficult exercises than these.

Weighed down by more than fifty dollars in change, the Hedonist walked into the fun house. The clear doors swung open in front of him. When they swung shut behind, the lights went out.

There was a disturbing moment of disorientation, as if he were floating aimlessly in space. It didn't help to identify the cause: an interrupter automatically canceling the wave lengths of light that should have reached him. Laughter poured in on him from all sides. Suddenly there was an apparition in front of him.

It was a satyr with dainty hoofs and shaggy legs and sharp little horns. Its red, sensual lips were curled into a joyful grin and its eyes were alight with laughter and lust. It hung upside down from the ceiling.

"Joy, sir, joy!" it cried. "Welcome to the Three Worlds. Name your pleasure. If it exists anywhere on the three worlds, you will find it here. What will you have?"

Before the Hedonist could speak, the satyr had disappeared. In a wink, it was back, floating horizontally.

"Joy, sir!" it shouted gleefully. "What will it be? Gambling?" He swept out an arm expansively, and a doorway opened in the darkness. The path led upward. At its end were glitter and movement and brilliance, fantastic machines doing incomprehensible things. "The very latest devices, sir. Those you saw in the arcade are only a poor sample of what we can provide in color, action, and thrill." His voice dropped to a confidential whisper. "Eight out of every ten players leave winners."

"It's surprising you can afford to remain open," the Hedonist commented wryly.

"It's a rich man's pleasure, sir," the satyr said quickly with a contagious laugh. "What shall it be? Sensies? We have all the latest tapes, sir. And many that won't be released to the public for months. The thrill of winning, sir, the ecstasy of success without the danger of failure. Create, achieve, enjoy, love! There is no limit to what the sensies can give you, effortlessly." His voice dropped again. "We can even offer you—real pain! Smuggled. Very rare and expensive. What will it be?"

The satyr and the pathway snapped out of existence. When the satyr reappeared, it was still horizontal, but its head and feet had been reversed.

"Joy, sir! How can we please you? Will it be girls?" As it spoke, doors opened in the darkness; behind each door was a different girl in a different pose. "We have all kinds: amateurs and professionals, ice maidens and nymphs; short ones, tall ones, thin ones, fat ones; girls of every shape and color, of every talent and desire. Name your delight, and she is yours!"

Helplessly, the Hedonist watched the satyr vanish. When it flashed back into view, it was standing on its feet. It threw out its arms dramatically.

"What shall it be, sir?" it demanded stridently. "The ethyloids? We have them all. List your flavor: Scotch, bourbon, Irish, rye, Canadian. . . . Describe your mixture; we will prepare it. Guaranteed to be without later unpleasure."

Its arms dropped and it looked cautiously to both sides and whispered, "We even have some real, vegetable-based, authentic Kentucky sour-mash. Distilled ourselves according to an ancient recipe—at fantastic risk. A most rare, raw flavor!"

Its voice lifted again. "Your pleasure, sir! Name it and you shall have it if it is available anywhere on three worlds. Narcotics? Of course! All the alkaloids. Neo-heroin. Whisper your addiction, and we will supply it in any form you desire. Or if you have none, let me recommend the unusual sensations of the latest craze—mescaline! It will slow time to a crawl. It will let you be beside yourself—legally and literally. Enjoy the symptoms of schizophrenia—that long-lost mental thrill—"

"A booth by the door," the Hedonist said quietly.

The satyr broke off in mid-declamation. It looked a little foolish. "Er—uh—your pleasure? A booth, sir?"

The Hedonist jingled the coins in his pocket.

The satyr recovered quickly. "Of course, sir. A booth. But here!" The Hedonist felt something slip over his face. "In the Three Worlds, identity is lost. Only pleasure is recognized! Only joy is unmasked!"

And it vanished.

X

There is only one way to achieve happiness
on this terrestrial ball,
And that is to have either a clear conscience,
or none at all.

OGDEN NASH

The Hedonist blinked as the darkness gave way to light. Half-blindly, he followed a small spot of light through a milling crowd of masked men and women. The spot led him to a dark, transparent door in a line of doors that were lighted and opaque. The booth was more like a good-sized room. There were two comfortable chairs, a table, and a pneumatic couch. Against the wall was a row of coin-operated dispensers. The usual things: drinks and narcotics.

The Hedonist sank wearily into one of the chairs and looked through the door. He could see the fun house entrance. Anyone could see him, too.

"For light and privacy," the table said, *"deposit one dollar for five minutes."*

Into a slot in the table top, the Hedonist fed five dollars in change. The room brightened. Around the edge of the door, a row of strong lights came on. They beamed against it. He could still see out, but no one could see in.

He bought a cup of Kafi from the dispenser and leaned back to sip it. It was the same bitter brew he had tasted in the morning. He shrugged and drank it and watched the entrance. It had been half an hour since his call to Lari. The hedonist should be coming into the fun house very soon.

Other people came through the door but not Lari. One girl came in already masked. Her mask was passion; below it was a young, curved body in revealing red satin. She didn't wait to have the fun-house wares described. She knew what she wanted and ignored the darkness as she brushed past the satyr's image—both of them invisible from this side—into the room.

A heavy-set man in a blue suit and a mask of thick-veined, red-faced rage grabbed her around the waist and tried to draw her close. She let herself be swung in against him while she deftly flicked back his mask and kept on turning right out of his arms. She disappeared in the surging throng.

After five minutes, Lari had not come in. The Hedonist watched the patrons of the Three Worlds stream past his door toward unknown destinations and unknown pleasures.

Some were dressed in rich, glittering clothes, and some were dressed in transparencies, and once a girl in a mask of agony and nothing else broke screaming through the mob and dashed across the floor pursued by a naked satyr.

Joy! the Hedonist thought. Pleasure! Here hedonism has reached its nadir. It can sink no lower.

It could, though. It could sink below saturnalia to madness. It could sink to delusion inanimately received, where nothing was important but the senses—the body useless (let it wither), the mind worthless (let it rot).

But wasn't this implicit in hedonism from the start? No. It wasn't. The pursuit of happiness need not be passive, could not be passive. And the freedom to be happy need not be license, could not be license, for license leads inevitably to unpleasure.

Hedonism was right. Pleasure was the only human good. But it had to be balanced against the total pleasure possible. Choice was necessary, and that demanded wisdom.

Like wisdom, happiness could not be a gift. You can teach a man, but you can't make him wise. You can show him the road to happiness, but he must travel alone.

Happiness was unique. Put it in a man's hands and it was ashes.

Lari stood in the doorway, blinking. His eyes were dark, troubled pools. His face was haggard and drawn. He pushed forward out of the darkness, and there was a mask on his face. The mask was fear.

The Hedonist glanced at his watch. Since he had put in the call, almost an hour had elapsed. He watched Lari work his way through the crowd, looking all around him with fear-widened eyes. Lari stopped the man with the mask of rage, but the man shook him off.

No one followed Lari. No one came through the entrance behind him. As Lari passed, the Hedonist swung the door open and caught his wrists.

"In here," he said softly, pulling.

Lari started and then let himself be tugged into the booth. As the door swung shut behind him, he stared at the Hedonist with terror-stricken eyes. It took a moment for the Hedonist to realize that the expression was in the mask.

But Lari kept staring. "Great sorrow, Morgan," he whispered, "is that you?"

"Yes," the Hedonist said. "What's the matter?"

Lari pointed toward the ceiling. "Look at yourself!"

The ceiling was a mirror. The Hedonist looked up. Gazing down at him was an idiot, loose-lipped and imbecilically happy. The Hedonist shuddered and jerked his head down. He started to lift the mask from his face.

"Never mind," Lari said, sinking down into the other chair. "Leave it on. It's safer that way."

Fear faced the Idiot across the table. "All right," Fear said. "Tell me what you want."

The Idiot smirked. Briefly he described what had happened to him that day, the summons, Gomer Berns, the Council. . . . But when he started to describe the Council's new devices and its plans for them, Fear cut him off impatiently. "I know all that," he said, fidgeting.

"You know and you haven't done anything?"

"What is there to do? So, you escaped. What do you plan to do now? I don't see how I can help—"

"I don't want you to help me," the Idiot said. "I'm not important. The important thing is to get the world back on the right road. We've got to replace the Council—"

Fear laughed nervously, choking. "How do you plan to do that?"

The Idiot outlined his plan for petition. "Once we have an emergency session, we can throw out the Council and get the world back to sanity. You and I know the proper hedonic techniques; we know that this way is madness. And once the situation is presented to the Congress in the proper light, it will defend the old standards. Well," he said as Fear was silent, "isn't it a good plan?"

"A fine plan, a beautiful plan," Fear said breathlessly. "It hasn't got a chance."

"Why not?"

"You're not a hedonist anymore. The Council revoked your license, destroyed your office and files. You're a criminal. You'll be picked up any minute and put to surgery."

The Idiot brushed it aside. "That doesn't matter. I can hide until the Congress has acted."

"Anyone who helps you is liable to the same penalties," Fear said suddenly. "But it doesn't matter. That's right. You'll never get an emergency session. And even if you did, it wouldn't do any good. There isn't a hedonist in the country who would sign your petition. The Congress is behind the Council, wholeheartedly."

"All?" the Idiot said dazedly.

"All! Every one!" Fear pounded hysterically on the table. Suddenly, frantically, he turned toward the wall and slipped a coin into one of the dispensers. A tiny syrette of neo-heroin dropped into his hand.

The Hedonist's eyes were incredulous as they watched Lari push up a sleeve, apply the syrette to a vein, and press the button. There was a quick, sharp, hissing sound. Lari dropped the empty syrette to the floor and leaned back, his eyes closed.

"Neo-heroin?" the Hedonist said.

"Yes, I'm an addict," Lari said calmly, his eyes still closed. "It's nothing to be ashamed of."

"For anyone but a hedonist, no. But how can you expect to help your dependents when your senses are dulled and your mind is depressed?"

"I'm a person, too," Lari said violently. "I have emotions and desires like everyone else. I need happiness too."

"You haven't been happy?"

"Happy?" Lari said softly. "I haven't been happy since I was a child. None of us have. We were brave and foolish, just a handful of hedonic therapists shouldering the burden of a world's happiness. It was mad. It was wonderful, but it was mad and impossible."

"But we did it," the Hedonist exclaimed. "We did it."

Lari sighed. "Yes, we did it. For a little while. Not perfectly, not completely, but we did it. And we paid for it. We sold ourselves to a thousand people each; we were their slaves. They brought their burdens to us, and we took them on. There are few nights I have had as much as five hours sleep, and most of that was allotted to therapy."

"You don't know what you're saying!"

"Oh, I know. I know too well. It was more than feeble tissue could endure, the labor and the sorrow. And when the Council offered us a chance at happiness, do you think we could turn it down? By then I'd already been on neo-heroin for two years."

The Hedonist clenched his fist. How could he convince Lari that he was wrong? It was so difficult because there was truth in what Lari said. A hedonist became a machine for making people happy; after a few years he even forgot that he had a name. "But it's wrong, Lari!" the Hedonist pleaded. "What the Council wants to do is wrong!"

"How can it be wrong," Lari said wearily, "to make people happy? How can it be wrong for me to be happy?"

"The wrong is the wrong we do ourselves," the Hedonist said quietly. "You've got to break the habit, Lari. You know how. And you know the techniques of happiness."

"Oh, I'll break it," Lari said distantly. "I'll break it in a few weeks. And I'll be happy." His eyes were sad behind the mask. "But you're lost. You've thrown your chance away."

Inside the booth, the lights dimmed. "For light and privacy," the table said, "deposit one dollar for five minutes."

The Hedonist was busy dropping coins into the table slot when the door opened. He moved smoothly to his feet. Standing in the doorway was the girl in the mask of passion and the red gown. She stared at him as she moved close. She lifted his mask, and he let her do these things, not knowing why.

She let the mask fall back and threw her arms around his neck. "It's you!" she sobbed.

It was Beth's voice. The Hedonist pulled down her mask. It was Beth's face. There was a glad smile on her lips, but there were tears in her eyes. They had a strange effect on the Hedonist. They made his heart pound and his knees weak.

"I've been hunting for you everywhere," she said.

"Where did you go? Why did you leave me?" the Hedonist asked, his eyes never leaving her face.

"There's no time for explanations," she said, drawing back and tugging at his arm. "We've got to get away from here."

"A little while after you left, the watchdogs came," he said, pulling back. "They almost caught me."

"You can't think I had anything to do with that!" she exclaimed. "I couldn't. Oh, you've got to trust me!"

"Why?" the Hedonist asked. "You've been acting very strangely."

"You're the hedonist," she reminded him sharply. "Don't you know?"

He shook his head in bewilderment.

"Oh, fury!" she exclaimed. And then, more softly, "I'm in love with you. I had no intention of marrying anyone but you. I wanted to look after you, to make you happy. I was no exception. All the women in the ward were in love with you, but I was the only one with the courage to do anything about it."

The Hedonist was suddenly aware that, under his mask, his jaw had dropped down. He closed it with a snap. "That's fantastic!" And he added, suddenly, "You made me sleep on the floor."

A smile slipped across her face. "You may be the hedonist," she said, "but you don't know anything about love. Some desires should be thwarted; it's like shading a flower that's used to the sun—it grows furiously to reach the light."

The Hedonist stared at her, wordless. "It's impossible," he said at last. "I'm a hedonist. I can't marry or love—"

"Fool! Fool!" she groaned. "How long do you think you can hold up the sky all by yourself? Just once, think of yourself. That's all over! Can't you see?"

Out of the corner of his eye, the Hedonist caught a flicker of movement. The walls of the booth fell through the floor. Behind the walls was the motley of clowns. A dozen black subduers were pointed toward them.

At first the Hedonist thought they were wearing masks, all of them the same: impassive blankness. But they were faces. The Hedonist realized, with a shock of recognition, that one of them belonged to the Council secretary.

"The girl's right," the secretary said. "It's all over."

His presence meant that it was a trap, carefully planned, skillfully executed. The Hedonist looked at Beth and the mask of passion dangling from her neck.

Slowly, painfully, she shook her head. "No, no!" she whispered. "You can't believe that. You mustn't—"

"I don't," he said suddenly. He turned to the secretary. "What are you going to do?"

"We're taking you in for treatment," the secretary said unemotionally. "Both of you."

Both of you. Beth and himself. Not Lari.

The Hedonist looked at Lari. Through the mask of fear, he could see his old friend's eyes. They were the eyes of a man who was lost, forever. He had damned himself, and his own private paradise would be his hell. No amount of pleasure would ever drown the pain.

"I'm sorry, Lari," the Hedonist said softly.

The eyes winced and closed. The mask turned aside.

"Let's go," the Hedonist said to the secretary.

For the second time that night, the lights went out.

XI

It is said an Eastern monarch once charged his wise men to invent him a sentence to be ever in view, and which should be true and appropriate in all times and situations. They presented him the words: "And this, too, shall pass away." How much it expresses! How chastening in the hour of pride! How consoling in the depths of affliction! . . . And yet, let us hope, it is not quite true. Let us hope, rather, that by the best cultivation of the physical world beneath and around us, and the best intellectual and moral world within us, we shall secure an individual, social, and political prosperity and happiness, whose course shall be onward and upward, and which, while the earth endures, shall not pass away.

ABRAHAM LINCOLN

The Hedonist threw his fist and felt the paralyzing shock go through it and up his arm. But in his shoulder he felt the solid impact of the fist against something that yielded. The secretary grunted and fell backward in a flurry of falling noises. There were shouts and groans and the clatter of feet.

But the Hedonist was too busy to listen to them, too busy even to enjoy the pleasure of striking back against the forces that had taken his life and his world and pulled them down together. He had swung on around, caught Beth, and pulled her through the door of the booth and into the shouting, milling crowd outside. There was laughter at first, as most of the patrons thought it was a joke, and then moans and screams and growing hysteria.

The darkness was absolute. They hadn't left it when they left the booth. Someone had an interrupter focused on the whole area.

The Hedonist held tightly to Beth's wrist and forced his way through the jostling, clutching, screaming crowd. He brought Beth close and yelled in her ear, "Are you all right?"

He could feel her head nod and then her lips were moving against his ear. "I can't fight this mob," she shouted. "You go ahead. I'll steer from behind."

"Where?" the Hedonist asked.

"Never mind! Quick! There's no telling how long the darkness will last."

The Hedonist hesitated, shrugged, and turned. He lowered his numbed shoulder and plunged into the squirming, clawing sea of humanity. She guided him with strong, sure movements of her hand. Fists bounced off his body and face and nails raked him, but he managed to get his partially paralyzed arm up in front of his face and forced his way onward, thankful for the first time that his body was big and strong.

It seemed as if the darkness had thickened, as if the night had arms and hands and feet to hold them back. The pressure increased and grew until, suddenly, it fell away before them and there was nothing.

The Hedonist reached with his foot and there were steps going down. He stumbled down them, dragging Beth behind. When they reached a level stretch again, the noise had faded in the distance, and they seemed to be alone. He brought Beth up beside him.

"What is this?" he demanded. "Where are we going? Who's using the interrupter? Who—?"

"No time now," she panted. "Come on. I'll try to tell you as we escape."

She led him through the darkness with a sure instinct. "The answer to most of your questions is, the Underground."

It was a strange new word. The Hedonist let it tumble around in his mind, and everywhere it touched it summoned up an exotic image: men tampering with hedometers; people meeting in dark, hidden places to share their illicit passions of grief, pain, and sorrow; saboteurs spreading infections of gloom. . . .

How could it have existed without his knowledge? "And you're a part of it," he said.

"Ever since I realized that what kept us apart was hedonics. Try to understand us! We aren't troubled about the great mass of the people; they're contented with what they have. We're concerned with the few malcontents who find happiness impossible and get into trouble."

She stopped. The Hedonist got an impression that there was something solid in front of them. In a moment he felt a sudden breath of cool air against his face. Beth led him down another flight of steps and into a straight, level passage.

"Then you aren't trying to overthrow the Council?" he asked, puzzled.

"Of course not. What would be the point? We don't want the responsibility for a world overpopulated with mediocrities. Let the Council have that. All we try to do is to rescue the few who are worth saving."

With one step they came out of the darkness into the

light. The Hedonist blinked at the brightness; the blindness wore off quickly. They were in a long, narrow passage lighted at infrequent intervals by bulbs in ceiling pits. The Hedonist could not see the end of it.

"Then you think hedonics is a failure?" he said.

The struggle through the mob had torn the red gown. Beth was trying, with only partial success, to hold it together. "No," she said with great seriousness—and the Hedonist would have smiled at her youthful gravity if it hadn't been so real. "For the great mass of the people, hedonics was a howling success. As a physiological and psychological discipline, it was a great step forward. But as a practical science, it was impossible. How many hedonists practiced it in those terms?"

The Hedonist looked blank.

"Very few," Beth said soberly. "Those few tried and of them only you and one or two others really succeeded. That is why the Council had to get rid of you. The rest bowed before the impossibility and compromised with the world. To be a hedonist, a man would have to be a god—and men aren't divine. Not yet. At least, not many of them." She looked at him with warm, dark eyes.

The Hedonist felt them melt a cold spot deep down inside him; it had been there for a long time, so long that he had forgotten all about it. "So you rescue the malcontents. Before they go to the surgeon?"

"All we can, and we get most of them."

"And then what?" the Hedonist asked, frowning.

Beth led the way up the few short steps. They came out into the night. The real night with the stars overhead.

"We bring them here," she said.

The Hedonist looked up from her shadowed face. Across the broad field was a towering, pointed shape, reaching up toward space and freedom. "The planets!" he said suddenly. "Mars and Venus."

"And Callisto and Ganymede," Beth added. "We send them out to be colonists. They make good ones. They can work out their discontent against their environment instead of themselves. That's the best therapy for them.

"And that's where we're going."

Before the Hedonist could recover his breath, a broad-shouldered man, who towered above the Hedonist like the ship across the field, had stepped out of the shadows behind them. The Hedonist looked up at the dark, scowling, bearded face. He had never seen more obvious self-torment. He itched to treat the man. *Devalue*, he longed to say, and *substitute*.

"You got him, did you?" the man said in a rumbling voice.

"Yes, Captain."

Captain. The association with the ship across the field was obvious.

"You helped us?" the Hedonist asked. "You're the one I should thank?"

The man nodded gloomily. "Me and some of the boys."

"I don't understand how you could take over a fun house so easily—"

The captain shrugged his massive shoulders. "We own it. We own most of the Strip. We still need things out there"—he waved his hand toward the sky—"that Earth can give us—men and tools—and for that we need money. So we give the rabbits what they really want, and they give us what we need. Used to shanghai a few colonists out of the place, but we stopped that. They were no good; died off too quick."

"Didn't the Council object?"

"Fat lot of good that would do." He chuckled at the idea. "They know what we could do if we took it in our minds to—and there's nothing those fat rabbits could do to stop us.

But we'd better be moving toward the ship. This might be the time the Council will decide to take a chance."

"They don't do anything about your aiding the escaped prisoners?"

"Why should they? Gets them off their hands, don't it? That's all they want. They're happy to leave us alone. Someday, maybe, we'll decide to come back and do something about the Council. Not now. We're too busy."

"Come on," Beth urged.

The Hedonist looked back the way they had come. On the horizon were the dark towers of the Old City, and in front of them was the ghostly radiance of the crater. They seemed like mute fingers trying to warm themselves before a cold, deadly fire. Their silence and pathos overwhelmed him.

"I can't," he groaned. "I can't go. I can't leave Earth like this and go seek my own happiness."

"But you can't help Earth," she pleaded. "There's nothing you can do. You have to accept reality."

The Hedonist was silent. Could he help? Could he overthrow the Council, all by himself? What was reality?

Deep down, he knew that he couldn't do anything. The black spires on the horizon were not fingers but gravestones. No one can raise the dead.

"Earth is happy as it is, I suppose," he said slowly. "It's overcrowded. There's no space left for modifying reality. Perhaps the self-discipline of hedonics demands too much. Maybe the only way to keep Earth from blowing apart from its own conflicting desires is the Council's way."

"I'm afraid it is," Beth said.

"All right," the Hedonist said. "Let's go." They started walking across the starlit field. "I suppose you need hedonists on Venus."

The captain stopped short. "Wait a minute," he growled. "You got the wrong idea. We don't want missionaries.

We're too busy to be happy. We've got a million things to do up there. We've got no use for any of your immorality." He turned viciously toward Beth. "I thought you said—"

"He'll be all right," she said frantically. "I tell you he'll be all right." She tugged at the Hedonist's arm.

Immorality, Captain? No, not immorality. The first truly moral society since man first began to congregate. The first society in which a man's instinct didn't conflict with the demands of society upon him.

Morality wasn't everything, of course. It was a little like death, the end of struggle and conflict. In that sense life was immoral, an eternal fight against the leveling forces, and the immoral, criminal, lawbreaking part of humanity was out there on the planets and the moons of Jupiter, some day to be lifting an illicit hand toward the stars.

That was all very true, but to give it all up! To surrender all he had labored to learn and practice! It was like dying.

What was it the captain had said? *We're too busy to be happy.* The Hedonist could see the truth of that. Happy men don't make good colonists. To tame a planet, to remold a world, takes hungry men, angry men. They had to be discontented, and they had to stay discontented. Otherwise, the world turned on them and broke them.

Devaluation was no good. Suppression was no good. Substitution was no good. You can't devalue the need for food. You can't suppress the desire for breathable air. You can't substitute for the necessities of shelter against the heat and the cold and the insects and the viruses. . . .

"I suppose," the Hedonist said, looking up, "that you could use a doctor. You need obstetricians and geriatricians, I guess. You have people who get sick, who break bones, who have babies, who grow old . . . I imagine the children need teachers. . . ."

A slow, brilliant smile spread across the captain's face. It reminded the Hedonist of the sun suddenly, joyfully breaking through the dark clouds. "Sure, Doc," he said. "Come on. We've got a million things to do and only a few hundred years to do them in."

So the Hedonist thought, his training would not be entirely wasted. His medical skill would be in great demand, and then there would be the children. There would be lots of children as humanity became prolific to populate a world. He would teach the children the hedonic disciplines without removing the angers that kept them alive. Hedonics wasn't finished, after all. It was only a new, finer beginning.

He took Beth's arm possessively, and they started walking toward the tall ship that would take them, without regret, from a world that, after the bitter ages, was going to be one hundred per cent happy.

A bright star hung just above the pointed nose of the ship. It was not Venus, but it was, perhaps, an omen.

There was a great deal to be said for the privilege of being just as unhappy as a man wanted to be.

NEW
BLOOD

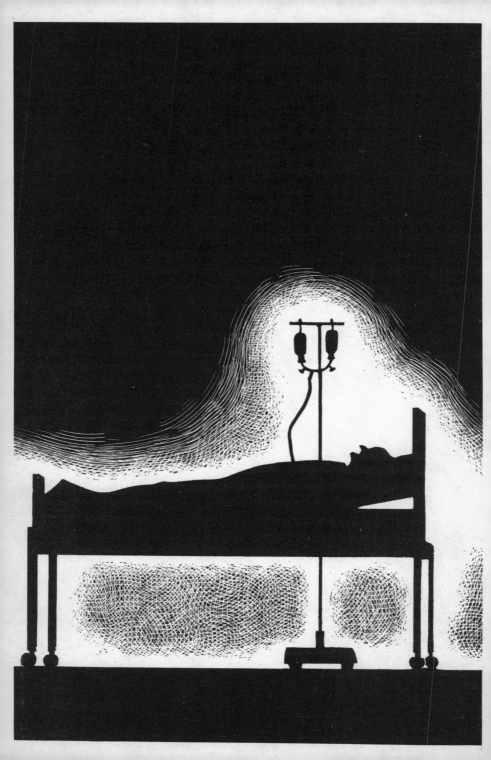

THE YOUNG MAN WAS stretched out flat on the padded hospital table, his bare left arm muscular and brown on the table beside him. The wide, flat band of a sphygmomanometer was tight around his bicep, and the inside of his elbow, where the veins were blue traceries, had been washed with soap and water, swabbed with alcohol, stained brown with iodine.

His eyes followed the quick efficiency of the technician. Her movements were as crisp as the white uniform.

She opened the left-hand door of the big old refrigerator and took a brown bottle from the second shelf. There was a handle at the bottom, fastened to the bottle by a metal band; it was raised now. Swishing below it was an inch of sodium citrate. The rest was vacuum.

The technician broke the tab, stripped off the metal cap, exposing the rubber gasket. From a cardboard box beneath the table she pulled a few feet of plastic tubing. At each end it had a needle. One went into the donor's procaine-deadened vein. The other was thrust through the gasket into the bottle.

Dark red blood raced through the tube, spurted into the bottle; the sodium citrate swirled pinkly. A moment later it was the color of grape juice, frothing at the top.

The technician printed the date and the donor's name in the spaces provided on the label. At the bottom she put her initials. She stuck a piece of adhesive tape above the label and wrote a number on it: 31,197; the same number was written on two small test tubes.

"Keep making a fist," she said, turning the bottle.

When the bottle was full, she closed a clamp on the tube and pulled the needle from the bottle. A square of gauze and a strip of tape was placed over the needle puncture in the donor's arm. She drained the blood in the tubing into the test tubes and slipped them into pockets in a tiny cloth apron hung over the neck of the bottle.

The tubing and needles were tossed away, and a strip of tape was pressed over the top of the bottle.

At the workbench by the window, the technician dabbed three blood samples onto two glass slides, one divided into sections marked A and B. She slipped the slides onto a light box with a translucent glass top; to one sample she added a drop of clear serum from a green bottle marked "Anti-A" in a commercial rack. "Anti-B" came from a brown bottle; "Anti-Rho" from a clear one.

She rocked the box back and forth on its pivots. The donor was sitting up now, watching her with interested eyes.

Sixty seconds later the red cells of the samples marked A and B were still evenly suspended. In the third sample, the cells had clumped together visibly.

"You're O neg all right," the technician said. She scribbled it across the label and on the strip of tape that sealed the top of the pint of blood.

The donor's young lips twisted at the corners.

"Valuable," the technician said briskly, making out a card and then a slip of paper. "Only kind we buy. Shall we put you on our professional donor's list?"

Without hesitation the young man shook his head.

The technician shrugged. She handed him the card. "Thanks anyway. Here's your blood type. Stay seated in the waiting room for ten minutes. The paper is a voucher for twenty-five dollars. You can cash it at the cashier's office—by the front door as you go out."

For a moment after the young man's broad back had disappeared from the doorway, the technician stared after him. Then she shrugged again, turned, and put the pint of blood onto the refrigerator's top left-hand shelf for serology tests.

A pint of whole blood—new life in a bottle for someone who might die without it. Within a few days the white cells will begin to die, the blood will decline in ability to clot. With the aid of refrigeration and the citrate solution, the red cells will last—some of them—for three weeks. After that the blood will be sent to the separator for the plasma, or sold to a commercial company for separation of some of the plasma's more than seventy proteins, the serum albumin, the gamma globulins. . . .

A pint of blood—market price: $25. In a few hours it will be on the second shelf from the top, right-hand side of the refrigerator, with the other pints of O-type blood.

But this blood was special. It had everything other blood had, and something extra that made it unique. There had never been any blood quite like it.

Twenty-five dollars? How much is life worth?

The old man was seventy years old. His body was limp on the hard hospital bed. In the sudden silence after the cutout of the air conditioner's gentle murmur, the harsh unevenness of his breathing was loud. The only movement in the private room was the spasmodic rise and fall of the sheet that covered the old body.

He was living—barely. He had used up his allotted three-score years and ten. It wasn't merely that he was dying—we all are. With him, it was imminent.

Dr. Russell Pearce held one bony wrist in his firm, young right hand. His face was serious, his dark eyes steady, his tanned skin well molded over strong bones.

The old man's face was yellow over a grayish blue, the color of death. It was bony, the wrinkled skin pulled back like a mask for the skull. Once he might have been handsome; now his eyes were sunken, the closed eyelids dark over them, and his nose was a thin, arching beak.

There is a kinship in old age, just as there is a kinship in infancy. Between the two, men differ, but at the extremes they are much the same.

Pearce had seen old men in the wards, charity cases most of them, picked up on the North Side, filthy, winos. The only differences with this man were a little care and a few million dollars. Where this man's hair was groomed and snow-white, the others' was yellowish-gray, long, scraggly on the seamed, thin necks. Where this man's skin was scrubbed and immaculate, the others had dirt in the wrinkles, sores in the crevices.

Pearce laid the arm gently down beside the body and slowly stripped back the sheet. The differences were minor. In dying we are much the same. Once this old man had been tall, strong, vital. Now the thin body was emaciated; the rib cage struggled through the skin, fluttered. The old veins stood out, knotted, ropy, blue, on the sticklike legs.

"Pneumonia?" Dr. Easter asked with professional interest. He was an older man, his hair gray at the temples, his appearance distinguished, calm.

"Not yet. Malnutrition. You'd think he'd eat more, get better care. Money is supposed to take care of itself."

"It doesn't follow. You don't order around a million dollars."

"Anemia," Pearce went on. "Bleeding from a duodenal ulcer, I'd guess. Pulse weak, rapid. Blood pressure low. Arteriosclerosis and all the damage that entails."

Beside him a nurse made marks on a chart. Her face was smooth and young; the skin glowed healthily.

"Let's have a blood count," Pearce said to her briskly. "Urinalysis. Requisition a pint of blood."

"Transfusion?" Easter asked, lifting an eyebrow.

"It'll help—temporarily, anyway."

"But he's dying." It was almost half a question.

"Sure. We all are." Pearce smiled grimly. "Our business is to postpone it as long as we can."

A few moments later, when Pearce opened the door and stepped into the hall, Dr. Easter was talking earnestly to a tall, blond, broad-shouldered man in an expensively cut business suit. The man was about Easter's age, somewhere between forty-five and fifty. The face was strange: it didn't match the body. There was a thin, predatory look to it which was accentuated by slate-gray eyes.

The man's name was Carl Jansen. He was personal secretary to the old man who was dying inside the room. Dr. Easter performed the introductions, and the men shook hands. Pearce reflected that the term "personal secretary" might cover a multitude of duties.

"Dr. Pearce, I'll only ask you one question," Jansen said in a voice as flat and cold as his eyes. "Is Mr. Weaver going to die?"

"Of course he is," Pearce answered. "None of us escape. If you mean is he going to die within the next few days, I'd say yes—if I had to answer yes or no."

"What's wrong with him?" Jansen asked suspiciously.

"He's outlived his body. Think of it as a machine. It's worn out, falling apart, one organ failing after another."

"His father lived to be ninety-one, his mother ninety-six."

Pearce looked at Jansen steadily, unblinking. "They didn't make a million dollars. We live in an age that has almost conquered disease, but that has inflicted its price.

The stress and strain of modern life tear us apart. Every million Weaver made cost him five years of living."

"What are you going to do—just let him die?"

Pearce's eyes were just as cold as Jansen's. "As soon as possible we'll give him a transfusion. Does he have any relatives, close friends?"

"There's no one closer than me."

"We'll need two pints of blood for every pint we give Weaver. Arrange it."

"Mr. Weaver will pay for whatever he uses."

"He'll replace it if possible. That's the hospital rule."

Jansen's eyes dropped. "There'll be plenty of volunteers from the office."

When Pearce was beyond the range of his low, penetrating voice, Jansen said, "Can't we get somebody else? I don't like him."

"That's because he's harder than you are," Easter said easily. "He'd be a good match for the old man when he was in his prime."

"He's too young."

"That's why he's good. The best geriatrician in the Middle West. He can be detached, objective. All doctors need a touch of ruthlessness. Pearce needs more than most; he loses every patient sooner or later. He's got it." Easter looked at Jansen, smiling. "When men reach our age, they start getting soft. They start getting subjective about death."

The requisition for one unit of blood arrived at the blood bank. The hospital routine began. A crisp technician came from the cluttered, makeshift cubicle on the first floor. From one of the old man's ropy veins she drew five cubic centimeters of blood, almost purple inside the slim barrel of the hypodermic.

The old man didn't stir. In the silence his breathing was a raucous noise.

Back at the workbench, she typed the blood sample quickly, efficiently. She wrote down the results on an 8½-by-11 printed form: patient's name, date, room, doctor. . . . Type: O. Rh: neg.

Divided by a double-ruled line was a section headed "Donors." The technician opened the right-hand door of the refrigerator and inspected the labels of the bottles on the second shelf from the top. She selected one and transferred to the sheet the name of the donor, bottle number, type, and Rh factor.

She put samples of the donor's and the patient's blood into two small test tubes.

A drop of donor's serum in a sample of the patient's blood provided the major crossmatch: it didn't make the red cells clump, and even under the microscope, after centrifuging, the cells were perfect, evenly suspended circles. A drop or two of patient's serum in a sample of the donor's blood and the minor crossmatch was done.

The technician signed the form and telephoned the nurse in charge that the blood was ready when needed. The nurse came for the blood in a few minutes. The technician took out a red-bordered label. She wrote:

> FOR
> LEROY WEAVER   9–4
> RM. 305   DR. PEARCE

She pasted it beside the original label on the bottle containing the pint of blood. The nurse, nodding her appreciation, carried the bottle away casually, familiarly.

Dr. Pearce studied the charts labeled "Leroy Weaver." He picked up the report from the hematology laboratory.

Red cell count: 2,360,000/cmm. Anemia, all right. Worse than he'd even suspected. That duodenal ulcer was losing a lot of blood.

The transfusion would help. It would be temporary, but everything is, at best. In the end, it is all a matter of time. Maybe it would revive Weaver enough to get some food down him. He might surprise them all and walk out of this hospital yet.

He picked up the charts and reports, and he walked down the long, quiet corridor, rubbery underfoot, redolent of the perennial hospital odors: alcohol and ether, antiseptic and anesthetic. He opened the door of room 305, and walked into the coolness.

He nodded distantly to the nurse on duty in the room, not one of the hospital staff. She was one of the three full-time nurses hired for Weaver by Jansen.

Pearce picked up the clipboard at the foot of the bed and looked at it. No change. He studied the old man's face. It looked more like death. His breathing was still stertorous; his discolored eyelids still veiled his sunken eyes.

What was he? Name him: Five Million Dollars. He was Money. He served no useful function; he contributed nothing to society, nothing to the race. He had been too busy to marry, too dedicated to father. His occupation: money-maker.

Pearce didn't believe that a man with money was necessarily a villain. But anyone who made a million dollars or a multiple of it was necessarily a large part predator and the rest magpie.

Pearce knew why Jansen was worried. When Weaver died, Money died, Power died. Money and Power are not immune from death, and when they fall they carry empires with them.

Pearce looked down at Weaver, thinking these things,

and it didn't matter. He was still one of us, still human, still alive. That meant he was worth saving. No other consideration was valid.

Two pint bottles hung from the metal "T"—the clear, antiseptic, saline solution and the dark life fluid. A glass T-joint reduced two plastic tubes into one. Below was a transparent filter. At the end of the tube was a 20-gauge needle.

The nurse released the clamp closing the tube just below the saline solution. The salt water ran, bubbling a little, through the tubing, the joint—backing up to the clamp below the blood—the filter, and spurted from the needle tip. The nurse clamped it off close to the needle.

Now the tubes were full. They were free of air bubbles that could be forced into the patient's veins to cause an embolism.

The clamp below the saline solution was closed off. The nurse waited while Pearce picked up the needle and studied Weaver's arm. No need bothering with procaine.

The antecubital vein was available, swollen across the inside of the elbow, Pearce swabbed it with alcohol and iodine, pushed in the needle with practiced ease, and taped it down. He nodded to the nurse.

She released the clamp under the blood. Slowly it stained the water, and then swirled darkly as she carefully eased open the bottom clamp. In a second it was all blood, running slowly through the long, transparent tubing into the receptive vein, new blood bringing new life to the old, worn-out mechanism on the hard hospital bed.

New blood for old, Pearce thought. *Money can buy anything.* "A little faster."

The nurse opened the bottom clamp a little wider. In the pint bottle, the level of the life fluid dropped faster.

Life. Dripping. Flowing. Making the old new.

The old man took a deep breath. The exhausted laboring of his chest grew easier.

Pearce studied the old face, the beaklike nose, the thin, bloodless lips, looking cruel even in their pallor. New life, perhaps. But nothing can reverse the long erosion of the years. Bodies wear out. Nothing can make them new.

Drop by drop the blood flowed from the pint bottle through the tubing into an old man's veins. Someone had given it or sold it. Someone young and healthy, who could make more purple life stuff, saturated with healthy red cells, vigorous white scavengers, platelets, the multiple proteins; someone who could replace it all in less than ninety days.

Pearce thought about Richard Lower, the seventeenth-century English anatomist who performed the first transfusion, and the twentieth-century Viennese immunologist, Karl Landsteiner, who made transfusions safe when he discovered the incompatible blood groups among human beings.

Now there was this old man, who was getting the blood through the efforts of Lower and Landsteiner and—he glanced inquisitively at the bottle and translated the upside-down printing into meaning—a donor named Cartwright; this old man who needed it, who couldn't make the red cells fast enough any longer, who couldn't keep up with the rate he was losing them internally.

What was dripping through the tubes was life, a gift of the young to the old, of the healthy to the sick.

The old man's eyelids flickered.

When Pearce made his morning rounds, the old man was watching him with faded blue eyes. Pearce blinked once and picked up the skin-and-bone wrist again and counted automatically. "Feeling better, eh?"

He got his second shock. The old man nodded.

"Fine, Mr. Weaver. We'll get a little food down you, and in a little while you'll be as good as new."

He glanced at his watch, looked away, and glanced back at it again. Gently, puzzledly, he lowered the old arm down beside the thin, sheeted body. He wrapped the wide, flat band of the sphygmomanometer around the stringy bicep and pumped it tight, listening at the inside of the elbow with his stethoscope. He looked at the gauge and let the air hiss out and listened for a moment at the old man's chest.

He sat back thoughtfully beside the bed, ignoring the bustling nurse. Weaver was making a surprising rally for a man in as bad shape as he had been. The pulse was strong and steady. Blood pressure was up. Somehow the transfusion had triggered hidden stores of energy and resistance.

Weaver was fighting back.

Pearce felt a strange and unprofessional sense of elation.

The next day Pearce thought the eyes that watched him were not quite so faded. "Comfortable?" he asked. The old man nodded. His pulse was almost normal for a man of his age.

On the third day, Weaver started talking.

The old man's thready voice whispered disjointed and meaningless reminiscences. Pearce nodded understandingly, and he nodded, inwardly, to himself. Arteriosclerosis had left its marks: chronic granular kidney, damage to the left ventricle of the heart, malfunction of the brain from a cerebral hemorrhage or two.

On the fourth day, Weaver was sitting up in bed talking to the nurse in a cracked, sprightly voice. "Yessirree," he said toothlessly. "That was the day I whopped 'em. Gave it to 'em good, I did. Let 'em have it right between the eyes. Always hated those kids. You must be the doctor," he said suddenly, turning toward Pearce. "I like you. Gonna see that you get a big check. Take care of the people I like. Take care of those I don't like, too." He chuckled; it was an evil, childish sound.

"Don't worry about that," Pearce said gently, picking up Weaver's wrist. "Concentrate on getting well."

The old man nodded happily and stuck a finger in his mouth to rub his gums. "You'll git paid," he mumbled. "Don't *you* worry about that."

Pearce looked down at the wrist he was holding. It had filled out amazingly. "What's the matter with your gums?"

"Itch," Weaver got out around his finger. "Like blazes."

On the fifth day Weaver walked to the toilet.

On the sixth day he took a shower. When Pearce came in he was sitting on the edge of the bed, dangling his feet. Weaver looked up quickly as Pearce entered, his eyes alert, no longer so sunken. His skin had a subcutaneous glow of health. Like his wrist and arm, his face had filled out. Even his legs looked firmer, almost muscular.

He was taking the well-balanced hospital diet and turning it into flesh and fat and muscle.

With his snowy hair, he looked like an ad for everybody's grandfather.

Next day, his hair began to darken.

"How old are you, Mr. Weaver?" Pearce asked sharply.

"Seventy," Weaver said proudly. "Seventy my last birthday, June 5. Born in Wyoming, boy, in a sod hut. Still Indians around then. Many's the time I seen 'em, out with my paw. Never give us no trouble, though. Timid bunch, mostly."

"What color was your hair?"

"Color of a raven's wing. Had the blackest, shiniest hair in the country. Gals used to beg to run their fingers through it." He chuckled reminiscently. "Used to let 'em. A passel of blackheaded kids in Washakie County before I left."

He stuck his finger in his mouth and massaged his gums ecstatically.

"Still itch?" Pearce asked.

"Like a Wyoming chigger." He chuckled. "You know what's wrong with me, boy? In my second childhood. That's what. I'm cutting teeth."

During the second week, Weaver's mind turned to business, deserting the long-ago past. A telephone was installed beside his bed, and he spent half his waking time in short, clipped conversations about incomprehensible deals and manipulations. The other half was devoted to Jansen, who was so conveniently on hand whenever Weaver called for him that Pearce thought he must have appropriated a hospital room.

Weaver was picking up the reins of empire.

While his mind roamed restlessly over possessions and ways of keeping and augmenting them, his body repaired itself like a self-servicing machine. His first tooth came through—a canine. After that they appeared rapidly. His hair darkened almost perceptibly; within the week it was as dark as he had described. His face filled out, the wrinkles smoothing themselves like a ruffled lake when the wind has gentled. His body became muscular and vigorous; the veins retreated under the skin to become blue traceries. The eyes darkened to a fiery blue.

The lab tests were additional proof of what Pearce had begun to suspect. Arteriosclerosis had never thickened those veins; or else, somehow, the damage of that fibrous tissue had been repaired. The kidneys functioned perfectly. The heart was as strong and efficient a pump as it had ever been. There was no evidence of a cerebral hemorrhage.

By the end of that week Weaver looked like a man of thirty. From birth, his body had aged no more than thirty years.

"Carl," Weaver was saying as Pearce entered the room, "I want a woman."

"That's easy," Jansen answered, shrugging. "Any particular one?"

"You don't understand," Weaver said bitingly. "I want one to marry. I made a mistake before; I'm not going to repeat it. A man in my position needs an heir. I'm going to have one. Yes, Carl—and you can hide that look of incredulity a little better—at my age!" He swung around quickly toward Pearce. "That's right, isn't it, doctor?"

Pearce shrugged. "There's no reason you can't father a child."

"Get this, Carl. I'm as strong and as smart as I ever was, maybe stronger and smarter. Some people are going to learn that very soon. I've been given a second chance, haven't I, doctor?"

"You might call it that. What are you going to do with it?"

"I'm going to do better. Better than I did before. This time I'm not going to make any mistakes. And you, doctor, do you know what you're going to do?"

"No. Tell me what I'm going to do."

Weaver's eyes twisted to Pearce's face. "You think I'm just talking. Don't make that mistake. You're going to find out why."

"Why?"

"Why I've recovered like I have. Don't try to kid me. You've never seen anything like it. I'm not seventy years old anymore. My body isn't. My mind isn't. Why?"

"What's your guess?"

"I never guess. I know. I get the facts from those who have them, and then I decide. That's what I want from you—the facts. I've been rejuvenated."

"You've been talking to Easter."

"Of course."

"But you never got that language from him. He'd never commit himself to that."

Weaver lowered at Pearce from under dark eyebrows. "What was done to me?"

"What does it matter? If you've been rejuvenated, that should be enough for any man."

"When Mr. Weaver asks a question," Jansen thrust in icily, "Mr. Weaver wants an answer."

Weaver brushed him aside. "Dr. Pearce doesn't frighten. But Dr. Pearce is a reasonable man. He believes in facts. He lives by logic. Understand me, doctor! I may be thirty now, but I will be seventy again. Before then I want to know how to be thirty again."

"Ah," Pearce sighed. "You're not talking about rejuvenation now. You're talking about immortality."

"Why not?"

"It's not for mortals. The human body wears out. Three-score years and ten. That—roughly—is what we're allotted. After that we start falling apart."

"I've had mine. Now I'm starting over at thirty. I've got forty to go. After that, what? Forty more?"

"We all die," Pearce said flatly. "Nothing can stop that. Not one man born has not come to the grave at last. There's a disease we contract at birth from which none of us recover; it's invariably fatal. Death."

"Suppose somebody develops a resistance to it?"

"Oh, I didn't mean that death was a specific disease," Pearce said quickly. "We die in many ways: accident, infection—" *And senescence*, Pearce thought. *For all we know, that's a disease. It could be a disease.* Etiology: *virus, unisolated, unsuspected, invades at birth or shortly thereafter—or maybe transmitted at conception.*

Incidence: *total.*

Symptoms: *slow degeneration of the physical entity, appearing shortly after maturity, increasing debility, failure of the circulatory system through arteriosclerosis and heart damage, malfunction of sense and organs, loss of cellular regenerative ability, susceptibility to secondary invasions. . . .*

Prognosis: *100% fatal.*

"Everything dies," Pearce went on smoothly. "Trees, planets, suns. . . . It's natural, inevitable. . . ." *But it isn't. Natural death is a relatively new thing. It appeared only when life became multicellular and complicated. Maybe it was the price for complexity, for the ability to think.*

Protozoa don't die. Metazoa—sponges, flatworms, coelenterates—don't die. Certain fish don't die except through accident. "Voles are animals that never stop growing and never grow old." Where did I read that? And even the tissues of the higher vertebrates are immortal under the right conditions.

Carrel and Ebeling proved that. Give the cell enough of the right food, and it will never die. Cells from every part of the body have been kept alive indefinitely in vitro.

Differentiation and specialization—that meant that any individual cell didn't find the perfect conditions. Besides staying alive, it had duties to perform for the whole. A plausible explanation, but was it true? Wasn't it just as plausible that the cell died because the circulatory system broke down?

Let the circulatory system remain sound, regenerative, and efficient, and the rest of the body might well remain immortal.

"Nothing's natural," Weaver said. "You gave me a transfusion. Immunities can be transferred with the blood, Easter told me. Who donated that pint of blood?"

Pearce sighed. "Someone named Marshall Cartwright."

The blood bank was in the oldest part of the building. Pearce led the way down the hot, narrow corridors, as far south on the east wing's second floor as possible, down a wandering stairway, to the square, cluttered little room.

"If you're smart," Jansen told him on the stairs, "you'll cooperate with Mr. Weaver. Do what he asks you. Tell him what he wants to know. You'll get taken care of. If not—" Jansen smiled unpleasantly.

Pearce laughed uneasily. "What can Weaver do to me?"

"Don't find out," Jansen advised.

The technician accepted the job without comment. She flipped the pages of a ledger, searching. "Weaver?" she said. "Oh, here it is. On the fourth." Her finger traveled across the sheet. "O neg. Hasn't been replaced, by the way."

Pearce turned on Jansen. "I thought you were going to take care of that."

"You'll get your blood tomorrow," the secretary growled. "Who was the donor?"

"Marshall Cartwright," said the technician. "O neg. Kline: Okay. Replaced— Now I remember. That was the day after our television appeal. We ran low on O neg, and our professional donor list was exhausted. Got a big response."

"Remember him?" asked Jansen.

She frowned and turned her head away to stare out the window. "That was the third. We have more than twenty donors a day. And that was over a week ago."

"Think!" Jansen demanded.

"I *am* thinking," she flared. "What do you want to know?"

"What he looked like. What he said. His address."

"Was there something wrong with the blood?"

Pearce grinned suddenly. " 'Contrariwise,' said Tweedle-dee."

A brief smile slipped across the technician's face. "We don't get many complaints like that. I can give you his address easy enough." She riffled through a box of 4-by-5 index cards. "Funny. He sold his blood once, but he didn't want to do it again." She walked across to the table against the east wall and opened a black, three-ring binder. She leafed through it.

"This is our registration and release form. Let's see, the third. Bean. Parker. Cartwright. Marshall Cartwright. Abbot Hotel. No phone listed."

"Abbot," Jansen said thoughtfully. "Sounds like a flop joint. Does that bring anything back?" he asked the technician insistently. "He didn't want his name on the donor's list."

Slowly, regretfully, she shook her head. "What's all this about anyway? Weaver? Isn't that the old boy up in 305 who made such a miraculous recovery?"

"Right," Jansen said, brushing the question away. "We'll want photostats of the two entries. Shall we take the books along now—"

"We'll see that you get them," Pearce cut in.

"Today," Jansen said.

"Today," Pearce agreed.

"That's all, then," Jansen said. "If you remember anything, get in touch with Mr. Weaver or me, Carl Jansen. There'll be something in it for you."

Something in it, something in it, Pearce thought. *The slogan of a class.* "What's in it for the human race? Never mind. You've got what you came for."

"I always do," Jansen said intently. "Mr. Weaver and I—we always get what we come for. Remember that!"

Pearce remembered while the young-old man named Leroy Weaver grew a handsome set of teeth, as white as his hair was black, and directed the course of his commercial empire from the hospital room, chafed at Pearce's delay in giving him the answer to his question, at the continual demands for blood samples, at his own enforced idleness, and slyly pinched the nurses during the day. Pearce did not inquire into what happened at night.

Before the week was over, Weaver had forced through his discharge from the hospital and Pearce had located a private detective.

The black paint on the frosted glass of the door said:

JASON LOCKE
CONFIDENTIAL INVESTIGATIONS

But Locke wasn't Pearce's preconception of a private eye. He wasn't tough—not on the outside. The hardness was inside, and he didn't let it show.

Locke was middle-aged, graying, his face firm and tanned, a big man dressed in a well-draped tropical suit in light cocoa; he looked like a successful executive. Business wasn't that good: the office was shabby, deteriorating, the furniture was little better, and there was no secretary or receptionist.

He was just the man Pearce wanted.

He listened to Pearce and watched him with dark, steady eyes.

"I want you to find a man," Pearce said. "Marshall Cartwright. Last address: Abbot Hotel."

"Why?"

"What difference does it make?"

"I have a license to keep—and a desire to keep out of jail."

"There's nothing illegal about it," Pearce said quickly, "but there might be danger. I won't lie to you; it's a medical problem I can't explain. It's important to me that you find Cartwright. It's important to him—it might mean his life. It might even be important to the world. The danger lies in the fact that other people are looking for him; if they spot you they might get rough. I want you to find Cartwright before they do."

"Who is 'they'?"

Pearce shrugged helplessly. "Pinkerton, Burns, International—I don't know. One of the big firms, probably."

"Is that why you didn't go to them?"

"One reason. I won't conceal anything, though. The man hiring them is Leroy Weaver."

Locke looked interested. "I heard the old boy was back on the prowl. Have you got any pictures, descriptions, anything to help me spot this man Cartwright?"

Pearce looked down at his hands. "Nothing, except the name. He's a young man. He sold a pint of his blood on the third. He refused to have his name added to our professional donor's list. He gave his address then as the Abbot."

"I know it," Locke said. "A fly trap on Ninth. That means he's left town, I'd say."

"Why do you say that?"

"That's why he sold the blood. To get out of town. He wasn't interested in selling it again; he wasn't going to be around. And anyone who would stay at a place like the Abbot wouldn't toss away a chance at some regular, effortless money."

"That's what I figured," Pearce said, nodding slowly. "Will you take the job?"

Locke swung around in his swivel chair and stared out the window across the light standards, transformers, and overhead power lines of Twelfth Street. It was nothing to look at, but he seemed to draw a decision from it. "Fifty dollars a day and expenses," he said, swinging back. "Sixty if I have to go out of town."

It was that afternoon Pearce discovered that he was being followed.

He walked along the warm autumn streets, and the careless crowds, the hurrying, anonymous shoppers, passed on either side without a glance and came behind, and conviction walked with him. He moved through the air-conditioned stores, quickly or dawdling over a display of deodorants at a counter, glancing surreptitiously behind, seeing nothing but sure that someone was watching.

The symptoms were familiar. They were usually those of hysterical women, most often in that wistful, tormented period of middle age, but occasionally in adolescence or early womanhood. Pearce had never expected to share them: the sensitivity in the back of the neck and between the shoulder blades that made him want to shrug it away, the leg-tightening desire to hurry, to run, to dodge into a doorway, into an elevator. . . .

Pearce nodded to himself and lingered. When he went to his car, he went slowly, talked to the parking lot attendant for a moment before he drove away, and drove straight home.

He never did identify the man or men who shadowed him, then or later. It kept up for weeks, so that when it finally ended he felt strangely naked and alone.

When he got to his apartment, the telephone was ringing. That was not surprising. A doctor's phone rings a hundred times as often as that of an ordinary citizen.

Dr. Easter was the caller. The essence of what he wanted to say was that Pearce should not be foolish; Pearce should cooperate with Mr. Weaver.

"Of course I'm cooperating!" Pearce exclaimed. "I cooperate with all my patients."

"That isn't what I meant," Dr. Easter said in an unctuous voice. "Work with him, not against him. You'll find it's worth your while."

"It's worth my while to practice medicine the best way I can," Pearce said evenly. "Beyond that no one has a call on me, and no one ever will."

"Very fine sentiments," Dr. Easter agreed pleasantly.

"The question is: will Mr. Weaver think you are practicing medicine properly? That's something to consider."

Pearce lowered the phone gently into the cradle, thinking about how it was practicing medicine, being a doctor—and he knew he could never be happy at anything else. He turned over in his mind the subtle threat Easter had made; it could be done. The specter of malpractice was never completely absent, and a powerful alliance of money and respectability could come close to lifting a license.

He considered Easter, and he knew that it was better to risk the title than to give away the reality.

The next week was a time of wondering and waiting, and of keeping busy—a problem a doctor seldom faces. It was a time of uneventful routine.

Then it seemed as if everything happened at once.

As he walked from his car toward the front door of the apartment house, a hand reached out of the shadows beside an ornamental fir and pulled him into the darkness.

Before he could say anything or struggle, a hand was clamped tight over his mouth, and a voice whispered in his ear, "Quiet now! This is Locke. The private eye, remember?"

Pearce nodded stiffly. Slowly the hand relaxed. As his eyes adjusted to the darkness, Pearce made out Locke's features. His face was heavily, darkly bearded, and something had happened to the nose. Locke had been in a brawl; the nose was broken, and the face was cut and bruised.

"Never mind me," Locke said huskily. "You should see the other guys."

As Pearce drew back a little, he could see that Locke was dressed in old clothes looking like hand-me-downs from the Salvation Army. "Sorry I got you into it," he said.

"Part of the job. Listen. I haven't got long, and I want to give you my report."

"It can wait. Come on up. Let me take a look at that face. You can send me a written re—"

"Nothing doing," Locke said heavily. "I'm not signing my name to anything. Too dangerous. From now on I'm going to keep my nose clean. I did all right for a few days. Then they caught up with me. Well, they're sorry, too. You wanta hear it?"

Pearce nodded.

For a while Locke had thought he might get somewhere. He had registered at the Abbot, got friendly with the room clerk, and finally asked about his friend, Cartwright, who had flopped there a couple of weeks earlier. The clerk was willing enough to talk. Trouble was, he didn't know much, and what little he knew he wouldn't have told to a stranger. Guests at the Abbot were liable to be persecuted by police and collection agents, and the clerk had suspicions that every questioner was from the health board.

Cartwright had paid his bill and left suddenly, no forwarding address given. They hadn't heard from him since, but people had been asking about him. "In trouble, eh?" the clerk asked wisely. Locke nodded gravely.

The clerk leaned closer. "I had a hunch, though, that Cartwright was heading for Des Moines. Something he said—don't remember what now."

Locke took off for Des Moines with a sample of Cartwright's handwriting from the Abbot register. He canvassed the Des Moines hotels, rooming houses, motels. Finally, at a first-class hotel, he noticed the name "Marshall Carter."

Cartwright had left the Abbot on the ninth. Carter had checked into the Des Moines hotel on the tenth. The handwritings looked identical.

Locke caught up with Carter in East St. Louis. He turned out to be a middle-aged salesman of photographic equipment who hadn't been near Kansas City in a year.

End of the trail.

"Can anyone else find him?" Pearce asked.

"Not if he doesn't want to be found," Locke said shrewdly. "A nationwide search—an advertising campaign —they'd help. But if he's changed his name and doesn't go signing his new one to a lot of things that might fall into an agency's hands, nobody is going to find him. That's what you wanted, wasn't it?"

Pearce looked at him steadily, not saying anything.

"He's got no record," Locke went on. "That helps. Got a name check on him from the bigger police departments and the F.B.I. No go. No record, no fingerprints. Not under that name."

"How'd you get hurt?" Pearce asked, after a moment.

"They were waiting for me outside my office when I got back. Two of 'em. Good, too. But not good enough. 'Lay off!' they said. Okay. I'm not stupid. I'm laying off, but I wanted to finish the job first."

Pearce nodded slowly. "I'm satisfied. Send me a bill."

"Bill, nothing!" Locke growled. "Five hundred is the price. Put it in an envelope and mail it to my office—no checks. I should charge you more for using me as a stake-out, but maybe you had your reasons. Watch your step, Doc!"

He was gone then, slipping away through the shadows so quickly and silently that Pearce started to speak before he realized that the detective was not beside him. Pearce stared after him for a moment, shrugged, and opened the front door.

Going up in the elevator, he was thoughtful. In front of his apartment door, he fumbled the key out absently and inserted it in the lock. When the key wouldn't turn he took it out to check on it. He noticed then that the door was half an inch ajar.

Pearce gave the door a little push. It swung inward

noiselessly. The light from the hall streamed over his shoulder, but it only lapped a little way into the dark room. He peered into it for a moment, hunching his shoulders as if that might help.

"Come in, Dr. Pearce," someone said softly.

The lights went on.

Pearce blinked once. "Good evening, Mr. Weaver. And you, Jansen. How are you?"

"Fine, doctor," Weaver said. "Just fine."

He didn't look fine, Pearce thought. He looked older, haggard, tired. Was he worried? Weaver was sitting in his favorite chair, a green leather one beside the fireplace. Jansen was standing beside the wall switch. "You've made yourself right at home, I see."

Weaver chuckled. "We told the manager we were friends of yours, and of course he didn't doubt us. But then we are, aren't we?"

Pearce looked at Weaver and then at Jansen. "I wonder. Do you have any friends—or only hirelings?" He turned his eyes back to Weaver. "You don't look well. I'd like you to come back to the hospital for a checkup—"

"I'm feeling fine, I said." Weaver's voice lifted a little before it dropped back to a conversational tone. "We wanted to have a little talk—about cooperation."

Pearce looked at Jansen. "Funny—I don't feel very talkative. I've had a hard day."

Weaver's eyes didn't leave Pearce's face. "Get out, Carl," he said quietly.

"But Mr. Weaver—" Jansen began, his gray eyes darkening.

"Get out, Carl," Weaver repeated. "Wait for me in the car."

After Carl was gone, Pearce sank down in the armchair facing Weaver. He let his gaze drift around the room, lingering on the polished darkness of the hi-fi record player and the slightly lighter wood of the desk in the corner. "Did you find anything?" he asked.

"Not what we were looking for," Weaver replied calmly.

"What was that?"

"Cartwright's location."

"What makes you think I'd know anything about that?"

Weaver clasped his hands lightly in his lap. "Can't we work together?"

"Certainly. What would you like to know—about your health?"

"What did you do with those samples of blood you took from me? You must have taken back that pint I got."

"Almost. Part of it we separated. Got the plasma. Separated the gamma globulin from it with zinc. Used it on various animals."

"And what did you find out?"

"The immunity is in the gamma globulin. It would be, of course. That's the immunity factor. You should see my old rat. As frisky as the youngest rat in the lab."

"So it's part of me, too?" Weaver asked.

Pearce shook his head slowly. "That's just the original globulins diluted in your blood."

"Then to live forever I would have to have periodic transfusions?"

"If it's possible to live forever," Pearce said, shrugging.

"It is. You know that. There's at least one person who's going to live forever—Cartwright. Unless something happens to him. That would be a tragedy, wouldn't it? In spite of all precautions, accidents happen. People get murdered. Can you imagine some careless kid spilling that golden blood into a filthy gutter? Some jealous woman putting a knife in that priceless body?"

"What do you want, Weaver?" Pearce asked evenly. "You've got your reprieve from death. What more can you ask?"

"Another. And another. Without end. Why should some nobody get it by accident? What good will it do him? Or the world? He needs to be protected—and used. Properly handled, he could be worth—well, whatever men will pay for life. I'd pay a million a year—more if I had to. Other men would pay the same. We'd save the best men in the world, those who have demonstrated their ability by becoming wealthy. Oh, yes. Scientists, too—we'd select some of those. People who haven't gone into business—leaders, statesmen. . . ."

"What about Cartwright?"

"What about him?" Weaver blinked as if recalled from a lovely dream. "Do you think anyone who ever lived would have a better life, would be better protected, more pampered? Why, he wouldn't have to ask for a thing! No one would dare say no to him for fear he might kill himself. He'd be the hen that laid the golden eggs."

"He'd have everything but freedom."

"A much overrated commodity."

"The one immortal man in the world."

"That's just it," Weaver said, leaning forward. "Instead of only one, there would be many."

Pearce shook his head from side to side as if he had not heard. "A chance meeting of genes—a slight alteration by cosmic ray or something even more subtle and accidental—and immortality is created. Some immunity to death—some means of keeping the circulatory system young, resistant, rejuvenated. 'Man is as old as his arteries,' Cazali said. Take care of your arteries, and they will keep your cells immortal."

"Tell me, man! Tell me where Cartwright is before all that is lost forever." Weaver leaned forward urgently.

"A man who knows he's got a million years to live is going to be pretty darned careful," Pearce said.

"That's just it," Weaver said, his eyes narrowing. "He

doesn't know. If he'd known, he'd never have given his blood." His face changed subtly. "Or does he know—now?"

"What do you mean?"

"Didn't you tell him?"

"I don't know what you're talking about."

"Don't you? Don't you remember going to the Abbot Hotel on the evening of the ninth, of asking for Cartwright, of talking to him? You should. The clerk identified your picture. And that night Cartwright left."

Pearce remembered the Abbot Hotel all right, the narrow, dark lobby, grimy, fly-specked. He had thought of cholera and bubonic plague as he crossed it. He remembered Cartwright, too—that fabulous creature, looking seedy and quite ordinary, who had listened, though, and believed and taken the money and gone. . . .

"I don't believe it," Pearce said.

"I should have known right away," Weaver said, as if to himself. "You knew his name that first day. When I asked for it."

"Presuming I did. If I did all that you say, do you think it was easy for me? To you he's money. What do you think he was to me? That fantastic laboratory, walking around! What wouldn't I have given to study him! To find out how his body worked, to try to synthesize the substance. You have your drives, Weaver, but I have mine."

"Why not combine them, Pearce?"

"They wouldn't mix."

"Don't get so holy, Pearce. Life isn't holy."

"Life is what we make it," Pearce said softly. "I won't have a hand in what you're planning."

Weaver got up quickly from his chair and took a step toward Pearce. "Some of you professional men get delusions of ethics," he said in a kind of muted snarl. "Not many. A few. There's nothing sacred about what you do. You're just craftsmen, mechanics—you do a job—you get paid for it. There's no reason to get religious about it."

"Don't be absurd, Weaver. If you don't feel religious about what you do, you shouldn't be doing it. You feel religious about making money. Money's sacred to you. Well, life is sacred to me. That's what I deal in, all day long, every day. Death is an old enemy. I'll fight him until the end."

Pearce propelled himself out of his chair. He stood close to Weaver, staring fiercely into the man's eyes. "Understand this, Weaver. What you're planning is impossible. What if we all could be rejuvenated? Do you have the slightest idea what would happen? Have you considered what it might do to civilization?

"No, I can see you haven't. Well, it would bring your society tumbling down around your pillars of gold. Civilization would shake itself to pieces like an unbalanced flywheel. Our culture is constructed on the assumption that we spend two decades growing and learning, a few more producing wealth and progeny, and a final decade or two decaying before we die.

"Look back! See what research and medicine have done in the past century. They've added a few years—just a few—to the average lifespan, and our society is groaning at the readjustment. Think what forty years would do! Think what would happen if we never died!

"There's only one way something like this can be absorbed into the race—gradually, so that society can adjust, unknowing, to this new thing inside it. All Cartwright's children will inherit the mutation. They must. It must be dominant. And they will survive, because this has the greatest survival factor ever created."

"Where is he?" Weaver asked.

"It won't work, Weaver," Pearce said, his voice rising. "I'll tell you why it won't work. Because you would kill him. You think you wouldn't, but you'd kill him as certainly as you're a member of the human race. You'd bleed him to death, or you'd kill him just because you couldn't stand having something immortal around. You or some other warped specimen of humanity. You'd kill him, or he'd get killed in the riots of those who were denied life, tossed to the wolves of death. What people can't have they destroy. That's been proved over and over."

"Where is he?" Weaver repeated.

"It won't work for a final reason." Pearce's voice dropped as if it had found a note of pity. "But I won't tell you that. I'll let you find out for yourself."

"Where is he?" Weaver insisted softly.

"I don't know. You won't believe that. But I don't know. I didn't want to know. I told him the truth about himself, and I gave him some money, and I told him to leave town, to change his name, hide—anything, but not be found; to be fertile, to populate the earth. . . ."

"I don't believe you. You've got him hidden away for yourself. You wouldn't give him a thousand dollars for nothing."

"You know the amount?" Pearce asked.

Weaver's lip curled. "I know every deposit you've made in the last five years, and every withdrawal. You're small, Pearce, and you're cheap, and I'm going to break you."

Pearce smiled, unworried. "No, you're not. You don't dare use violence, because I just might know where Cartwright is hiding. Then you'd lose everything. And you won't try anything else because if you do I'll release the article I've written about Cartwright—I'll send you a copy—and then the fat would really be in the fire. If everybody knew about Cartwright, you wouldn't have a chance to control it, even if you could find him."

At the door, Weaver turned and said, calmly, "I'll be seeing you again."

"That's right," Pearce agreed, and thought, *I've been no*

*help to you, because you won't ever believe that I haven't
got a string tied to Cartwright.*

But you're not the one I pity.

Two days after that came the news of Weaver's marriage,
an elopement with a twenty-five-year-old girl from the
country club district, a Patricia Warren. It was the weekend
sensation—wealth and beauty, age and youth.

Pearce studied the girl's picture in the Sunday paper and
told himself that surely she had got what she wanted. And
Weaver—Pearce knew him well enough to know that he
had got what he wanted. Weaver's heir would already be
assured. Otherwise, Weaver would never risk himself and
his empire in a woman's hands. There were reliable tests
even this early.

The fourth week since the transfusion passed unevent-
fully, and the fifth week was only distinguished by a
summons from Jansen, which Pearce ignored. The beginning of the sixth week brought a frantic call from Dr.
Easter. Pearce refused to go to Weaver's newly purchased
mansion.

They brought him to the hospital in a screaming ambulance, clearing the streets ahead of it with its siren and its
flashing red light, dodging through the traffic with its
precious cargo: Money, personified.

Pearce stood beside the hard hospital bed, checking the
pulse in the bony wrist, and stared down at the emaciated
body. It made no impression in the bed. In the silence, the
harsh unevenness of the old man's breathing was loud. The
only movement was the spasmodic rise and fall of the sheet
that covered the old body.

He was living—barely. He had used up his allotted
three-score years and ten. It wasn't merely that he was
dying. We all are. With him it was imminent.

The pulse was feeble. The gift of youth had been taken

away. Within the space of a few days, Weaver had been drained of color, drained of forty years of life.

He was an old man, dying. His face was yellowish over grayish blue, the color of death. It was bony, the wrinkled skin pulled back like a mask for the skull. Once he might have been handsome. Now his eyes were sunken, the closed eyelids dark over them, and his nose was a thin, arching beak.

This time, Pearce thought distantly, there will be no reprieve.

"I don't understand," Dr. Easter muttered. "I thought he'd been given forty years—"

"That was his conclusion," Pearce said. "It was more like forty days. Thirty to forty days—that's how long the gamma globulin remains in the bloodstream. It was only a passive immunity. The only person with any lasting immunity to death is Cartwright, and the only ones he can give it to are his children."

Easter looked around to see if the nurse was listening and whispered, "Couldn't we handle this better? Chance needs a little help sometimes. With semen banks and artificial insemination we could change the make-up of the human race in a couple of generations—"

"If we weren't all wiped out first," Pearce said, and turned away.

He waited, his eyes closed, listening to the harshness of Weaver's breathing, thinking of the tragedy of life and death—the being born and the dying, entwined, all one, and here was Weaver who had run out of life, and there was his child who would not be born for months yet. It was a continuity, a balance—a life for a life, and it had kept humanity stable for millions of years.

And yet—immortality? What might it mean?

He thought of Cartwright, the immortal, the hunted man. While men remembered they would never let him rest, and if he got tired of hiding and running, he was doomed. The search would go on and on—crippled a little, fortunately, now that Weaver had dropped away—and Cartwright, with his burden, would never be able to live like other men.

He thought of him, trying to adjust to immortality in the midst of death, and he thought that immortality—the greatest gift, surely, that a man could receive—demanded payment in kind, like everything else. For immortality, you must surrender the right to live.

God pity you, Cartwright.

"Transfusion, Dr. Pearce?" the nurse repeated.

"Oh, yes," he said hastily. "Might as well." He looked down at Weaver once more. "Send down a requisition. We know his type already—O negative."

THE
MEDIC

HE WOKE TO PAIN. It was a sharp, stabbing sensation in the pit of his stomach. It pulled his knees up toward his chest and contorted his gaunt, yellowed face with an involuntary grimace that creased the skin along familiar lines, like parchment folded and refolded.

The pain stabbed again. He grunted; his body jerked. Slowly it ebbed, flood waters retreating, leaving its detritus of tormented nerve endings like a promise of return. "Coke!" shouted the man on the twenty-ninth floor.

The word echoed around the big room, bounced off the tall ceiling and the wood-paneled walls. There was no answer. "Coke!" he screamed. "COKE!"

Footsteps pattered distantly, clapped against marble floors, muffled themselves in carpeting. They stopped beside the broad, silken bed. "Yes, boss?" The voice cringed. The man cringed, too. It made him even shorter. The little eyes wavering in the monkey face refused to focus.

The sick man writhed on the bed. "The medicine!"

Coke snatched up the brown bottle from the gray metal nightstand and shook out three pills into a trembling hand. One of them dropped to the floor and he retrieved it. He held them out, and the sick man grabbed them greedily, popped them into his mouth. Into his hand Coke put a glass of water he had poured from a silver pitcher. The sick man drank, his Adam's apple jerking convulsively.

In a few minutes the sick man was sitting up. He hugged

his knees to his chest and breathed in exhausted pantings. "I'm sick, Coke," he moaned. "I've got to have a doctor. I'm going to die, Coke." Terror was in his voice. "Call the doctor!"

"I can't," Coke squeaked. "Don't you remember?"

The sick man frowned as if he were trying to understand, and then his face writhed and his left hand swung out viciously. It caught Coke across the mouth and hurled him into the corner. He crouched there, one hand pressed to his bleeding lips, watching the sick man with a rodent's wary eyes.

"Be here!" the sick man snarled. "Don't make me call you!" He forgot Coke. His head dropped. He hammered futilely against the bed with a knotted fist. "Damn!" he moaned.

In that position, he sat, graven, for minutes. Coke huddled in the corner, unmoving, watchful. At last the sick man straightened, threw back the heavy comforter, and stood up. He walked painfully to the curtained windows. As he walked he whimpered. "I'm sick. I'm going to die."

He tugged on a thick, velvet cord; the curtains whispered apart. Sunlight flooded into the room, spilled over the sick man; it turned his scarlet pajamas into flame, his face into dough.

"It's a terrible thing," said the sick man, "when a dying man can't get a doctor. I need the elixir, Coke. I need treatment for this pain. I can't stand it any longer."

Coke watched; his eyes never left the tall, thin man who stood in the sunlight and stared blindly out over the city. Coke took his hand away from his mouth; the back was smeared and red, and blood welled through three cuts in the lips.

"Get me a doctor, Coke," the sick man said. "I don't care how you do it. Just get him."

Coke got his feet under him and scuttled out of the room. The sick man stared out of the window, not hearing.

From here the ruins were not so apparent. The city looked almost as it had fifty years ago. But if a man looked closely he could see the holes in the roofs, the places where the porcelain false fronts had fallen and the brick behind them had crumbled and toppled into the streets.

Twelfth Street was blocked completely. Mounds of rubble made many other streets impassable. The hand of Time is not as swift as that of man, but it is inexorable.

The distant, arrowing sweep of Southwest Trafficway drew the eye like movement, bright through the drabness of decay. Medical Center was out of sight behind the rising ground to the south, but the complex, walled entity on Hospital Hill was brilliant in the sunlight.

It was an island rising out of a stinking sea, an enclave of life within the dying city.

The sick man stared out the window at the first tendrils of smog thrusting up the streets from the river, climbing toward the twenty-block-square fortress on Hospital Hill. But they would never get that far.

"Damn them!" the sick man whimpered. "Damn them!"

Flowers peered out the slit-windows of the one-man ambulance into the sooty night. The misting rain was mixed with smog now. It was a live thing against which the fog lamp struggled helplessly. It shifted constantly, there was no place to grab it, and the amber beam retreated in defeat, let itself be rolled back.

Ever since Flowers had left the trafficway with its lights and its occasional patrols, he had been lost and uneasy. Even the trafficway wasn't safe any more. A twenty-millimeter shell caroming from the ambulance's armored roof made a fearful din.

Where had the police been then?

The maps that listed Truman Road as "passable" were out of date. This had to be Truman Road; it was too wide to be anything else. But he had only a vague notion how far east he had come. On either side of the street was darkness; possibly it was a shade denser on the right.

Unless that was a strip razed by wind, fire, or dynamite, it was a park. He visualized the city map. It was either The Parade or The Grove.

Something exploded under the front wheel. The ambulance leaped, shuddering, into the air. It came down hard. Before the shocks absorbed it, the chauffeur lost control and the ambulance slewed toward the left.

Flowers grabbed the emergency wheel and took over from the chauffeur, turning the ambulance in the direction of the skid. Like the muffled wail of a parturient woman came the sound of screaming tires.

Lights loomed up unexpectedly, dim-red lanterns in the night, almost invisible in the swirling smog. They were about waist-high to a man standing in the street. That meant there was something supporting them.

Flowers twisted the wheel to the right this time, sharp, clutched his seat with taut legs as the ambulance took the curb, fought the crazy tilt as it lit in mud and skidded again. It was a park, all right. He raced through it, fighting desperately for control, dodging trees and bent telephone poles with their tangles of old webs, until he jogged the ambulance back into the street. He was blocks past the beginning of madness. He pulled up.

In the ambulance, balanced at the side of the road, Flowers sat and sweated. He rubbed the back of a hand across his forehead and fought the twitching nerves across his shoulders.

Damn the city! he thought savagely. *Damn the street*

department! Damn the Resident who would send out a medic on a night like this.

But it was nobody's fault.

The night traveler went at his own risk. There weren't enough of them to waste scarce taxes on street repairs, and it was no trick to avoid the holes, ruts, and uprooted slabs of concrete by daylight.

He thought back over the near-accident. That hadn't felt so much like a hole. It had felt more like a landmine. And those lanterns could have been sitting on a barricade which sheltered a band of hijackers.

Flowers shivered and stepped on the accelerator and wished fervently that he were back at the Center, working out his shift in the antiseptic, bullet-proof comfort of the emergency ward.

The chauffeur seemed to have settled down again. As Flowers eased the ambulance back into the middle of the road, he relaxed his grip on the wheel.

The smog shifted, and he saw the light. It glimmered far down the street like something lost in the night.

Flowers coasted past the café without lights. Inside was a waiter behind a long counter, and a single customer. Flowers swung the ambulance around the corner into a puddle of darkness.

Before he opened the door, he broke open a fresh filter packet and slipped the filters into his nostrils, taking time to see that they were a good fit. He slid the needle gun out of the holster on the ambulance door. The magazine was full. He set the controls for automatic defense and stepped into the night.

He sniffed the air tentatively. It wasn't conditioned, not by a wild stretch of the imagination, but the odor wasn't unbearable. A few minutes shouldn't cut down his life expectancy appreciably.

The smog swirled around him, clutching, trying to insinuate its deadly tendrils down into his lungs. Boyd was right: *We swim in a sea of carcinogens.*

There were two ways to deal with the problem. You could climb out of the sea, or you could filter out the carcinogens. But while you were about the first, the ideal solution, you had to do your best for those who had to live in the sea.

The rain had almost stopped, but Flowers pulled his coat tight at the collar. The black bag was in the ambulance, but even a flash of his white jacket was dangerous here. There was always a chance of running into hijackers or Antivivs, or just an ordinary citizen with a grudge.

Flowers passed quickly in front of the broad, patched window, through the pool of yellow light, his cropped, bare head bent. His hand rested on the right-hand coat pocket where he could feel the comfortable shape of the needle gun.

The street number was long gone from above the door. Flowers pushed his way through the airlock and into the brightness.

The waiter was a thick-necked urban with a battered nose and a scar starting at his hair line and seaming the left side of his face down to his neck. He wore a filthy white jacket in obvious imitation of a doctor's uniform.

The man puffed carelessly on a cigarette that was almost lost between his fingers. Flowers' brief thrill of horror turned to disgust. It wasn't enough that the urbans had to live in the sea; they had to add their own carcinogens.

Flowers diagnosed the thin weasel-faced customer automatically: *Thyroid. Hypertension.* He gave the man five years. The customer eyed Flowers slyly as he spooned something out of a bowl into his crooked mouth.

"What's for you?" asked the waiter eagerly. "Got a new health-food menu. Got a new tonic fresh from the lab—all the known vitamins, plus trace minerals, iron, and a new secret ingredient in an oral suspension of medicinal alcohol. You wanta see the lab sheets, analysis, testimonials?"

"No," Flowers began; "what I—"

"Augmented fruit juice?" the waiter continued doggedly. "Vegetables? Got a drink contains the liquified whole vegetable, eighteen different kinds. One glassful gives you your weekly requirements of eleven vitamins, eight minerals, and—"

"All I want to—"

"Say now," said the waiter, his voice dropping conspiratorially, "I got some stuff under the counter—straight Kentucky bourbon, no vitamins, no minerals, just plain rotgut."

"All I want to know is the address here," Flowers said.

The waiter looked at him blankly. Suspicion was something solid between them.

The waiter jerked a thumb back the way Flowers had come. "That way," he said, "that's Benton."

"Thanks," Flowers said coldly. He turned toward the door, danger at the back of his neck, prickling. He went out into the night.

"Pssst!" something hissed behind him.

Flowers glanced back. It was Thyroid, his weasel face screwed up ingratiatingly. Flowers stopped. The man sneaked close. "Where you going? I can maybe tell you."

Flowers hesitated. "Tenth," he said. "Thirty-four hundred block." What possible harm?

"Two blocks east, turn left. It's straight north," the man whispered huskily. Flowers muttered his thanks and turned away. He had just noticed that the man had no filters in his nose; he felt embarrassed. "Look!" the man said quickly. "Want some penicillin?"

Flowers stood rooted for a moment, too surprised to act. Then his right hand went casually into his pocket to grab the pistol butt while his left hand pressed two studs on his belt buckle. Faintly, listening for it, he heard the ambulance motor rev up. "What did you say?" he asked.

"Penicillin," the shover repeated urgently. "Hot stuff. Straight from the lab, and the price is right."

"How much?"

"A buck per hundred thousand. Look!" He stuck out a grimy hand; the yellow restaurant light filtered over it, over the metal-capped ampule that nestled in the palm. "Here's three hundred thousand units all ready to go to work. Suppose you get an infection tonight. It can lay you away for good. With this little ampule here, you catch it yourself. Three bucks, okay? Save a day's work, and you got your money back."

Flowers looked curiously at the 10 cc. ampule. Any penicillin in it was cut heavily. A dollar per hundred thousand units was less than wholesale.

The shover rolled the ampule across his palm in a gesture he meant to be irresistible. "Three bucks, and I throw in a hypodermic. You can't beat that. Well"—he pulled his hand back as if he were going to thrust it into his pocket and walk away—"it's your life. End up in a hospital."

Flowers stepped backwards into the darkness, closer to the ambulance, and listened for the beat of rotors. The night was silent. "There's worse places," he said.

"Name one," the shover challenged, and edged closer. "Tell you what. I'll make it two-fifty. How about it now—two-fifty, eh? Two-fifty and the hypo?"

Finally the price dropped to two bucks. By then the shover was close. Too close, Flowers thought. He backed away. The shover grabbed at the coat to hold him. The coat fell open.

Flowers damned the fool who had failed to magnetize the closure properly. The shover staggered back from the white jacket and looked wildly around for help that was unavailable.

Flowers pulled out the pistol. "That's far enough," he said firmly.

The shover came back immediately, like a ball on a string. "Look, say. I mean there's no reason we can't do business. I give you the penicillin, you forget we ever met, eh?"

"How much have you got?"

The shover looked as if he wanted to lie but didn't dare. "Ten million. Take it. Take it all."

"Keep your hands out of your pockets." Ten million. A hundred bucks. That was a load for a shover of his caliber. "Where did you get it?"

The man shrugged helplessly. "You know how it is. Somebody passes it to me, and how do I know where it comes from? Stolen maybe. Diverted at the factory. Like that."

"Bone?"

The shover looked startled. He glanced apprehensively into the shadows. "What do you think? Come on, medic, give me a break. You wouldn't really shoot me, would you? A medic and all?"

"Sure I would," Flowers said evenly. "Who'd care?"

The light came on like a detergent spray, cleansing the darkness. Flowers heard the rotors overhead and blinked blindly.

"Don't move," said the bull voice. "You're under arrest."

The shover dashed for the darkness. Flowers aimed carefully. The needle caught him in the back of the neck, just below the basi-occipital bone. He took one more step and crumpled, half in darkness. The police sergeant listened to Flowers' description of events with unconcealed impatience. "You shouldn'ta shot him," he said. "What's the man done, he should get shot?"

"Shoving," Flowers began firmly, counting on his fingers with the muzzle of the needle gun. "Bribery. Adulterating, too, if you'll analyze that ampule." It was in the middle of the broken sidewalk, miraculously whole. The sergeant stooped for it reluctantly.

"That's no proof," he said sourly. "You think we got nothing better to do than answer false alarms? I ought to run you in for disturbing the peace and false arrest." He glanced again at the ambulance, speculatively, and back to the needle gun.

"Proof?" Flowers echoed, scowling darkly. "What do you need? There's a man with ten million units of penicillin. There's my testimony. There's this." He pressed the play-back button on his belt buckle.

The voice was rich and cultured. "Contra-indications are known ilotycin sensitivity and—"

Flowers hit the stud hastily and reeled off a few feet of tape before he started it again. "Penicillin," said the shover's husky whisper. "Hot stuff. Straight from the lab, and the price is right. . . ."

When it was finished, Flowers erased the tag end of Dr. Curry's lecture on internal medicine and added his own affidavit, "I, Benjamin Flowers, seventh-year medic, do hereby swear by Aesculapius and Hippocrates that . . ."

The officer's reluctant confirmation made it legal, and Flowers dropped the bobbin-sized spool into the officer's meaty hand. "That should be plenty. There's your prisoner."

The shover was on his hands and knees, weaving his head back and forth like a sleepy elephant. Flowers put one foot on his back and shoved him over. "I'm going to follow up this case," he said. "I want to see this man get the full penalty. I've got your badge number. I wouldn't let him escape or lose any of the evidence."

The sergeant's voice dropped to a whine. "You don't have

to get tough. I'll do my job. You should understand, though—a man's got to live. These is hard times. Why, that man's probably trying to meet payments on a medical contract! Look at it from our angle. If we was to run in every shover in town we'd have 'em stacked eight deep in the city jail. How'd we feed 'em? How'd we keep 'em there if they didn't want to stay?"

"That's your problem, sergeant. It's rats like that who are slashing the throat of the medical profession. If drugs and antibiotics circulate without supervision, the lifespan will plummet to seventy or lower. We have enough trouble with antibiotic sensitivity and resistant bacteria strains without this."

Flowers looked down again at the shover. He was sitting up, bewildered. He rubbed the back of his neck and pulled his hand away to stare at it. "I ain't dead," he said.

"My business is saving life, not taking it," Flowers said harshly.

The shover looked up at the voice and snarled. "You! You lousy body snatcher! Quack! You ain't gonna get away with this! John Bone'll take care of you, butcher!"

"Here, now!" the sergeant broke in sharply, hauling the shover to his feet. "That's enough out of you."

But his hands were surprisingly gentle. Flowers' lips twisted wryly.

Over the muffled throb of the helicopter's rotors, the shover shouted at him, "You and your kind—you're responsible for all this!"

The searchlight swept along the front of the porch roof and picked out two numbers hanging rusty and askew. Luckily they were the last two.

The house stood beside a vacant lot crammed with disintegrating pipe and machinery and the decaying derrick of a gas-drilling outfit. At one time the yard had been paved;

now it was little better than powdery gravel as Flowers drove up to the front steps.

He turned off the lights and sat in the darkness staring up at the place. There were two stories and an attic. A dilapidated porch reached across the front. The windows stared dark and blind into the night.

Had the Resident made a mistake? It would be typical.

Then he saw a dim flicker behind the west second-floor window.

Carefully Flowers climbed the rotten wooden steps. The light built into the black bag splashed against the old door. Flowers knocked. There was no answer. The only sound was the comforting vibration of the ambulance motor.

He tried the antique brass handle. The door swung open. He pulled out the needle gun and entered cautiously. To the right an archway had been boarded off with worm-eaten plywood. Ahead was a flight of stairs.

As he climbed noiselessly, the light gleamed from hand-turned spindles, polished by generations of small hands. When he could afford a place of his own in the country, he told himself, he would have something in it like that—old, haunted by a thousand memories of the past. If he found some really good examples of early woodwork, he could buy the place or have it condemned by the public health department.

At the top of the stairs were several doors. Flowers turned right. The door he tried was locked. It rattled under his hand.

He listened uneasily to the noises of the house. It creaked and squeaked and stirred as if it had acquired a life of its own over the centuries. His shoulders twitched.

The door opened.

The light from the black bag spilled over the girl like quicksilver. She stared into it, unblinking. Flowers stared back. She was perhaps five feet five. Her dark hair would have been very long, he thought, if it had been allowed to fall free, but it was braided and wound around her head like a coronet.

Her face was delicate and slender, the skin very white, the features regular. Her dress was yellow, flowing, belted in to a small waist; it was impractical and unflattering and completely unlike the straight, narrow fashions women were wearing these days. But there was something suggestive about the hint of figure beneath the cloth and the bare, white feet. His pulse climbed ten beats per minute.

Only then did he notice that she was blind. Her corneas were opaque, darkening the pale blue of her eyes.

"Are you the medic?" Her voice was low and gentle.

"Yes."

"Come in before you arouse our roomers. They might be dangerous."

As the girl bolted the door behind him, Flowers surveyed the room, which was fairly large. Once it had been a bedroom; now it was a one-room apartment containing two chairs, a gas burner, an upended crate serving as a table for a smoking kerosene lamp, and a cot made of wood and canvas.

On the cot was a middle-aged man, sixtyish, his eyelids closed, his breathing noisy in the bare room.

"Philip Shoemaker?" Flowers asked.

"Yes," the girl said.

He noticed her eyes again. In the sun they would be the color of wild hyacinth. "Daughter?"

"No relation."

"What are you doing here?"

"He's sick," she said simply.

Flowers studied her face. Its peace and calmness told him nothing.

As he sat down on the chair beside the cot he unlocked his black bag. Quickly, without wasted motion, he brought out a handful of instruments, trailing their wires. One small pickup went over the old man's heart; another was fastened to his wrist, a third to the palm. He wrapped a sphygmomanometer band around the bicep and watched it grow taut, slipped a mouthpiece between pale lips, fitted something like a skullcap to the head. . . .

When he was finished, Shoemaker was a fly caught in a web, transmitting feeble impulses to the spider lurking in the bag. This spider, though, was linked to the ambulance below by intangible lines, and together they would pour life back into the fly, not suck it away.

It took one minute and twenty-three seconds. During the next second, Flowers noticed the adhesive tape on the patient's forearm. He frowned and tore it loose. Beneath it was a compress dark with blood and a small, welling slit in the median-basilic vein.

"Who's been here since this man fell ill?"

"Me," the girl said clearly. One hand was resting gently on the box that held the lamp.

Beneath the head of the cot was a quart jar. In it was a pint of blood, clotting now but still warm. Flowers put it down slowly. "Why did you perform a phlebotomy on this man?"

"There was no other way to save his life," she said gently.

"This isn't the Dark Ages," Flowers said. "You might have killed him."

"Study your lessons better, medic," she told him softly. "In some cases blood-letting is effective when nothing else will work—in cerebral hemorrhage, for instance. It lowers the blood pressure temporarily and gives the blood in the ruptured vessel a chance to clot."

Involuntarily, Flowers glanced into the bag. From the bottom, the diagnosis was shining up fluorescently. It was cerebral hemorrhage, all right, and the prognosis was hopeful. The hemorrhage had stopped.

He took a compress out of a pocket in the bag, pulled the tab, and watched the wrapper disintegrate. He pressed it firmly over the cut. It clung to the skin as he took his hand away.

"There are laws against practicing medicine without a license," he said slowly. "I'll have to report this."

"Should I have let him die?"

"There are doctors to treat him."

"He called one. It took you an hour and a half to get here. If I had waited, he'd have died."

"I came as fast as I could. It's no joke to find a place like this at night."

"I'm not criticizing." She put her hand back until she felt the chair behind her and sank down into it, lightly, gracefully, and folded her white hands in her lap. "You asked me why I bled him. I told you."

Flowers was silent. The girl's logic was impeccable, but she was wrong all the same. There weren't any reasonable excuses for breaking the law. The practice of medicine had to be the monopoly of men who were carefully, exactingly trained for it and indoctrinated in the ancient ethics. No one else could be permitted to tamper with the most sacred thing in the world.

"You were lucky," he said. "You might have guessed wrong."

"There are no degrees to death."

"He'll probably die anyway."

She rose and walked toward him confidently, put a hand on his shoulder, and leaned past him to touch Shoemaker's forehead. "No," she said, and her voice was firm with an odd certainty. "He'll get well now. He's a good man. We mustn't let him die."

The girl's nearness was a warm fragrance, stirring, provocative. Flowers felt his blood pressure mount. *Why not?* he thought; *she's only an urban.* But he couldn't, and it wasn't just a medic's honor or even, perhaps, that she was blind.

He didn't move, but she drew away, took back her hand, as if she sensed the emotions fermenting inside him.

"I've got to get him to the hospital," Flowers said. "Besides the hemorrhage, there'll be infection."

"I scrubbed the arm with soap and then with alcohol," she said. "I sterilized the knife in the lamp flame and scorched the bandage over the lamp chimney."

Her fingers looked blistered. "You were lucky," he said coldly. "Next time someone will die."

She turned her face toward his voice. Flowers found the movement strangely appealing. "What can you do when they need you?"

It was too much like a physician's response to the world's plea for help. A doctor had the right to respond to the plea; she didn't. He turned brusquely back to Shoemaker and began stripping off the instruments and stowing them away. "I'll have to carry him down to the ambulance. Can you carry the bag for me to light the way?"

"You mustn't take him. He hasn't kept up payments on his contract. You know what they'll do."

Flowers stopped in the act of snapping the bag shut. "If he's a defaulter . . ." he began, his voice trembling on the verge of anger.

"What would you do," she asked quietly, "if you were dying and alone? Wouldn't you call for help? Any help? Would you stop to weigh legalities? He had a contract once, and the payments ruined him, cost him his home in the county, drove him here to the sustenance life. But when he was sick, he turned to his old faith, as a dying Catholic calls for his priest."

Flowers recoiled from the comparison. "And he deprived several people of vital, lawful attention. The chances are he traded his life for that of someone else. That's why the laws were passed. Those who pay for medical treatment shouldn't be penalized by those who can't—or won't, which is usually the case. If Shoemaker can't pay, he ought to be repossessed." He stooped toward the old man.

She pulled him back with surprising strength and slipped between them, bent backwards, one arm thrown back protectively toward Shoemaker. Her eyes were cloudy embers in the lamplight. "Surely you've got enough blood, enough organs. They'll kill him."

"There's never enough," Flowers said. "And there's research, after that." He put an impatient hand on her shoulder to push her aside. Under the dress material, the flesh felt warm and soft. "You must be an Antiviv."

"I am, but that's only part of it. I'm asking for him, because he's worth saving. Are you so inflexible, so perfect, that you can't—forget?"

He stopped pushing, looked down at his hand for a moment, and let it drop. He refused to fight with the girl for the man's body.

"All right," he said.

He picked up the black bag with a snap that locked it shut and started toward the door.

"Wait!" she said.

He looked back at her as she moved toward him blindly, her hand outstretched until her fingers touched the arm of his coat. "I want to thank you," she said gently. "I thought there wasn't any mercy left in the medical profession."

For a moment his viscera felt cold, anesthetized, and then the icy feeling melted in a surge of anger. "Don't misunderstand me," he said brutally, shrugging her hand away. "I'm going to turn in his name to the Agency. I'm going to report you, too. That's my duty."

Her hand fell to her side in a gesture of apology, for her own mistake and perhaps also for the nature of humanity. "We do what we must."

She moved forward past him, unbolted the door, and turned toward him, her back against the door. "I don't think you're as hard as you pretend to be."

That stopped him. He wasn't hard. He resented the implication that he was, that medics in general were incapable of understanding, were devoid of sympathy.

Those who must live in the midst of sickness and death, upon whose skill and judgment rest health and life and their concomitant, happiness, can't be touched by the drama, the poignancy, the human values of every situation. It would be unendurable.

"There's an old man downstairs who needs help," she said hesitantly. "Would you see him?"

"Out of the question," he answered sharply.

Her head lifted for a moment. That was pride, he thought. Then she nodded. "I'm sorry," she said softly.

The light was dangerous, she said, and offered to lead him. Her hand was warm and firm and confident. Three-quarters of the way down there was a landing, where the stairs turned left. A door opened in the darkness to the right of the landing.

Flowers tore his hand loose and stuck it into his coat pocket onto the solid reassurance of the needle gun.

Glimmering whitely in the dark rectangle of the door was a ghost of a face. "Leah?" it said. It was a girl's voice. "I thought it was you. Give me your hand. Let me hold it for a moment. I thought I would never get through the night. . . ."

"There now," said Leah. She put out a hand toward the face. "You're going to be all right. Don't let yourself believe anything else."

Flowers snapped on the light of the black bag. It hit the girl in the doorway like a blow; she recoiled, moaning, her arm over her eyes.

Flowers turned the light off—he had seen enough. The

girl, in her thin, mended nightdress, was a bundle of bones wrapped tautly in pale skin. Except for two feverish spots of color in her cheeks, her face was dead-white.

She was dying of tuberculosis.

Tuberculosis. Today! Why do they do it!

"Go up and stay with Phil," Leah said. "He needs you. He's had a stroke, but he's better now."

"All right, Leah," the girl said. Her voice seemed stronger, more confident. She slipped past them silently and climbed the stairs.

"What's the matter with them?" Flowers' voice was strained and puzzled. "Tuberculosis is no problem. We can cure it easily. Why do they let themselves die?"

She stopped in front of the worm-eaten plywood partition and raised her face toward him. "Because it's cheaper. It's all they can afford."

"Cheaper to die?" Flowers exclaimed incredulously. "What kind of economy is that?"

"The only kind of economy they know. The only kind the hospitals will let them practice. You've made good health too expensive. A few months of bed rest," she said wearily, "a hundred grams of dihydrostreptomycin, a thousand grams of PAS, perhaps some collapsed-lung therapy, some rib resections. That girl has never seen more than fifty dollars all at once. If she lived to be a hundred she couldn't save half the money necessary for the treatment. She's got children to support. She can't stop working for a day, much less for months—"

"There are clinical contracts," Flowers said impatiently.

"They don't cover the kind of treatment she needs," Leah said wistfully. A door opened behind her. "Good night, medic." Then she was gone.

At the door he turned back impetuously, words pouring to his lips: *If there isn't enough to go around, who are you*

*going to treat—the indigent or the prosperous, the wasters or
the savers, the bottomless pits or those who can finance the
future, more medicine, more health for everyone?*

But the words died on his lips. The panel in the partition
had come ajar. In the room behind it was a battered old
aluminum chaise longue—Twentieth Century Modern. An
old man was propped upright in it, so straight and still that
Flowers thought for a moment the man was dead.

He was a very old man. Flowers thought that he had
never seen a man as old, although geriatrics was one of
Medical Center's leading specialties. His hair was pure
white and thick; his face was seamed, like old leather, the
flesh sagging away from the strong facial bones.

Beside the chair Leah had sunk to her knees. She had one
of the bony hands in hers, pressed to her cheek, her eyelids
closed over their clouded corneas.

Flowers found himself standing in the doorway, the panel
swinging noiselessly away from him. There was something
familiar about that old face, something he couldn't place,
pin down. He noticed with a shock that the old man's eyes
were open now.

It was like a return from the dead. There was life in the
old eyes, faded blue though they were, and the wrinkled old
skin seemed to grow firm. The body warmed, grew strong as
the face smiled gently.

"Come in, medic," the old man whispered.

Leah's face came up, her sightless eyes open; she turned
toward him. She smiled, too. It was a warming thing, like
sunlight.

"You came back to help," Leah said.

Flowers shook his head slowly and then remembered that
she couldn't see. "There's nothing I can do."

"There's nothing anyone can do," the old man whispered.
"Even without your gadgets, medic, you know what's wrong

with me. You can't mend a whole body, not with all your skill and all your fancy instruments. The body wears out. With most of us it happens part by part. With a few it goes all at once.

"You could give me a new heart from some unfortunate defaulter, but my arteries would still be thickened with arteriosclerosis. And if, somehow, you replaced those without killing me, I would still have a fibrotic liver, scarred lungs, senile ductless glands, probably a few carcinomas. And even if you gave me a new body, you still couldn't help me, because down deep, where your knives can't reach and your instruments can't measure, is the me that is old beyond repair."

When Leah turned her face back toward Flowers, he was shocked to see tears trickling from the blind eyes. "Can't you do something?" Her voice broke. "Aren't you good for anything?"

"Leah!" Even the old man's whisper was reproof.

"It leaves a permanent recording in the ambulance library," Flowers explained reasonably. "I can't afford that; neither can you."

She pressed her forehead fiercely against the back of the old man's hand. "I can't stand it, Russ. I can't bear to lose you."

"Tears are wasted for a man who has outlived his generation," Russ said, "and almost his own era." He smiled at Flowers; it was almost a benediction. "I'm one hundred and twenty-five years old." He drew his hand gently from Leah's firm young hands and folded his across his lap. They lay there as if they no longer belonged to him. "That's a long time."

Leah stood up angrily. "There must be something you can do—with all your magnificent knowledge, all the expensive gadgets we bought you!"

"There's the elixir," he said thoughtlessly.

Russ smiled again, reminiscently perhaps. "Ah, yes—the elixir. I had almost forgotten. *Elixir vitae.*"

"Would it help?" Leah demanded.

"No," Flowers said firmly.

He had said too much already. Laymen weren't equipped for medical information; it confused them; it blurred the medical picture. What the patient needed more than anything else was not an understanding of his condition but implicit faith in his doctor. When every treatment is familiar, none is effective. It is better for medicine to be magic than to be commonplace.

Besides, the elixir was still only a laboratory phenomenon. Perhaps it would never be more than that. The stuff was a synthesis of a rare blood protein—a gamma globulin— which had been discovered in the bloodstreams of no more than a handful of persons in the whole world. This protein, this immunity factor, seemed to pass on its immunity as if death itself were a disease. . . .

"A tremendously complicated process," he said. "Prohibitively expensive." He turned accusingly toward Russ. "I can't understand why you didn't have new corneas grafted onto her eyes."

"I couldn't take the sight of anyone else," Leah said softly, reproachfully.

"There's accidental deaths," Flowers pointed out.

"How are you going to know?"

"Don't you want her to see?" Flowers demanded of Russ.

"If wanting were enough," the old man whispered, "she would have had my eyes many years ago. But there's the expense, my boy. It all comes back to that."

"Stupidity!" Flowers turned to leave.

"Wait, boy," Russ whispered. "Come here a moment."

Flowers turned and walked to the old man's chair; he looked down at Leah and back to Russ. The old man held out his hand, palm up. Automatically, Flowers put out his hand to meet it, let his hand rest upon it. As the hands met, Flowers felt a curious electrical sensation, as if something had stimulated a nerve into sending a message up his arm to his brain and carrying an answer back.

Russ's hand dropped back limply. He lowered his head wearily against the back of the chaise longue, his eyes closed. "A good man, Leah, troubled but sincere. We might do worse."

"No," Leah said firmly, "he must not come here again. It wouldn't be wise."

"Don't worry about that," Flowers said. He wouldn't be back; he hadn't felt like this since he was a little boy listening to his father tell him about medicine.

"Some empty time," Russ said distantly, "you might think of this, a conclusion I reached many years ago: *There are too many doctors and not enough healers.*"

Leah rose gracefully from the floor. "I'll see you to the door."

Her unconscious use of the phrase brought pity chokingly into Flowers' throat. It was tragedy because she was beautiful—he thought of her now as beautiful—and peacefully beautiful inside. Reporting her was going to be painful.

He wondered how his hand had felt to her: hot, sweaty, nervous? How had he seemed to her?

He paused at the outside door. "I'm sorry I couldn't help your grandfather."

"He's my father. I was born the year he was one hundred. He wasn't old then. He was middle-aged, everyone thought. It's only these last few months he's grown old. I think it's a surrender we make when we grow very tired."

"How do you live—with him sick, and—"

"And me blind? People are generous."

"Why?"

"They're grateful, I suppose. For the times when we can

help them. I collect old remedies from grandmothers and make them up; I brew ptisans; I'm a midwife when I'm needed; I sit up with the sick, help those I can, and bury those I can't. You can report this, too, if you wish."

"I see," Flowers said, turning away and swinging back, irresolute. "Your father—I've seen him somewhere. What's his name?"

"He lost it more than fifty years ago. Here in the city, people call him *healer.*" She held out her hand toward him. Flowers took it reluctantly. This was the end of it. The hand was warm; his hand remembered the warmth. It would be a good hand to hold if you were sick..

"Good-by, medic," she said soberly. "I like you. You're human. So few of them are. But don't come back. It wouldn't be good for any of us."

Flowers cleared his throat noisily. "I said I wouldn't," he said; even to him it sounded petulant and childish. "Good-by."

She stood in the doorway as he turned, shifted the bag into his right hand, and picked his way down the porch stairs. It was a good bag, and it felt solid in his hand. It was on semi-permanent loan from the Center. Against its black side were two words imprinted in gold: BENJ. FLOWERS. Someday there would be two more letters added: M.D.

A few months more and he would have earned them; he would buy the bag, make a down payment on his library, pass the state examination. He would have a license from the state to practice medicine upon the bodies of its citizens. He would be a doctor.

For the first time since he could remember, the prospect didn't excite him.

A man was lying almost under the front wheel of the ambulance. Beside him, on the broken pavement, was a crowbar. Flowers rolled the man over. His eyes were closed, but he was breathing easily. He had got too close and the supersonics had knocked him out.

He should call the police about this, too, but he felt too tired for another battle with the police.

He pulled the body out of the path of the wheels and opened the ambulance door. There was a whisper of movement behind him.

"Medic!" Leah screamed. Her voice was distant and frightened.

Flowers started to turn, but it was too late. The night came down and covered him.

He opened his eyes to darkness, and the thought was instantaneous: *This is what it is to be blind. This is what Leah knows always.*

His head throbbed. There was an egg-sized lump on the back of it, where someone had hit him. The hair was matted with dried blood. He winced as his fingers explored the depth of the cut, but it wasn't too bad. He decided that there was no concussion.

He didn't feel blind. Probably there was no light.

He had a faded, uncertain memory—as of something lost in childhood mists—of a wild ride through city streets; of a heavy door that swung upwards, clanging; of an entrance into a place cavernous, musty, echoing; of being carried— on what? the ambulance stretcher?—up a short flight of stairs, through something awkward, up more steps, down dark halls, and being put down.

Someone had said something. "He's coming around. Shall I tap him again?"

"Never mind. Just roll him out until we need him. He won't go anywhere."

Thump! Blackness again.

There was concrete under him, cold and hard. He got to his feet, feeling shaky, aching all over, not just his head. He took a cautious step forward, and another, holding one hand straight out in front, fingers extended, the other arm curled protectively over his face.

At the fifth step, his fingers touched a vertical surface. Concrete again. A wall.

He turned and moved along the wall to a corner and along a second wall that was shorter and had a door in it. The door was solid metal; it had a handle, but the handle wouldn't turn. The other walls were unbroken. When he had finished the circuit, he had a mental picture of a windowless room about fifteen feet long by nine feet wide.

He sat down and rested.

Somebody had booby-trapped him, knocked him out, brought him to this concrete box, locked him in.

There was only one person it could have been. The man he had pulled from under the wheel. He had crept in close to the ambulance, so slowly that the detectors hadn't reacted. When Flowers had come, they had clicked off, and the man had been released to club him. A crowbar might make a wound like that.

If he was a hijacker, if he wanted the drugs and the instruments, why had he bothered to bring along the medic?

He went through his pockets—futilely. There was nothing in the coat or the jacket underneath. They had taken the needle gun.

He would hide behind the door, he decided. When it opened—it opened inward—he would be behind it. He had fists. He was big enough; maybe he was strong enough. He would have a good chance of taking the hijackers by surprise.

Meanwhile, he sat in the dark silence, remembering the dream he had wakened from. It had seemed to him that he was a little boy again, and his father was talking to him in the grown-up fashion he had affected with his son. It had always embarrassed Flowers, even when he was very young.

"Ben," his father said, "there may be more important things than medicine, but you can't be sure of any of them." He put his hand on the boy's shoulder. It was heavy and Ben wanted to shrug it off, but he didn't dare.

"It's different with medicine. You deal with life, and life is always important. You'll feel it every day, because every day you'll have a personal fight with death, you'll beat him back a foot, surrender a few inches, and come back to the battle. Because life is sacred, Ben. No matter how mean it is or crippled, it's sacred. That's what we bow down to, Ben."

"I know, dad," Flowers said, his voice high and a little frantic. "I want to be a doctor. I want to—"

"Then bow down, boy. Bow down!"

But why should he think of Leah's father? Why should the memory of something that had probably never happened make him think of Russ?

Was it what the dying man had said: "Some empty time . . . ?"

What time could be emptier than this?

Too many doctors and not enough healers! That's what the old man had said.

Absurd. It was like so many meaningless phrases which seem portentous because of their vagueness. It reminded him of arguments with the other medics.

In the darkness, the hospital incense seemed to drift to him—ether and alcohol. The good smell. The reverent smell. Anyone who criticized medicine just didn't know what he was talking about.

He remembered standing by the dormitory's bullet-proof window, staring out at the block of houses being razed to make room for the two new wings, geriatrics and the premature section of obstetrics. It seemed to him that the twin processes of destruction and construction never stopped. Somewhere on the Center's periphery there were always new wings growing over the old ruins.

How many square blocks did the Center's walls enclose? Forty? Forty-five? He had forgotten.

He must have said it aloud, because Charley Brand answered from his desk. "Sixty and three-fourths." Brand was a strange person, an accretion of miscellaneous information waiting to be mined, a memory bank awaiting only the proper question. But he lacked something; he was cold and mechanical; he couldn't synthesize.

"Why?" asked Hal Mock.

"No reason," Flowers said, vaguely irritated. "I went on a call a few days ago—into the city."

" 'Thus conscience does make cowards of us all,' " Brand quoted, not looking up from the desk where he flipped the frames in the viewer, one every second. Mechanical, mechanical.

"What does that mean?" Flowers snapped.

"Sometimes," Mock mused, "I wish something would happen to a few medics in our class. Like getting sick—not seriously, you understand—or breaking a leg. The school can only graduate so many, you know. It has a quota. But we're all so healthy, so careful. It's disgusting." He brooded over it. "Think of it. Seven years of torture, grinding my brains to a sharp point, and the prize depends on the right answers to a few stupid questions. It makes me sick to think about it."

Brand shifted uneasily and changed the subject. "What are you going to specialize in, Ben? After you graduate."

"I don't know," Flowers said. "I haven't thought about it."

"I have," said Brand. "Psychiatry."

"Why be a head-shrinker?" Mock asked scornfully.

"Simple economics," Brand said. "The incidence of mental disease in this country is sixty-five point three per cent. Almost two out of every three persons needs the services of a psychiatrist during his lifetime. On top of that are the neuroses and the stress diseases like stomach cramps, rheumatoid arthritis, asthma, duodenal ulcers, hypertension, heart disease, ulcerative colitis. And life doesn't get any simpler. You can't beat those figures."

"How about geriatrics?" Mock asked slyly. "The incidence of senescence is one hundred per cent. That's the well that never runs dry."

"Until they bring out the elixir in quantity!"

"They'll never do that," Mock said shrewdly. "They know which side—"

Flowers listened intently in the darkness. Was that a noise on the other side of the door? A rattling, clanging sort of noise?

He sprang to his feet, but the noise—if it had been a noise—wasn't repeated. There was no use taking chances. He felt his way into the corner, behind the door, and leaned against the wall, waiting.

"There's more to medicine than money," he repeated softly.

"Sure," Mock said, "but economic facts are basic. Ignore them and you can't do an acceptable job at your profession. Look at the income tax rate: it starts at fifty per cent. On ten thousand a year, it's eighty per cent. How are you going to pay for your bag, your instruments, your library? You can't practice medicine without them. How are you going to pay your dues in the county medical society, in the A.M.A., special assessments . . . ?"

"Why are the income taxes so high?" Flowers demanded. "Why are instruments so expensive? Why are a hundred million people without adequate medical facilities, condemned to a lingering death in a sea of carcinogens, unable to afford what the orators call 'the finest flower of medicine'?"

"It's the cost of living," Mock said, curling his lip. "Whatever you want, you have to pay for. Haven't you figured it out?"

"No," Flowers said savagely. "What do you mean?"

Mock glanced cautiously behind him. "I'm not that foolish," he said slyly. "You never know who might be listening. Some medic might have left his recorder on in his desk on the off chance of catching somebody with his ethics down. I'll say this, though: *We can be too healthy!*"

"Nuts!" Flowers muttered in the darkness of the concrete cell. He let himself sink down the wall until he reached the floor.

They were all wrong, Mock and Russ and Leah and the rest of them who hinted at dark things. In another age they would have been burned at the stake. He had seen Dr. Cassner refute them brilliantly in a beautiful three-hour display of microsurgical virtuosity.

It began as an ordinary arterial resection and transplant. The overhead shadowless light was searching and cold on the draped body of the old man. The assistant surgeons and nurses worked together with that exquisite precision which is the result of years of training and experience.

The air conditioners murmured persistently, but sweat beaded Cassner's broad forehead and trickled down beneath his mask before the nurse could mop it away with sterile cotton.

But Cassner's hands never stopped. They were things in motion, disembodied, alive. His fingers manipulated the delicate controls of the surgical machine with a sureness, a dexterity unmatched in this part of the country, perhaps anywhere. Genius is incomparable.

Flowers watched with a hypnotized fascination that

made time meaningless. The scalpels sliced through the skin with unerring precision, laying bare the swollen old arteries; deft metal fingers tied them off, snipped them in two, accepted a lyophilized transplant, and grafted the healthy young artery to the stump of the old; the suture machine moved swiftly after, dusting the exposed area with antibiotics, clamping together the edges of the incision, sealing them with a quick, flattening movement. . . .

Cassner's eyes flickered from the patient on the operating table to the physiological monitor on the wall behind it, absorbing at a single glance the composite picture of the patient's condition: blood pressure, heartbeat, respiration. . . .

The microsurgeon saw the danger first. The operation was, comparatively, a speedy thing, but there were disadvantages. The area involved was large, and even the chlorpromazine-promethazine-Dolosal cocktail and the chilling could not nullify shock entirely. And the heart was old.

It was impossible to transfer the instruments to the new area swiftly enough. Cassner took the scalpel in his own fingers and opened up the chest cavity with a long, sure stroke. "Heart machine," he said in his quick, high voice to no one in particular.

It was pumping within thirty seconds, its tubes tied to the aorta and the left atrium. Two minutes later a new heart, still palpitating, was in the old chest; Cassner grafted the arteries and veins to it. Ten minutes after the monitor had signaled the heart stoppage, Cassner pulled out the old heart and held it, a dead thing of worn-out muscle. He motioned wearily for his first assistant to inject the digitalis.

As the chest cavity was closed, the new heart began squeezing powerfully, forcing the blood through the arteries.

Cassner would have had a good excuse for turning the

more routine job over to the assistant, but he completed the arterial job before he turned away toward the dressing room. . . .

That's what the scoffers forgot, Flowers thought—what a man got for his money: the skill, the drugs, the instruments. Without modern medicine the man on the operating table would have died twenty years earlier.

That man wasn't too healthy. If he were any less healthy, he'd be dead. Now he was good for five to ten years more.

"That's nothing," Mock said. "I saw Smith-Johnson save a five-month fetus. It made me wonder: why?"

Flowers looked scornful. He knew why: it was because life was sacred, any life, all life.

"Sometimes in the night," Mock said distantly, "I can hear their voices wailing, muffled by the incubators, all the premies that were too weak to live, that nature wanted to be rid of, and we saved—for blindness and disease and perpetual care. Oh, Cassner's good, but I wonder: how much did the operation cost?"

"How should I know?"

"Why don't you find out?"

Flowers shivered in the darkness, although the room was hot, and pushed his hands into his pockets. He touched his belt buckle.

He started, and wondered why he hadn't thought of it before. He pushed the alarm button hastily.

It was a chance, and any chance was worth trying. He supposed that the hijackers had turned off the ambulance motor when they parked it.

Flowers sank back against the wall, remembering how he had gone to the business office. They had taken down his name, but they had shown him the statement. The old man had put down a $200,000 deposit. The business office had figured it pretty shrewdly. The total bill was only a few hundred less.

He glanced down the "Debit" column with its four- and five-digit numbers:

Operating Room $40,000

Well, why not? The heart machine alone had cost $5,000,000, and that microsurgery had been the marvel of the Middle West when it had been constructed and equipped. Someone had to pay for it.

After that was the room fee, anesthesia, laboratory fees, X-ray, tissue exam, EKG-EEG-BMR fees, drugs and dressings, and, most prominently, the prices for new organs and arteries:

New Arteries (1 set) $30,000
New Heart (1) $50,000

Some poor devil of a defaulter had paid his bill.

Flowers sat in the concrete cell and told himself that a medic shouldn't have to weigh questions of relative value. So the operation had cost the old man $30,000 to $40,000 for each year of life it promised him. It was worth it—from the old man's viewpoint. Was there another viewpoint? Was someone else footing the bill?

Society, maybe. Was it worth it to society? Maybe not. The old man was a consumer now, eating up and using up what he had been smart enough or strong enough or ruthless enough to have produced when he was younger.

So it wasn't worth it to society!

That was a brutal, inhuman viewpoint. That was the reason nobody wanted society to be the judge of what was worthwhile. Medicine had been fighting that possibility for centuries; on that point the A.M.A. was immovable. A man had an inalienable right to the doctor of his choice and the medical treatment he could afford.

Of course, of course. It illustrated the danger of looking at the problem all backwards, as Hal Mock might. The knowledge was there; the skill was there; the equipment was there. If it wasn't used, it would be an outrageous waste.

But maybe, he thought sharply, the mistake came earlier, in developing the knowledge, the skill, and the equipment in the first place. That was when society footed the bill.

Society puts a price on everything. In every era there are limited quantities of intelligence, energy, and that inheritance from the thought and labor of the past, capital. Society's value system determines how these assets are distributed among a thousand different enterprises.

It was like a budget: so much for food, so much for shelter, so much for clothing, education, research, entertainment; so much for the doctor.

What was more valuable than good health? Nothing, said society. Without it, all is worthless.

What did Mock mean when he said we can be too healthy?

Was there an optimum beyond which medicine consumed more than it produced in benefits? And was there a point past that at which medicine became a monster, devouring the society that produced it?

Maybe the cost of living could be too high. Maybe a society could be too healthy, like a hypochondriac, spending itself into bankruptcy in a vain effort to cure small or fancied ills.

"Charley," he asked Brand one day, "what percentage of the national income went into medicine last year?"

"Therapy, education, research, production, or construction?"

"Everything."

"Let's see—fifteen point six, ten point one, twelve point nine, five point two, eight point seven—that's—what does that add up to?"

"Fifty-two point five," said Flowers.

In the darkness of the concrete room, he repeated the figure to himself. "Nonsense," he muttered.

It was a relief from thought to discover that the recorder was running. He had only to press the playback stud to discover the identities of his captors.

He pressed the stud and listened, engrossed, to the voices of Leah and Russ and himself. . . . But before the tape reached Leah's frightened cry, the door swung open and a blinding light dazzled his eyes.

He stabbed the recorder into silence and cursed silently. He had lost his chance.

"Who are you?" he demanded.

"Police officers," said a harsh voice. "Didn't you send out an alarm?"

"Get that light out of my eyes," Flowers said suspiciously. "Let me see you."

"Sure."

The light, turned away, splashed against dark trousers, lighter tunics, glittered on badges, exposed faces, caps.

One of the two officers looked familiar. Surely that was the sergeant to whom he had turned over the shover?

"Well, medic," the sergeant said, "we meet again, eh? Come on, we'd better get out of here."

"Certainly, but where's the ambulance? Did you find it? Did you catch the hijackers? Did you—"

"Hold it." The sergeant chuckled. "We ain't got time for everything now. The hijackers might come back, eh, Dan?"

"You bet," said Dan.

They went down long marble corridors, echoing with their footsteps, opening before them as the flashlight moved forward into the darkness. They reached a wide hall. On each side were three sets of heavy brass doors, one set standing open. Behind it was an elevator. Flowers followed the officers into the car. The sergeant pushed a button. They started up with a jerk.

The elevator creaked and rattled and wheezed until Flowers wondered whether it would ever make it. That was the sound he had heard in the concrete room, he thought. He leaned back wearily against the ornate brasswork of the wall and thought, *I'm lucky.*

In his moment of safety he found time to wonder about Leah. Was the blind girl all right? Surely she hadn't been hurt. And her father—what was familiar about his face?

It reminded him of a picture, of the time he had wandered through the hall of past presidents in the court house headquarters of the county medical society. There were dozens of the portraits, all done in dark oils, all with their solemn faces and their stern eyes that seemed to watch him as he passed, to say, "We received the great Aesculapian tradition intact, unblemished; we hand it down to you, unchanged. Live up to it if you can."

It was a pretty grim business, Flowers thought, this presidency of the county medical society. No occasion for laughter.

No, that was wrong. One of them had worn a ghost of a smile, the vague possibility around the painted lips that they once had smiled, that they did not take this matter quite as seriously as the painter.

He had bent over, curiously, to read the name on the tarnished brass plate fastened to the bottom of the frame, but he had forgotten it. He bent again, in imagination, trying to read the memory engraved on his brain. He visualized it, getting closer, clearer. He read the name:

DR. RUSSELL PEARCE
PRESIDENT, 1972–1983

Russell Pearce—of course, how could he forget? Discoverer of *elixir vitae*, developer of the synthesis which bore his name, dying now of senescence in a rotting house in the middle of the city.

Dr. Russell Pearce—Russ—Leah's father.

The door opened in front of them. Hesitantly Flowers stepped out into the hall. It was almost identical with the one below.

To the left were tall windows opening on a graying night. Dawn was not far away. "Where are we?" Flowers asked fretfully.

"City Hall," said the sergeant. "Come on."

"What am I doing in City Hall? I'm not going anywhere until you answer my questions."

"Hear that, Dan? He ain't going anywhere. Ain't that the truth? Go tell Coke we're here."

The other officer, big and sullen-faced, slipped through a pair of glass doors at the other end of the hall. The sergeant grinned and ostentatiously adjusted a pistol in the holster at his side.

That one, Flowers thought with a shudder, wouldn't be loaded with anesthetic slivers. "You've got no right to keep me here against my will."

"Who's keeping you here against your will?" the sergeant asked, surprised. "You want to leave? Go. Of course, you gotta be careful about little accidents on the way, like tripping on the stairs. It's a long way down."

This degradation of the police power of the city paralyzed Flowers' will.

The wizened little man who came back with Dan peered at Flowers speculatively. "He's just a medic," he said petulantly, his bruised mouth curving down in disappointment.

"You expect us to be choosy?" the sergeant complained.

"Well," Coke said timidly, "I hope it's all right. Follow me." He motioned to Flowers.

The medic compressed his lips defiantly. "No!"

The sergeant's hand moved in a blur of speed. It hit Flowers' face, palm open, with a solid, meaty sound. The room reeled; Flowers' knees buckled. Anger burst over him redly, and he straightened, his arms ready for battle.

Dan stepped forward, grinning, and kicked him in the groin.

The pain blurred everything as Flowers lay curled on the floor, sobbing. Gradually it ebbed, and his muscles relaxed enough to let his legs fall away from his belly. Flowers forced himself to his knees on the cold marble floor and struggled up. He found the sergeant's arm around him, helping him stand.

"There now," the officer said casually, "we're going to be sensible, aren't we?"

Flowers gritted his teeth and did not groan. He let himself be led through swinging glass doors into a large room bisected by a long, darkly polished counter. Against the right wall was a bench. On the bench was a thin, weasel-faced man.

The weasel face smirked at Flowers. *Thyroid*, Flowers thought dazedly. The shover. Free. Laughing. While he was held by the police, in agony.

By the time they reached the heavy walnut door in the right wall, Flowers could walk without crippling pain. "Where are we going?" he got out between clenched teeth.

"The Boss needs a doctor," Coke said, trotting past him to open the door. Beyond was darkness. "It's about time he should wake up."

The Boss? "Who's he?"

The gray little man stared at him incredulously. "John Bone!"

"Coke!" screamed a voice thinned with pain. "Coke! Where are you?"

"Here, boss!" Coke said in a frightened voice. "Here with a medic!"

He scurried across the room to draw curtains away from tall windows. The light crept in grayly across the floor, onto the wide bed with its tumbled covers. A man was sitting upright among them. He was cadaverously thin, his face a blade, his arms and legs mere sticks.

"A medic!" he screamed. "Who wants a medic? I'm dying. I need a doctor!"

"This is all we could get," Coke squeaked.

"Oh, all right," Bone said. "He'll have to do." He swung his feet over the edge of the bed and fitted them into baby-blue mules. "Come, medic. Treat me!"

"Where's your contract?" Flowers asked.

"Contract!" Bone screamed wildly. "Who's got a contract? If I had a contract do you think I'd be hijacking medics?"

"No contract, no treatment."

The hand hit him on the back of the neck like a club. Flowers sagged and almost fell. Distantly he heard his own voice saying, "That won't do any good."

When the blackness went away, he was sitting in a chair near the bed. He turned his head painfully. The policemen were standing behind him, one on each side. In the doorway, the shover was lurking, watching eagerly. Coke was in front of him. Pacing back and forth between the chair and the window was Bone, his mules clacking against the marble floor and then clumping on the thick carpeting.

"I want treatment, medic! Can't you see I'm dying?"

"We're all dying," Flowers said.

Bone stopped and stared fiercely at Flowers. "Sure. But some of us can put it off longer if we're smart. I'm smart. I want treatment. I can pay. Why shouldn't I have treatment? Why should I be discriminated against? You think nobody ever got treatment who wasn't entitled to it?"

"The only thing I know is that there are ethical standards and I'm bound to them. What difference does it make?" Flowers said defiantly. "You don't need a doctor; you need a psychiatrist. The only disease you've got is hypochondria. Everybody knows that."

Bone turned to stare at Flowers with dark, unreadable eyes. "So," he said softly. "A hypochondriac, am I? I am not dying, eh? Who is to say? These pains in my belly, they are imaginary? My head is sick? Well, maybe. Come here. I want to show you something."

Flowers didn't move quickly enough. A rough hand shoved him out of the chair, propelled him across the room. He stopped beside Bone in front of one of the tall windows. The dawn had come in earnest, and the city lay beneath them, gilded, the signs of decay hidden.

"Look!" Bone said, encompassing the city within the sweep of his arm. "My city! I am the last of a dying breed, the political boss. After me, the deluge. There will be no more city. It will fall apart. Is that not a sad thing?"

Flowers looked at the city, knowing its ruins, and thought it would be a very good thing if it were all destroyed by fire or flood, wiped off the earth just as medicine had wiped out smallpox, diphtheria, malaria, and a hundred other infectious diseases—only in a different way, of course.

"The City," Bone mused. "It is a strange thing. It has a life of its own, a personality, emotions. I woo her, I rage at her, I beat her. But underneath it all there is love. She is dying, and there is no medicine to save her." There were real tears in Bone's eyes.

"I can't help her," Bone said softly, beating his fist gently against the paneled wall beside the window. "I can only weep. What has killed her? That cancer there upon the hill! The doctors have killed her. Medicine has killed her."

Flowers looked where the skeletal finger pointed, toward the hill rising like an island of sunlight out of a sea of night.

The reddish, slanting rays gleamed on the stout walls and sky-reaching towers of Hospital Hill.

"You killed it," Bone said, "with your talk of carcinogens and urban perils. 'Get out of the city!' you said, and wealth left, moved into the country, built its automatic factories, and left us bloodless, leukemia eating at our veins. And inside, the hospitals grew, gobbling block after block, taking a quarter of the city off the tax rolls and then a third. Medicine killed her."

"All medicine did was present the facts and let the public act upon them as it saw fit," Flowers said stiffly.

Bone beat at his own forehead with the side of a fist. "You're right, you're right. We did it ourselves. I wanted you to see that. We gave ourselves into the hands of the physicians, saying, 'Save us! Make us live!' And you did not ask, 'How live? Why?'

"Take these pills, you said, and we swallowed them. You need X-rays, you said, and radioactive iodine and antibiotics and specifics for this and that, and we took them with our tonics and our vitamins." His voice dropped into a chant. "Give us this day our daily vitamins. . . . With microsurgery we can give you another year of life, you said; with blood banks another six months; with organ and artery banks a month, a week. We forced them on you because we were afraid to die. What do you call this morbid fear of disease and death? Give it a name: hypochondria!

"Call me a hypochondriac," Bone went on, "and you are only saying that I am a product of my environment. More intimately than you, than anyone, I am connected to my city. We are dying together, society and I, and we will die crying out to you, 'Save us! Save us or we die!' "

"I can't do anything," Flowers insisted. "Can't you understand that?"

Bone took it with surprising calm as he turned his dark eyes toward Flowers. "Oh, you will," he said, off-hand.

"You think now that you won't, but there will come a time when the flesh conquers, when it screams that it can endure no more, when the nerves will grow weary of pain and the will agonized with waiting, and you will treat me."

He studied Flowers casually, from head slowly toward the feet. His eyes grew bright. Flowers thought he would not look, but he couldn't resist. He glanced down. His jacket had come open. Below its immaculate whiteness was the button-and-spool of the belt buckle.

Bone reached curiously toward the buckle. Before Flowers' tension could achieve action, his arms were caught from behind, pinned back.

"A spool," Bone said, "and something on it." With an experienced finger, he punched the button for rewind and then playback. As the voices came disembodied into the room, he leaned back against the paneled wall, listening with a thin, speculative smile on his pale lips. When it ended, his smile broadened lazily. "Pick up the girl and the old man. I think they might be useful."

Flowers understood him instantly. "Don't be foolish," he said. "They mean nothing to me. I don't care what happens to them."

"Then why protest?" Bone asked blandly. He turned his eyes toward the police officers. "Keep him close. In the broken elevator, there's an idea."

A minute later, the big brass doors clanged behind Flowers, and he was in the darkness again.

But this was darkness with a difference. This was night gingerly supported above a pit of nothingness. It gave him a prickling, swelling feeling of terror. . . .

He found himself trembling in front of the doors, hammering against them with futile, aching fists, screaming. . . .

He forced himself to sit down in a corner of the car. He

forced himself to forget that it was a car, hanging broken over a void. There was no escape.

He remembered punching the old buttons of the control panel. In his frenzy he had torn off a fingernail trying to pry the door open.

He found the black bag and flipped on the light. He rummaged for a bandage, pressed it across the finger where the nail had been.

Then he sat in the dark. It was uncomfortable; he didn't like it. But it was better to sit in darkness with the knowledge of light available if it was needed than to be without any chance of light at all.

Two hours later the doors swung open, and Leah was thrust between them. His watch told him the time; otherwise he would not have believed that a day had not passed.

The girl staggered blindly, and Flowers was as blind as she. He sprang to his feet, though, caught her before she fell, and held her tightly. She fought against him, twisting in his arms, lashing out wildly with her arms and feet.

"It's me," Flowers said repeatedly, "the medic." When she stopped struggling, Flowers started to release her, but she stiffened, clutched at his arm, and held herself, trembling, against him.

It was a curious sensation for Flowers to hold her. It was a comforting thing, not professional, skillful, or impersonal like his medical skill. This was clumsy; it offered part of himself.

"Where are we?" she whispered.

"A broken elevator car in City Hall," he said huskily. "John Bone."

"What does Bone want?" she asked. Her voice was almost steady; it made him feel stronger, abler, listening to it.

"Treatment."

"And you won't." It was a statement. "You're consistent, anyway. I reported your kidnaping to Medical Center. Maybe they'll help."

Hope flamed up, but reality put it out. Center would have no way of locating him, and they wouldn't tear apart the city for one minor medic. He was on his own.

"Did Bone get your father, too?"

"No," Leah said evenly. "The Agency got him. They saw Russ when they came about the kidnaping. One of them recognized him. They took him in."

"That's fantastic!" Flowers exclaimed incredulously. "But where did they take him?"

"The Experimental Ward."

"Not Dr. Pearce!"

"You remember now who he was. So did they. They used his old, reciprocal contract as an excuse because the terminating date was set arbitrarily at one hundred. Doctors didn't use to live that long. I guess they still don't."

"But he's famous!"

"That's why they want him; he knows too much, and too many people remember him. They're afraid the Antivivisection Party will get hold of him and use him against the Profession in some way. They've been looking for him sixty years now—ever since he walked out of the hospital and went into the city and never came out."

"I remember now," Flowers said quickly. "It was like Ambrose Bierce, they said. He was lecturing to a class—on hematology, I think—and he stopped in the middle of a sentence, and he said, 'Gentlemen, we have gone too far; it is time to retrace our steps and discover where we went astray.' Then he walked out of the classroom and out of the hospital and no one ever saw him again. No one ever knew what he meant."

"Those days are forgotten. He never talks—talked about them. I thought the hiding was over. I thought they had finally given him up. . . . Why does John Bone want me?"

"He hopes he can force me to treat him—by—"

"Torturing me? Did you laugh at him?"

"No. No, I didn't do that."

"Why not?"

"Maybe I didn't think fast enough."

Slowly Leah pulled her hand away, and they sat silently in the darkness. Flowers' thoughts were painful; he could scarcely bear to consider them.

"I'm going to look at your eyes," he said suddenly.

He got out his ophthalmoscope and leaned toward the girl, focusing the spot of light on the clouded cornea. She sat still, let him pull up her eyelids, pull down the soft skin of her cheek. He nodded slowly to himself and put the instrument away.

"Is there any hope, doctor?" she asked.

He lied. "No," he said.

It was unethical; it gave him a queer, dizzy feeling, as if he had thrown mud at the hospital wall, but it was mixed with a strange feeling of elation. It was mercy. Of course she could see—if she had an operation costing several thousand dollars more than she would ever have. It was mercy to kill that hope quickly and finally.

Maybe it wasn't ethical, but he'd just begun to realize there were times when a doctor must treat the patient and not the disease. In spite of what the professors said. Each patient was an individual with his own problems and his own treatment, and only part of both were medical.

"I don't understand," he said abruptly, "why the people let John Bone continue here with his corruption and his graft and his violence."

"That is only one side, and a side few people see. To most

of them he is the patron—or, in longer translation, the one who does things for us. What are you going to do about him?"

"Treat him," Flowers said quietly. "There's no point in being quixotic about this."

"But, medic—" she began.

"Ben," he said. "Ben Flowers. I don't want to talk about it. Someone might be listening."

After that there was more silence than talking, but it was a warm sort of silence, warmer perhaps than speech, and her hand came creeping back into his.

When the policeman opened the door, it was night again. Flowers had only a glimpse of the hall before they were hustled in to see Bone in the dark-paneled room. The political boss had a warm red robe wrapped around his body, but he still looked chilled.

Bone watched Flowers' eyes studying the office, and he said: "This used to be the city manager's office. The mayor's office is on the other side. I use that one for business, this one for pleasure, although there isn't much business any more—or pleasure, either, for that matter. So this is the girl. Blind. I should have known that. Well, medic, what is it to be?"

Flowers shrugged. "I'll treat you, of course."

Bone rubbed his thin hands together with a dry, sand-paper sound. "Good, good." Suddenly he stopped and smiled. "But how can I be sure that you will treat me properly? Maybe we should show the medic what my lack of treatment will mean to the girl?"

"That isn't necessary," Flowers said hastily. "I'm not a fool. You're filming this. After I treat you, you'll use it as blackmail to get future treatment. If you aren't satisfied, you can turn it over to the county society. Besides"—his voice deepened suddenly, surprisingly—"touch the girl, and I won't lift a finger to save your life!"

The light in Bone's eyes might have been admiration. "I like you, medic," he said. "Throw in with me. We'd make a pair."

"No, thanks," Flowers said scornfully.

"Think it over. Let me know if you change your mind," Bone said. "But let's get down to business." His voice was eager.

"Have the ambulance motor started," Flowers said.

Bone nodded at the sergeant. "Do it!"

They waited, the four of them, stiff with a watchful uncertainty. When the depths of the bag glowed dimly, Flowers began fastening the instruments to Bone's emaciated body.

Where's Coke? he wondered.

He read the diagnosis, removed the instruments, and slowly stowed them away. Thoughtfully, he explored the pockets of the bag.

"What is it?" Bone asked anxiously. "Tell me what's wrong!"

Flowers' face was sober. "It's nothing to be concerned about," he said, trying to hide his concern, but failing. "You need a tonic. You're taking vitamins already, I'm sure. Double the dose." He pulled out a bottle of pink pills. "Here's some barbiturate-amphetamine pills to put you to sleep at night and wake you up in the morning. And here's some extra ones." He handed Bone a second bottle; in it the pills were round, flat, and green. "Take one of these three times a day."

Bone frowned cautiously. "What's in them?"

"Nothing to hurt you." Flowers shook out a couple into his hand, tossed them into his mouth, swallowed. "See?"

Bone nodded, satisfied. "Okay. Take the two of them back," he said to the policeman.

"Wait a minute," Flowers objected. "Aren't you going to turn us loose?"

"Where'd you get that idea?" Bone chuckled. "I like having a medic around. Gives me a feeling of security."

Flowers sighed, accepting it. "Well, I guess there's nothing I can do." He bent to pick up the bag and noticed the expression of disappointment that flickered across Leah's face. His hand strayed past Bone's neck. "Here," Flowers said to the officer watching them suspiciously, "I suppose you'll want to keep this."

The policeman stepped forward to accept the bag and moved back with it in his hand. With the hand that held the gun, he reached down to scratch the back of his other hand.

Slowly Bone collapsed behind Flowers. It made a rustling sound. The policeman tried to lift the gun, but it was too heavy. It pulled him down. As he fell, he half turned.

"What's happened?" Leah asked, startled. "What are those noises?"

Flowers caught up her hand and scooped up the black bag in one swift motion. "I knocked out Bone with supersonics and the cop with a hypodermic of neo-curare. Come on."

As they went through the glass doors into the hall, he wondered again: *Where's Coke?* There were probably stairs, but he couldn't run down them leading a blind girl. He thumbed the elevator call button and waited in a frenzy of impatience. Leah held his hand firmly, confidently.

"Don't worry. You'll get us out."

Cool certainty flooded over him. His shoulder straightened.

"What medicine did you give him?" she asked.

Flowers chuckled. "Sugar pills. Placebo. Imaginary medicine for an imaginary illness."

When the elevator doors opened, the sergeant was behind them. He stared at them, surprised, and his hand dropped to his gun.

Flowers stepped forward confidently. "Bone said to let us loose."

"That don't sound like Bone," the sergeant growled. He tugged his gun loose. "Let's go check."

Flowers shrugged, released Leah's hand so that he could shift the bag into that one, and swung around so that the bag bumped the sergeant's leg. The sergeant brushed the spot casually, took two steps, and fell, heavily.

As Flowers and Leah stepped out of the elevator into the basement hall, the lights went out. *Coke,* Flowers thought, and groaned.

"What's the matter?" Leah asked, alarmed.

"The lights went out."

"I could help if I knew what you were trying to do."

"Find the ambulance. It should be somewhere in the basement."

"They must have brought me in that way," Leah said thoughtfully. "There was a door that clanged, some steps, another door, some more steps, and then a straight stretch to the elevator. Come on."

Flowers held back for a moment and then let her pull him into the darkness. "There are steps," she said. They walked down carefully. Flowers found the handle of the door and held it open. A moment later they were going down more steps.

"This way," Leah said confidently.

Within seconds they were beside the ambulance, climbing through the door, switching on the light. Flowers swung the responsive vehicle around with a feeling of elation approaching giddiness. Even the sight of the closed garage door didn't bother him. He eased the ambulance as close as possible, swung out, touched the door gingerly, and tugged at the handle. It rose with well-oiled ease.

After that it was nothing. Flowers headed north for Sixth

Street Trafficway, to avoid ambush and shake off pursuers. On the road, he could outdistance anything. After a few minutes they hit Southwest Trafficway. Flowers turned the driving over to the chauffeur, and swung around to look at Leah. She was sitting on the cot.

"Look!" he began. "I—" He stopped.

"Don't you know what to do with me?" she asked gently.

"Well, I—I guess that's right. I can't leave you alone out here, and if I take you to your home, Bone might pick you up again. There are rules against taking one into the Center—" He took a deep breath. "The hell with the rules. Listen! You're a patient. For—an eye operation, replacement of an opaque cornea. You've been transferred from the Neosho County Hospital—that's just outside Chanute, Kansas, in case they ask questions—and you don't know why your records haven't got here yet. Understand?"

"Won't that mean trouble for you?" she asked.

"Nothing I can't get out of. If anyone sees us together—why, I was fooled, too, that's all. No argument now. It'll give us an extra day to decide what to do with you."

"Will I be able to see my father?"

"Of course not," Flowers said. "Not if he's in Experimental, anyway. The only ones allowed in are doctors and attendants on duty."

"I understand. All right, I'll leave it up to you."

Again Flowers felt that quick, irrational flood of happiness. It was inappropriate. He shoved it down, deep, as the walls of Medical Center opened and took them in.

They were lucky. There was no one around as Flowers parked the ambulance in the vast underground garage and led Leah cautiously to the subway. They waited in the shadows until an empty car swung into view.

"Move quickly," he said. "Trust me."

He led her onto the moving belt, holding her forearm in a sure grip. Even so, she swayed and almost fell. He pulled her up and led her swiftly after the car moving on the belt beside them. Just as they reached the end of the approach-way, Flowers helped her into the car and swung himself after her.

He was sweating. The subway wasn't built for the blind.

Getting off was much less difficult. The sign above the archway said: EENT. They walked into an elevator and let it lift them to the fifth floor. Flowers watched from the concealment of a cross-corridor while Leah walked blindly down the hall, feeling her way to the glass enclosure of the duty office.

"Is there anyone here?" she asked out of her darkness. "There was a medic, but he had to leave. I'm from the Neosho County Hospital. . . ."

As Flowers faded down the hall, he saw the nurse come out of the office with a look of concern. He sighed. Leah was safe for the moment.

He walked through the dark halls wondering where everybody was. It was only eight o'clock in the evening.

The floor under his feet was yielding and resilient. He breathed in the hospital smells of ether and alcohol, the old odors, omnipresent, eternal. They were his first memory of his father. It was a good smell. He filled his lungs with it, held it in tightly, as if he could hold onto everything he valued if only he could keep this from escaping.

This was his place, his home. This was his job. This was his life. He had to believe that. Otherwise everything was worthless, seven years of study and labor were wasted, and a lifetime of dreams was turned into nightmare, and everything that was to come, the dedication, the re-wards. . . .

Charley Brand looked up from his desk, surprised. "My God, man! Where've you been?"

"A long story," Flowers said wearily. "First I've got to have some food and some rest."

"They'll have to wait. There's a royal request on your desk."

There was a message glowing on the plate set into the top of his desk. He read it with a cold, shrinking feeling.

> Your presence is requested at the meeting of the Wyandotte County Medical Society this evening and at the meeting of the Political Action Committee to follow.
>
> *J. B. Hardy, M.D.*
> *Secretary*

Flowers looked around the dormitory with frantic eyes; he had to discuss this with someone. "Where's Hal?"

"Do you think he'd miss a meeting?" Brand asked sardonically and added a good imitation of Mock's knowing voice. " 'These things look good on your record.' Better run along. If you hurry you can still make the convoy."

It was more of a tradition than anything else—this convoy detail with the minesweepers snuffling ahead, the tanks lumbering heavily on either side, and helicopters hovering above. No one was foolish enough to attack anything stronger than a lone ambulance.

They drove north on Seventh Street Trafficway over the Armourdale Industrial District that flamed below them in the night, past the ruins of the old stockyards where no man went by night and few dared to go by day. Flowers looked out, unseeing, his fatigue and his hunger conquered by anxiety.

Why did the PAC want to see him?

Few medics and fewer doctors got summons to appear before the committee. It was not an invitation to be envied. It was followed, frequently, by the person involved quietly collecting his personal belongings from the hospital and disappearing from the purview of medicine.

When the convoy pulled up in front of the court house

and parked within the protection of the concrete pillboxes on the lawn and the anti-aircraft emplacements on the roof, Flowers was still tormenting himself with possibilities.

As usual, the meeting was a bore. When the anxiety ebbed, Flowers dozed in his chair, jerking himself upright occasionally to hear a few fragments of the minutes of the last meeting, the treasurer's report, the mumbling of research records. . . .

There was a moving speech by the A.M.A. field representative on the danger to ethical standards in new legislation pending before Congress. Its inevitable result was socialized medicine.

Funny, Flowers mused, how that Hydra was never scotched. Cut off one head and two more grew in its place. Doctors should know enough to cauterize the stump.

By unanimous voice vote, $325,000 was turned over to the Washington lobby for legislative action.

When the chairman of the Political Action Committee stood up, Flowers studied him curiously. He was a tall, fleshy man with bushy, black hair, crouching eyebrows, and a ruddy complexion. Flowers didn't know him. That wasn't unusual in a four-county census of 10,000 doctors.

According to the PAC, the political situation was under control at state and county levels. The Antivivisection Party had closed alliances with a number of quasi-religious groups during the last months, but this was expected to amount to no more than usual. Everyone had been given a mimeographed slate of the state and county candidates. They had all received PAC approval.

The slate was accepted without dissent. A sum of $553,000 was voted for campaign expenses.

There was more.

When the general meeting had been adjourned, Flowers wandered slowly toward the door of the room announced for the meeting of the PAC.

"Flowers?"

It was the chairman of the committee. Flowers followed him numbly into the big room. There were five of them, the chairman taking his place in the middle. They sat solemn-faced behind a long, heavy desk made of real wood darkened by centuries of use.

"You're in trouble, boy," the chairman began.

The doctor on the chairman's right leaned forward, a small memoreader in his hand. "Last night, while on an emergency call into the city, you turned over to the police an alleged shover named Crumm.

"Crumm was dismissed at 9 A.M. He had a license. And the penicillin in the ampule tested a full three hundred thousand units."

"A typical Bone trick! He took out a license and backdated it. And they're lying about the penicillin. They couldn't sell it at that price; it was less than wholesale."

"If you had been listening to the reports tonight, you would have learned that penicillin is worthless. When it was first introduced, immune bacterial strains averaged five per cent. Now they are ninety-five per cent and still climbing."

Flowers thought of the money shoveled into research and production for antibiotics which developed more virulent bacterial strains for which newer and better antibiotics had to be discovered.

"How are we going to put a stop to it," Flowers asked, "if we don't punish them when we have a chance?"

The doctor smiled. "That's what the PAC is for. We've refused to renew John Bone's contract. That will bring him to his senses." His face hardened. "At least, we thought it would until today."

"What do you mean?" Flowers felt vaguely frightened.

"Until Bone released you this evening."

Flowers stared at the five immobile faces with a feeling of frozen horror. "He didn't release me. I escaped!"

"Now, Flowers, don't waste our time with stuff like that," the chairman said impatiently. "Men don't escape from John Bone. And we have evidence—a film of the examination and treatment you gave him!"

"But I did," Flowers broke in. "I used the supersonic anesthetizer and a hypodermic of neo-curare and I escaped—"

"Fantastic! After treating Bone—"

"I gave him sugar pills—"

"Just as bad. For Bone, they're as effective as anything else."

"Don't you see why Bone sent you the films? If I'd really treated him, he'd have held these films over my head as a blackmail threat."

The committee members exchanged glances. "We might be able to accept that," the chairman said, "except that we have other evidence to prove that you hold the Profession and its ethics rather lightly."

He switched on a recorder. Incredulously, Flowers listened to his voice mouthing questions about medicine and fees and social problems. It was skillfully edited. It was damning.

Hal, he thought, *Hal, why did you do it?*

But he knew why. Hal Mock was worried that he might not graduate. One less in the class was one more chance for Hal.

The chairman was speaking to him. "You will submit your resignation in the morning. As soon after that as possible, you will collect your personal effects and leave the Center. If you are ever discovered practicing medicine or treating the sick in any way . . ."

When it was finished, Flowers asked quietly, "What are you going to do with Dr. Russell Pearce?"

The chairman's eyes narrowed and then he turned to the doctor on his right. "Dr. Pearce?" he said. "Why, he disappeared sixty years ago, didn't he? He must have died long ago. If he were alive, he'd be over one hundred and twenty-five. . . ."

Flowers stopped listening. Something had snapped inside him like a carbon-steel scalpel, and he didn't have to listen any more. A man spends his life searching for the truth. If he's lucky he learns before he dies that no one has it all. We have little pieces, each of us, Flowers thought. The danger was in assuming our fragment was the whole. Medicine could not be both political and irresponsible. Dr. Pearce could not be both hero and villain.

Flowers had finally found his way to the back of the statue and learned—in time—that half an ideal is worse than none at all. *Father*, he thought, *you never got there. I'm sorry, father.*

He turned and walked out of the room. There was a phone in the court house lobby. He called his number and waited and then spoke briefly and urgently into the pickup. While the chauffeur guided the ambulance back toward Medical Center, he fished around in the black bag for a couple of amphetamine pills and ate them like candy.

But his feeling of exhilaration and purpose began minutes before the stimulant hit him. It was all very well to be an integral part of a great social and ethical complex, but occasionally a man had to do his own thinking. And then, of course, the great social and ethical complex had to watch out for itself.

He wasn't even disturbed to discover that he was being followed. He shook off the distant white jacket in the subway.

"Look," he said to the pharmacist on duty, "it must get pretty boring here at night. Don't you ever get an over-whelming yen for a cup of coffee?"

"I sure do."

"Go ahead," Flowers said. "I'll watch the pharmacy."

The pharmacist hesitated, torn between duty and desire. The decision to go resulted from a reluctance to appear timid before the medic.

As soon as he was gone, Flowers went straight through the pharmacy to the vault. The heavy door was ajar. In the farthest corner was a modest cardboard carton. Its contents has been estimated, conservatively, as worth $10,000,000. Flowers pocketed an ampule, hesitated, and removed the eleven others from their cotton nests—he suddenly was doubtful that the hospital should be trusted with them. . . .

"Thanks for the break," said the pharmacist gratefully a few minutes later.

Flowers waved carelessly as he left. "Any time."

At the barred door of Experimental Ward, the guard stopped him. "I don't see your name here anywhere," he growled, his finger moving down the duty list.

"No wonder," Flowers said, pointing his own finger. "They misspelled it. Powers instead of Flowers."

It worked. Inside, he walked quickly past the blood bank with its rows of living factories, the organ bank with its surgery and automatic heart machines. . . . The part of the experimental rooms devoted to geriatrics was at the very end.

Dr. Pearce made scarcely a dent in the firm hospital mattress. Flowers shook him, but the smudged eyelids wouldn't open. He filled a hypodermic from the ampule in his jacket pocket and injected it into a vein.

Flowers waited anxiously in the near darkness. Finally Dr. Pearce's eyelids flickered. "Dr. Pearce," he whispered, "this is the medic. Remember?" Pearce nodded, barely perceptibly. "I'm going to try to get you out of here, you and Leah. She's here, too. Will you help?"

Pearce nodded again, stronger this time. Flowers brought

the long cart beside the bed and lifted Pearce's bone-light body onto it. He pulled a sheet up over the face. "Here we go."

He engaged the clutch and guided the cart back the way he had come, past the rooms with their burdens of human tragedy, through the door, past the startled guard. The guard acted as if he were going to say something, but he waited too long.

When they were entering the elevator, Pearce whispered in a dust-dry voice, "What was the shot, medic?"

"*Elixir vitae.* Isn't that justice?"

"So seldom do we get it."

"When did you have your last shot?"

"Sixty years ago."

So, Flowers thought, *I was wrong about that, too.* It wasn't the elixir keeping the old man alive. "You said you'd give Leah your eyes. Did you mean it?"

"Yes. Can you do it?"

The years had desiccated the body, but they hadn't dimmed the mind, Flowers thought. Pearce had realized instantly what Flowers meant. "I don't know," he admitted. "It's a chance. I'll have to do it all alone in haste. I could give her some from the bank, but she would hate it. With yours it would be different."

"A gift of love," Pearce whispered. "It can never be refused. It enriches him who gives and him who receives. That is how it should be done always, with love. Don't tell her. Afterwards she'll understand, how it made me happy to give her what I could not give her as a father—the world of light. . . ."

The duty office was vacant. Flowers ran his finger down the room list until he found Leah's name. He found another cart, ran it silently into the room, and stopped beside the bed. "Leah?"

"Ben?" she said instantly.

For a moment it blunted the cold edge of his determination. It had been a long time since anyone had called him "Ben" like that. "Onto the cart. I've got your father. We're going to make a break for it."

"You'll be ruined."

"It was done for me," he said. "Funny. You have an ideal—maybe it looks like your father—and you think it exists inside you like a marble statue in a hidden niche. And one day you look and it isn't there any more. You're free."

The cart was rolling toward the elevator. On the floor below, he guided the cart into the EENT operating room. As it bumped gently against the cart on which Pearce was lying, Leah put out a hand, touched her father's arm, and said, "Russ!"

"Leah!"

For a moment it stabbed Flowers with jealousy; he felt left out, alone. "You were right," Leah said, and she put out another hand to catch hold of Flowers and pull him close. "He is the man. Better even than we thought."

"Find a great deal of happiness, children," Pearce said.

Flowers chuckled. "I think you two planned the whole thing."

Leah blushed slowly. *She's really beautiful,* Flowers thought in sudden surprise. "No, we only hoped it," she said.

Flowers injected the anesthetic, felt her fingers relax, droop away. Motionless, he stared at her face and then held up his hands in front of his eyes. They were trembling. He looked around at the gleaming whiteness of the walls, the delicate microsurgical tools, the suturing machine, the bandages, and he knew how easy it would be to slip, to make the fatal mistake.

"Courage, medic," said Pearce. His voice was getting

stronger. "You've studied for seven years. You can do this simple thing."

He took a deep breath. Yes, he could do it. And he went at it, as it should be done—with love.

"Medic Flowers," said the hidden speaker in the ceiling, "report to the dormitory. Medic Flowers. . . ."

They had discovered that Pearce was missing. The old man talked to him while his hands were busy and helped take his mind off the terrifying consequences. He told Flowers why he had walked out on his class sixty years before.

"It suddenly came to me—the similarity between medicine and religion. We fostered it with our tradition-building, our indecipherable prescriptions, our ritual. Gradually the public had come to look upon us as miracle workers. The masses called the new medicines wonder drugs because they didn't know how they worked. Religion and medicine —both owed their great periods to a pathological fear of death. He is not so great an enemy."

Flowers made depth readings of the cloudy corneas and set them into the microsurgical machine.

"Oh, the doctors weren't to blame. We were a product of our society just as John Bone is a product of his. But we forgot an ancient wisdom which might have given us the strength to resist. 'A sound mind in a sound body,' the Greeks said. And even more important, 'Nothing in excess.' "

Flowers positioned the shining scalpel over Leah's right eye.

"Anything in excess will ruin this society or any other. Even the best of things—too much wealth, too much piety, too much health. We made a fetish of health, built it shrines in our medicine cabinets, built great temples for worship."

The blade slipped into the eye without resistance, slicing away the cornea.

"The lifespan can be extended to a reasonable length without overburdening the society. Then we run into the law of diminishing returns, and it takes just as much again to push it a year further, and then six months, three months, a week, a day. There is no end, and our fear is such that no one can say, 'Stop! We're healthy enough!' "

The scalpel retracted and moved to the left eye.

"The lives we were saving were peripheral: the very young, the very old, and the constitutional inadequates. We repealed natural selection, saved the weak to reproduce themselves, and told ourselves that we were healthier. It was a kind of suicide. It was health out of bottles. When the bottles break, the society will die."

Both corneas were gone. Flowers looked at his watch. It was taking too long. He turned to Pearce.

"No anesthetic," Pearce said. As the microsurgical machine came over his face, he went on, "We called it humanitarian, but it was only another name for folly. Medicine became dependent upon the very thing it was destroying. Vast technologies were vital to its maintenance, but that level of civilization fostered its own diseases."

The empty sockets were bandaged.

"We destroyed the cities with our doom-sayings, and we amassed a disproportionate amount of capital with our tax-exemptions, our subsidies, our research grants. Like religion again, in medieval Europe, when piety accumulated wealth exempt from levies."

The corneas were in place.

"It couldn't last in Europe, and it can't last here. Henry the Eighth found an excuse to break with the Pope and appropriate the Church lands. In France it helped bring the Revolution. And thus this noble experiment will end. In ice or fire, by the degeneration of technology below the level necessary to sustain it, or by rebellion. And that's why I went into the city."

The suturing machine drove its tiny needles into the edges of the cornea, stitching it to the eye in a neat graft.

"That's where the future will be made, where the people are surviving because they are strong. There we are learning new things—the paranormal methods of health that are not so new after all, but the age-old methods of healers. Their merit is that they do not require complexity and technology, but only a disciplined mind that can discipline the body. When the end comes, the fine spacious life in the county will end like the May fly. The city will survive and grow again. Outside they will die of diseases their bodies have forgotten, of cancer they cannot resist, of a hundred different ailments for which the medicine has been lost."

As the bandages were fastened over Leah's eyes, the speaker in the ceiling spoke again. "Emergency squads report to stations. Heavily armed forces are attacking St. Luke's."

The time for caution was past. Flowers taped together the cart legs and guided them across the hall into the elevator. They dropped to the subway level. Clumsily, Flowers maneuvered the two carts across the approachway into one of the cars and swung himself aboard after them.

In seconds the garage would be swarming with the emergency squads.

Another speaker boomed: "Snipers on buildings along Main Street are shelling St. Luke's with five-inch mortars. No casualties reported. Emergency squads, on the double."

"Has it started already?" Pearce asked softly.

Flowers smiled grimly.

As they reached the garage, men were racing past them. No one paid any attention to the medic guiding the two carts. Flowers stopped at the first unoccupied ambulance, opened the back, and lifted Leah's unconscious body onto one of the stretchers. He lifted Pearce onto the other one. He slammed the door shut and ran around to the front.

Just as the engine caught, a startled medic raced up and pounded futilely against the door. Flowers pulled away from him in a burst of speed.

The ambulance was only one vehicle among many; they streamed from the Center, ambulances, half-tracks, tanks. At Southwest Trafficway, Flowers edged out of the stream and turned north. North into the city.

John Bone was waiting beside the garage door under City Hall. "Okay," he told Coke, "you can call off the diversion now. Come on in," he said to Flowers.

"Said the spider to the fly," Flowers said, smiling. "No, thanks. You'll get healed, and better than I can do. But not now."

Bone's face wrinkled angrily. "By whom?"

"These," Flowers said, waving his hand toward the back of the ambulance.

"An old man? A blind girl?"

"A blind old man, and a girl who might see. Yes. They can do more for you than I can. We'll get along, Bone."

Bone grimaced. "Yes. Yes, I suppose we will."

Leah was stirring. Flowers reached back and put a hand on her forehead. She grew quiet. He turned back to Bone and stripped off his white jacket and tossed it to the political boss of the city. "Here, maybe this will do you some good. You can have the ambulance, too, when it's taken us home."

Home. He smiled. He had thrown in his lot with the city. He had even forgotten his filters. There was brutality in the city, but you could tame it, put its misdirected vitality to use.

But the only thing to do with an ideal that has outworn its necessity is to turn your back on it, to leave it behind.

There is no division between men; there aren't men, and

men in white jackets. A doctor is only a man with special skills. But a healer is something more than a man.

They would make the beginning, the old man, and the blind girl who might see, and the medic who had found a new ideal. "I spent seven years learning to be a doctor," Flowers said. "I guess I can spend seven years more learning to heal."